Richard A. Proctor

The Great Pyramid

observatory, tomb, and temple

Richard A. Proctor

The Great Pyramid
observatory, tomb, and temple

ISBN/EAN: 9783337406547

Printed in Europe, USA, Canada, Australia, Japan

Cover: Foto ©Andreas Hilbeck / pixelio.de

More available books at **www.hansebooks.com**

"KNOWLEDGE" LIBRARY

THE

GREAT PYRAMID

OBSERVATORY, TOMB, AND TEMPLE

BY

RICHARD A. PROCTOR

EDITOR OF 'KNOWLEDGE'
AUTHOR OF 'SATURN AND ITS SYSTEM' 'THE SUN' 'THE MOON'
'OTHER WORLDS THAN OURS' ETC.

WITH ILLUSTRATIONS

LONDON
LONGMANS, GREEN, AND CO.
AND NEW YORK: 15 EAST 16th STREET
1888

PREFACE.

THE mystery of the Great Pyramid resides chiefly in this: that while certainly meant to be a tomb, it was obviously intended to serve as an observatory, though during the lifetime only of its builder, and was also associated with religious observances. Minor difficulties arise from the consideration of the other pyramids. In this treatise I show that there is one theory, which, instead of conflicting with other theories of the pyramid, combines all that is sound in them with what has hitherto been wanting, a valid and sufficient reason (for men who thought as the builders of the pyramid certainly did) for erecting structures such as these, at the cost of vast labour and enormous expense. The theory here advanced and discussed shows—(1) why the Great Pyramid was an astronomical observatory while Cheops lived ; (2) why it was regarded as useless as such after his death ; (3) why it was worth his while to build it ; (4) why separate structures were required for his brother, son, grandson, and other members of his family ; (5) why it would naturally be used for his tomb; and (6) why it would be the scene of religious observances. All that is necessary by way of postulate, is that he and his dynasty believed fully in astronomy as a means (1) of predicting the future, and (2) of ruling the planets, in the sense of selecting right times for every action or enterprise. If there is one thing certain about Oriental nations in remote past ages, it is that this belief was universally prevalent.

The remaining portion of the work shows how potent were those ancient superstitions about planetary influences—and their bearing first on Jewish, and later on Christian festivals and ceremonial.

RICHARD A. PROCTOR.

CONTENTS.

CHIEF ILLUSTRATIONS.

PLATES.

WOODCUTS IN TEXT.

GREAT PYRAMID.

CHAPTER I.

HISTORY OF THE PYRAMIDS.

FEW subjects of inquiry have proved more perplexing than the question of the purpose for which the pyramids of Egypt were built. Even in the remotest ages of which we have historical record, nothing seems to have been known certainly on this point. For some reason or other, the builders of the pyramids concealed the object of these structures, and this so successfully that not even a tradition has reached us which purports to have been handed down from the epoch of the pyramids' construction. We find, indeed, some explanations given by the earliest historians; but they were professedly only hypothetical, like those advanced in more recent times. Including ancient and modern theories, we find a wide range of choice.   Some have thought that these buildings were associated with the religion of the early Egyptians; others have suggested that they were tombs; others, that they combined the purposes of tombs and temples, that they were astronomical observatories, defences against the sands of the Great Desert, granaries like those made under Joseph's direction, places of resort during excessive overflows of the Nile; and many other uses have been suggested for them.   But none of these ideas are found on close examination to be tenable as representing the sole purpose of the pyramids, and few of them have strong claims to be regarded as presenting even a chief object of these remarkable structures.   The significant and perplexing history of the three oldest pyramids—the Great Pyramid of Cheops, Shofo, or Suphis, the pyramid of Chephren, and the pyramid of Mycerinus; and the most remarkable of all the facts known respecting the pyramids generally, viz. the circumstance that one pyramid after another was built as though each had become useless soon after it was finished, are left entirely unexplained by all the theories above mentioned, save one only, the tomb theory, and that does not afford by any means a satisfactory explanation of the circumstances.

I propose to give here a brief account of some of the most suggestive facts known respecting the pyramids, and, after considering the difficulties which beset the theories heretofore advanced, to indicate a theory (new, so far as I know) which seems to me to correspond better with the facts than any heretofore advanced; I suggest it, however, rather for consideration than because I regard it as very convincingly supported by the evidence. In fact, to advance any theory at present with confident assurance of its correctness, would be simply to indicate a very limited acquaintance with the difficulties surrounding the subject.

Let us first consider a few of the more striking facts recorded by history or tradition, noting, as we proceed, whatever ideas they may suggest as to the intended character of these structures.

It is hardly necessary to say, perhaps, that the history of the Great Pyramid is of paramount importance in this inquiry. Whatever purpose pyramids were originally intended to subserve must have been conceived by the builders of *that* pyramid. New ideas may have been superadded by the builders of later pyramids, but it is unlikely that the original purpose can have been entirely abandoned. Some great purpose there was, which the rulers of ancient Egypt proposed to fulfil by building very massive pyramidal structures on a particular plan. It is by inquiring into the history of the first and most massive of these structures, and by examining its construction, that we shall have the best chance of finding out what that great purpose was.

According to Herodotus, the kings who built the pyramids reigned not more than twenty-eight centuries ago; but there can be little doubt that Herodotus misunderstood the Egyptian priests from whom he derived his information, and that the real antiquity of the pyramid-kings was far greater. He tells us that, according to the Egyptian priests, Cheops 'on ascending the throne plunged into all manner of wickedness. He closed the temples, and forbade the Egyptians to offer sacrifice, compelling them instead to labour one and all in his service, viz. in building the Great Pyramid.' Still following his interpretation of the Egyptian account, we learn that one hundred thousand men were employed for twenty years in building the Great Pyramid, and that ten years were occupied in constructing a causeway by which to convey the stones to the place and in conveying them there. 'Cheops reigned fifty years; and was succeeded by his brother Chephren, who imitated

the conduct of his predecessor, built a pyramid—
but smaller than his brother's—and reigned fifty-
six years. Thus during one hundred and six years
the temples were shut and never opened.' Moreover, Herodotus tells us that 'the Egyptians so
detested the memory of these kings, that they do
not much like even to mention their names. Hence
they commonly call the pyramids after Philition, a
shepherd who at that time fed his flocks about the
place.' 'After Chephren, Mycerinus, son of Cheops,
ascended the throne. He reopened the temples,
and allowed the people to resume the practice of
sacrifice. He, too, left a pyramid, but much inferior in size to his father's. It is built, for half of
its height, of the stone of Ethiopia,' or, as Professor Smyth (whose extracts from Rawlinson's
translation I have here followed) adds, 'expensive
red granite.' 'After Mycerinus, Asychis ascended
the throne. He built the eastern gateway of the
Temple of Vulcan (Phtha); and being desirous of
eclipsing all his predecessors on the throne, left as
a monument of his reign a pyramid of brick.'

This account is so suggestive, as will presently
be shown, that it may be well to inquire whether
it can be relied on. Now, although there can be
no doubt that Herodotus misunderstood the Egyptians in some matters, and in particular as to the

chronological order of the dynasties, placing the pyramid-kings far too late, yet in other respects he seems not only to have understood them correctly, but also to have received a correct account from them. The order of the kings above named corresponds with the sequence given by Manetho, and also found in monumental and hieroglyphic records. Manetho gives the names Suphis I., Suphis II., and Mencheres, instead of Cheops, Chephren, and Mycerinus; while, according to the modern Egyptologists, Herodotus's Cheops was Shofo, Shufu, or Koufou; Chephren was Shafre, while he was also called Nou-Shofo or Noun-Shufu as the brother of Shofo; and Mycerinus was Menhere or Menkerre. But the identity of these kings is not questioned. As to the true dates there is much doubt, and it is probable that the question will long continue open; but the determination of the exact epochs when the several pyramids were built is not very important in connection with our present inquiry. We may, on the whole, fairly take the points quoted above from Herodotus, and proceed to consider the significance of the narrative, with sufficient confidence that in all essential respects it is trustworthy.

There are several very strange features in the account.

In the first place, it is manifest that Cheops
(to call the first king by the name most familiar
to the general reader) attached great importance
to the building of his pyramid.   It has been said,
and perhaps justly, that it would be more interesting to know the plan of the architect who devised
the pyramid than the purpose of the king who
built it.   But the two things are closely connected.
The architect must have satisfied the king that
some highly important purpose in which the king
himself was interested would be subserved by the
structure.   Whether the king was persuaded to
undertake the work as a matter of duty, or only
to advance his own interests, may not be so clear.
But that the king was most thoroughly in earnest
about the work is certain.   A monarch in those
times would assuredly not have devoted an enormous amount of labour and material to such a
scheme unless he was thoroughly convinced of its
great importance.   That the welfare of his people
was not considered by Cheops in building the
Great Pyramid is almost equally certain.   He
might, indeed, have had a scheme for their good
which either he did not care to explain to them or
which they could not understand.   But the most
natural inference from the narrative is that his
purpose had no reference whatever to their wel-

fare. For though one could understand his own
subjects hating him while he was all the time
working for their good, it is obvious that his
memory would not·have been hated if some important good had eventually been gained from his
scheme. Many a far-seeing ruler has been hated
while living on account of the very work for which
his memory has been revered. But the memory of
Cheops and his successors was held in detestation.

May we, however, suppose that, though Cheops
had not the welfare of his own people in his
thoughts, his purpose was nevertheless not selfish,
but intended in some way to promote the welfare
of the human race? I say his purpose, because,
whoever originated the scheme, Cheops carried it
out; it was by means of his wealth and through
his power that the pyramid was built. This is the
view adopted by Professor Piazzi Smyth and
others, in our own time, and first suggested by
John Taylor. 'Whereas other writers,' says Smyth,
'have generally esteemed that the mysterious persons who directed the building of the Great Pyramid
(and to whom the Egyptians, in their traditions,
and for ages afterwards, gave an immoral and
even abominable character) must therefore have
been very bad indeed, so that the world at large
has always been fond of standing on, kicking, and

insulting that dead lion, whom they really knew not; he, Mr. John Taylor, seeing how religiously bad the Egyptians themselves were, was led to conclude, on the contrary, that those *they* hated (and could never sufficiently abuse) might, perhaps, have been pre-eminently good; or were, at all events, of *different religious faith* from themselves.'   'Combining this with certain unmistakable historical facts,' Mr. Taylor deduced reasons for believing that the directors of the building designed to record in its proportions, and in its interior features, certain important religious and scientific truths, not for the people then living, but for men who were to come 4,000 years or so after.

I consider at length, further on, the evidence on which this strange theory rests. But there are certain matters connecting it with the above narrative which must here be noticed.   The mention of the shepherd Philition, who fed his flocks about the place where the Great Pyramid was built, is a singular feature of Herodotus's narrative.   It reads like some strange misinterpretation of the story related to him by the Egyptian priests.   It is obvious that if the word Philition did not represent a people, but a person, this person must have been very eminent

and distinguished—a shepherd-king, not a mere
shepherd. Rawlinson, in a note on this portion of
the narrative of Herodotus, suggests that Philitis
was probably a shepherd-prince from Palestine,
perhaps of Philistine descent, ‘ but so powerful and
domineering, that it may be traditions of his
oppressions in that earlier age which, mixed up
afterwards in the minds of later Egyptians with
the evils inflicted on their country by the subsequent shepherds of better known dynasties, lent so
much force to their religious hate of Shepherd times
and that name.’ Smyth, somewhat modifying this
view, and considering certain remarks of Manetho
respecting an alleged invasion of Egypt by shep-
herd-kings, ‘ men of an ignoble race (from the
Egyptian point of view) who had the confidence to
invade our country, and easily subdued it to their
power without a battle,’ comes to the conclusion
that some Shemite prince, ‘ a contemporary of, but
rather older than, the Patriarch Abraham,’ visited
Egypt at this time, and obtained such influence
over the mind of Cheops as to persuade him to
erect the pyramid. According to Smyth, the
prince was no other than Melchizedek, king of
Salem, and the influence he exerted was supernatural. With such developments of the theory
we need not trouble ourselves. It seems tolerably

clear that certain shepherd-chiefs who came to Egypt during Cheops's reign were connected in some way with the designing of the Great Pyramid, It is clear also that they were men of a different religion from the Egyptians, and persuaded Cheops to abandon the religion of his people. Taylor, Smyth, and the Pyramidalists generally, consider this sufficient to prove that the pyramid was erected for some purpose connected with religion. ' The pyramid,' in fine, says Smyth, ' was charged by God's inspired shepherd-prince, in the beginning of human time, to keep a certain message secret and inviolable for 4,000 years, and it has done so ; and in the next thousand years it was to enunciate that message to all men, with more than traditional force, more than all the authenticity of copied manuscripts or reputed history ; and that part of the pyramid's usefulness is now beginning.'

There are many very obvious difficulties surrounding this theory ; as, for example, (i.) the absurd waste of power in setting supernatural machinery at work 4,000 years ago with cumbrous devices to record its object, when the same machinery, much more simply employed now, would effect the alleged purpose far more thoroughly ; (ii.) the enormous amount of human misery and its attendant hatreds brought about by this alleged

divine scheme ; and (iii.) the futility of an arrangement by which the pyramid was only to subserve
its purpose when it had lost that perfection of
shape on which its entire significance depended,
according to the theory itself.   But apart from
these, there is a difficulty, nowhere noticed by
Smyth or his followers, which is fatal, I conceive,
to this theory of the pyramid's purpose.   The
second pyramid, though slightly inferior to the
first in size, and probably far inferior in quality of
masonry, is still a structure of enormous dimensions, which must have required many years of
labour from tens of thousands of workmen.   Now,
it seems impossible to explain why Chephren built
this second pyramid, if we adopt Smyth's theory
respecting the first pyramid.   For either Chephren
knew the purpose for which the Great Pyramid
was built, or he did not know it.   If he knew that
purpose, and it was that indicated by Smyth, then
he also knew that no second pyramid was wanted.
On that hypothesis, all the labour bestowed on the
second pyramid was wittingly and wilfully wasted.
This, of course, is incredible.   But, on the other
hand, if Chephren did not know what was the
purpose for which the Great Pyramid was built,
what reason could Chephren have had for building a pyramid at all?   The only answer to this

question seems to be that Chephren built the second pyramid in hopes of finding out why his brother had built the first, and this answer is simply absurd. It is clear enough that, whatever purpose Cheops had in building the first pyramid, Chephren must have had a similar purpose in building the second ; and we require a theory which shall at least explain why the first pyramid did not subserve for Chephren the purpose which it subserved or was meant to subserve for Cheops. The same reasoning may be extended to the third pyramid, to the fourth, and in fine to all the pyramids, forty or so in number, included under the general designation of the Pyramids of Ghizeh or Jeezeh. The extension of the principle to pyramids later than the second is especially important as showing that the difference of religion insisted on by Smyth has no direct bearing on the question of the purpose for which the Great Pyramid itself was constructed. For Mycerinus either never left or else returned to the religion of the Egyptians. Yet he also built a pyramid, which, though far inferior in size to the pyramids built by his father and uncle, was still a massive structure, and relatively more costly even than theirs, because built of expensive granite. The pyramid built by Asychis, though smaller still, was remarkable as built of brick ; in fact, we are expressly told that Asychis desired to eclipse all his predecessors in such labours, and accordingly left this brick pyramid as a monument of his reign.

We are forced, in fact, to believe that there was some special relation between the pyramid and its builder, seeing that each one of these kings wanted a pyramid of his own. This applies to the Great Pyramid quite as much as to the others, despite the superior excellence of that structure. Or rather, the argument derives its chief force from the superiority of the Great Pyramid. If Chephren, no longer perhaps having the assistance of the shepherd-architects in planning and superintending the work, was unable to construct a pyramid so perfect and so stately as his brother's, the very fact that he nevertheless built a pyramid shows that the Great Pyramid did not fulfil for Chephren the purpose which it fulfilled for Cheops. But, if Smyth's theory were true, the Great Pyramid would have fulfilled finally and for all men the purpose for which it was built. Since this was manifestly not the case, that theory is, I submit, demonstrably erroneous.

It was probably the consideration of this point, viz. that each king had a pyramid constructed for himself, which led to the theory that the pyramids were intended to serve as tombs. This theory was once very generally entertained. Thus we find Humboldt, in his remarks on American pyramids, referring to the tomb theory of the Egyptian pyramids as though it were open to no question. 'When we consider,' he says, 'the pyramidical monuments of Egypt, of Asia, and of the New Continent, from the same point of view, we see that, though their form is alike, their destination was altogether different. The group of pyramids of Ghizeh and at Sakhara in Egypt; the triangular pyramid of the Queen of the Scythians, Zarina, which was a stadium high and three in circumference, and which was decorated with a colossal figure; the fourteen Etruscan pyramids, which are said to have been enclosed in the labyrinth of the king Porsenna, at Clusium—were reared to serve as the sepulchres of the illustrious dead. Nothing is more natural to men than to commemorate the spot where rest the ashes of those whose memory they cherish, whether it be, as in the infancy of the race, by simple mounds of earth, or, in later periods, by the towering height of the tumulus. Those of the Chinese and of Thibet have only a few metres of elevation. Farther to the west the dimensions increase; the tumulus of the king Alyattes, father of Crœsus, in Lydia, was six stadia, and that of

Ninus was more than ten stadia in diameter. In the north of Europe the sepulchre of the Scandinavian king Gormus, and the queen Daneboda, covered with mounds of earth, are three hundred metres broad, and more than thirty high.'

But while we have abundant reason for believing that in Egypt, even in the days of Cheops and Chephren, extreme importance was attached to the character of the place of burial for distinguished persons, there is nothing in what is known respecting earlier Egyptian ideas to suggest the probability that any monarch would have devoted many years of his subjects' labour, and vast stores of material, to erect a mass of masonry like the Great Pyramid, solely to receive his own body after death. Far less have we any reason for supposing that many monarchs in succession would do this, each having a separate tomb built for him. It might have been conceivable, had only the Great Pyramid been erected, that the structure had been raised as a mausoleum for all the kings and princes of the dynasty. But it seems utterly incredible that such a building as the Great Pyramid should have been erected for one king's body only —and that, not in the way described by Humboldt, when he speaks of men commemorating the spot where rest the remains of those whose memory

they cherish, but at the expense of the king himself whose body was to be there deposited. Besides, the first pyramid, the one whose history
must be regarded as most significant of the true
purpose of these buildings, was not built by an
Egyptian holding in great favour the special religious ideas of his people, but by one who had
adopted other views, and those not belonging, so
far as can be seen, to a people among whom
sepulchral rites were held in exceptional regard.

A still stronger objection against the exclusively tombic theory resides in the fact that this
theory gives no account whatever of the characteristic features of the pyramids themselves. These
buildings are all, without exception, built on special
astronomical principles. Their square bases are so
placed as to have two sides lying east and west,
and two lying north and south ; or, in other words,
so that their four faces front the four cardinal
points. One can imagine no reason why a tomb
should have such a position. It is not, indeed,
easy to understand why any building at all, except
an astronomical observatory, should have such a
position. A temple perhaps devoted to sun-
worship, and generally to the worship of the
heavenly bodies, might be built in that way. For
it is to be noticed that the peculiar figure and

position of the pyramids would bring about the following relations:—When the sun rose and set south of the east and west points, or (speaking generally) between the autumn and the spring equinoxes, the rays of the rising and setting sun illuminated the southern face of the pyramid; whereas during the rest of the year—that is, during the six months between the spring and autumn equinoxes—the rays of the rising and setting sun illuminated the northern face. Again, all the year round the sun's rays passed from the eastern to the western face at solar noon. And lastly, during seven months and a half of each year—namely, for three months and three quarters before and after midsummer—the noon rays of the sun fell on all four faces of the pyramid; or, according to a Peruvian expression (so Smyth avers), the sun shone on the pyramid 'with all his rays.' Such conditions as these might have been regarded as very suitable for a temple devoted to sun-worship. Yet the temple theory is as untenable as the tomb theory. For, in the first place, the pyramid form— as the pyramids were originally built, with perfectly smooth slant faces, not terraced into steps, as now, through the loss of the casing-stones—was entirely unsuited for all the ordinary requirements of a temple of worship. And further, this theory gives no explanation of the fact that each king built a pyramid, and each king only one. Similar difficulties oppose the theory that the pyramids were intended to serve solely as astronomical observatories. For, while their original figure, however manifestly astronomical in its relations, was quite unsuited for observatory work, it is manifest that if such had been the purpose of pyramid-building, so soon as the Great Pyramid had once been built, no other would be needed. Certainly none of the pyramids built afterwards could have subserved any astronomical purpose which the first did not subserve, or have subserved nearly so well as the Great Pyramid those purposes which that building may be supposed to have fulfilled as an astronomical observatory.

Of the other theories mentioned at the beginning of this paper none seem to merit special notice, except perhaps the theory that the pyramids were made to receive the royal treasures, and this theory rather because of the attention it received from Arabian literati, during the ninth and tenth centuries, than because of any strong reasons which can be suggested in its favour. 'Emulating,' says Professor Smyth, 'the enchanted tales of Bagdad,' the court poets of Al Mamoun (son of the far-famed Haroun al Raschid) 'drew gorgeous pictures of the contents of the pyramid's interior. . . . All the treasures of Sheddad Ben Ad the great Antediluvian king of the earth, with all his medicines and all his sciences, they declared were there, told over and over again. Others, though, were positive that the founder-king was no other than Saurid Ibn Salhouk, a far greater one than the other; and these last gave many more minute particulars, some of which are at least interesting to us in the present day, as proving that, amongst the Egypto-Arabians of more than a thousand years ago the Jeezeh pyramids, headed by the grand one, enjoyed a pre-eminence of fame vastly before all the other pyramids of Egypt put together; and that if any other is alluded to after the Great Pyramid (which has always been the notable and favourite one, and chiefly was known then as the East pyramid), it is either the second one at Jeezeh, under the name of the West pyramid; or the third one, distinguished as the Coloured pyramid, in allusion to its red granite, compared with the white limestone casings of the other two (which, moreover, from their more near, but by no means exact, equality of size, went frequently under the affectionate designation of " the pair ").'

The report of Ibn Abd Alkokm, as to what

was to be found in each of these three pyramids, or rather of what, according to him, was put into them originally by King Saurid, runs as follows: 'In the Western pyramid, thirty treasuries filled with store of riches and utensils, and with signatures made of precious stones, and with instruments of iron and vessels of earth, and with arms which rust not, and with glass which might be bended and yet not broken, and with strange spells, and with several kinds of *alakakirs* (magical precious stones) single and double, and with deadly poisons, and with other things besides. He made also in the East' (the Great Pyramid) 'divers celestial spheres and stars, and what they severally operate in their aspects, and the perfumes which are to be used to them, and the books which treat of these matters. He put also into the Coloured pyramid the commentaries of the priests in chests of black marble, and with every priest a book, in which the wonders of his profession and of his actions and of his nature were written, and what was done in his time, and what is and what shall be from the beginning of time to the end of it.' The rest of this worthy's report relates to certain treasurers placed within these three pyramids to guard their contents, and (like all or most of what I have already quoted) was a work of imagination.

Ibn Abd Alkokm, in fact, was a romancist of the first water.

Perhaps the strongest argument against the theory that the pyramids were intended as strongholds for the concealment of treasure, resides in the fact that, search being made, no treasure has been discovered. When the workmen employed by Caliph Al Mamoun, after encountering manifold difficulties, at length broke their way into the great ascending passage lending to the so-called King's Chamber, they found 'a right noble apartment, thirty-four feet long, seventeen broad, and nineteen high, of polished red granite throughout, walls, floor, and ceiling, in blocks squared and true, and put together with such exquisite skill that the joints are barely discernible to the closest inspection. But where is the treasure—the silver and the gold, the jewels, medicines, and arms? These fanatics look wildly around them, but can see nothing, not a single *dirhem* anywhere. They trim their torches, and carry them again and again to every part of that red-walled, flinty hall, but without any better success. Nought but pure polished red granite, in mighty slabs, looks upon them from every side. The room is clean, garnished too, as it were, and, according to the ideas of its founders, complete and perfectly ready for its visitors so long expected, so long delayed. But the gross minds who occupy it now, find it all barren, and declare that there is nothing whatever for them in the whole extent of the apartment from one end to another ; nothing except an empty stone chest without a lid.'

It is, however, to be noted that we have no means of learning what had happened between the time when the pyramid was built and when Caliph Al Mamoun's workmen broke their way into the King's Chamber. The place may, after all, have contained treasures of some kind ; nor, indeed, is it incompatible with other theories of the pyramid to suppose that it was used as a safe receptacle for treasures. It is certain, however, that this cannot have been the special purpose for which the pyramids were designed. We should find in such a purpose no explanation whatever of any of the most stringent difficulties encountered in dealing with other theories. There could be no reason why strangers from the East should be at special pains to instruct an Egyptian monarch how to hide and guard his treasures. Nor, if the Great Pyramid had been intended to receive the treasures of Cheops, would Chephren have built another for his own treasures, which must have included those gathered by Cheops. But, apart from this, how

inconceivably vast must a treasure-hoard be supposed to be, the safe guarding of which would
have repaid the enormous cost of the Great Pyramid in labour and material! And then, why
should a mere treasure-house have the characteristics of an astronomical observatory? Manifestly,
if the pyramids were used at all to receive treasures, it can only have been as an entirely subordinate though perhaps convenient means of
utilising these gigantic structures.

Having thus gone through all the suggested
purposes of the pyramids save two or three which
clearly do not possess any claim to serious consideration, and not having found one which appears
to give any sufficient account of the history and
principal features of these buildings, we must
either abandon the inquiry or seek for some explanation quite different from any yet suggested.
Let us consider what are the principal points of
which the true theory of the pyramids should give
an account.

In the first place, the history of the pyramids
shows that the erection of the first great pyramid
was in all probability either suggested to Cheops
by wise men who visited Egypt from the East, or
else some important information conveyed to him
by such visitors caused him to conceive the idea of

building the pyramid. In either case we may suppose, as the history indeed suggests, that these learned men, whoever they may have been, remained in Egypt to superintend the erection of the structure. It may be that the architectural work was not under their supervision; in fact, it seems altogether unlikely that shepherd-rulers would have much to teach the Egyptians in the matter of architecture. But the astronomical peculiarities which form so significant a feature of the Great Pyramid were probably provided for entirely under the instructions of the shepherd chiefs who had exerted so strange an influence upon the mind of King Cheops.

Next, it seems clear that self-interest must have been the predominant reason in the mind of the Egyptian king for undertaking this stupendous work. It is true that his change of religion implies that some higher cause influenced him. But a ruler who could inflict such grievous burdens on his people, in carrying out his purpose, that for ages afterwards his name was held in utter detestation, cannot have been solely or even chiefly influenced by religious motives. It affords an ample explanation of the behaviour of Cheops, in closing the temples and forsaking the religion of his country, to suppose that the advantages which he hoped to secure by building the pyramid, depended in some way on his adopting this course. The visitors from the East may have refused to give their assistance on any other terms, or may have assured him that the expected benefit could not be obtained if the pyramid were erected by idolaters. It is certain, in any case, that they were opposed to idolatry; and we have thus some means of inferring who they were and whence they came. We know that one particular branch of one particular race in the East was characterised by a most marked hatred of idolatry in all its forms. Terah and his family, or, probably, a sect or division of the Chaldæan people, went forth from Ur of the Chaldees, to go into the land of Canaan—and the reason why they went forth we learn from a book of considerable historical interest (the book of Judith) to have been because 'they would not worship the gods of their fathers who were in the land of the Chaldæans.' The Bible record shows that members of this branch of the Chaldæan people visited Egypt from time to time. They were shepherds, too, which accords well with the account of Herodotus above quoted. We can well understand that persons of this family would have resisted all endeavours to secure their acquiescence in any scheme associated with idolatrous rites. Neither promises nor threats would

have had much influence on them. It was a distinguished member of the family, the patriarch
Abraham, who said: 'I have lifted up mine hand
unto the Lord, the most high God, the possessor of
heaven and earth, that I will not take from a thread
even to a shoe-latchet, and that I will not take
anything that is thine, lest thou shouldest say, I
have made Abram rich.' Vain would all the
promises and all the threats of Cheops have been
to men of this spirit. Such men might help him
in his plans, suggested, as the history shows, by
teachings of their own, but it must be on their own
conditions, and those conditions would most certainly include the utter rejection of idolatrous worship by the king in whose behalf they worked, as
well as by all who shared in their labours. It
seems probable that they convinced both Cheops
and Chephren, that unless these kings gave up
idolatry, the purpose, whatever it was, which the
pyramid was erected to promote, would not be
fulfilled. The mere fact that the Great Pyramid
was built either directly at the suggestion of these
visitors, or because they had persuaded Cheops of
the truth of some important doctrine, shows that
they must have gained great influence over his
mind. Rather we may say that he must have been
so convinced of their knowledge and power as to

have accepted with unquestioning confidence all that they told him respecting the particular subject over which they seemed to possess so perfect a mastery.

But having formed the opinion, on grounds sufficiently assured, that the strangers who visited Egypt and superintended the building of the Great Pyramid came from the land of the Chaldæans, it is not very difficult to decide what was the subject respecting which they had such exact information. They were doubtless learned in all the wisdom of their Chaldæan kinsmen. They were masters, in fact, of the astronomy of their day, a science for which the Chaldæans had shown from the earliest ages the most remarkable aptitude. What the actual extent of their astronomical knowledge may have been it would be difficult to say. But it is certain, from the exact knowledge which later Chaldæans possessed respecting long astronomical cycles, that astronomical observations must have been carried on continuously by that people for many hundreds of years. It is highly probable that the astronomical knowledge of the Chaldæans in or long before the days of Terah and Abraham was much more accurate than that possessed by the Greeks even after the time of Hipparchus.[1] We

---

[1] It has been remarked that, though Hipparchus had the

see indeed, in the accurate astronomical adjustment of the Great Pyramid, that the architects must have been skilful astronomers and mathematicians ; and I may note here, in passing, how strongly this circumstance confirms the opinion that the visitors were Chaldæans. All we know from Herodotus and Manetho, all the evidence from the circumstances connected with the religion of the pyramid-kings, and the astronomical evidence given by the pyramids themselves, tends to suggest that members of that particular branch of the Chaldæan family which went out from Ur of the Chaldees because they would not worship the gods of the Chaldæans, extended their wanderings to Egypt, and eventually superintended the erection of the Great Pyramid so far as astronomical and mathematical relations were concerned.

But not only have we already decided that the pyramids were not intended solely or chiefly to subserve the purpose of astronomical observatories,

enormous advantage of being able to compare his own observations with those recorded by the Chaldæans, he estimated the length of the year less correctly than the Chaldæans. It has been thought by some that the Chaldæans were acquainted with the true system of the universe, but I do not know that there are sufficient grounds for this supposition. Diodorus Siculus and Apollonius Myndius mention, however, that they were able to predict the return of comets, and this implies that their observations had been continued for many centuries with great care and exactness.

but it is certain that Cheops would not have been
personally much interested in any astronomical information which these visitors might be able to
communicate. Unless he saw clearly that something was to be gained from the lore of his visitors,
he would not have undertaken to erect any astronomical buildings at their suggestion, even if he
had cared enough for their knowledge to pay any
attention to them whatever. Most probably the
reply Cheops would have made to any communi-
cations respecting mere astronomy, would have run
much in the style of the reply made by the Turkish
Cadi, Imaum Ali Zadè, to a friend of Layard's who
had apparently bored him about double stars and
comets: 'Oh my soul! oh my lamb!' said Ali
Zadè, 'seek not after the things which concern thee
not. Thou camest unto us, and we welcomed
thee: go in peace. Of a truth thou hast spoken
many words; and there is no harm done, for the
speaker is one and the listener is another. After
the fashion of thy people thou hast wandered from
one place to another until thou art happy and content in none. Listen, oh my son! There is no
wisdom equal unto the belief in God! He created
the world, and shall we liken ourselves unto Him
in seeking to penetrate into the mysteries of His
creation? Shall we say, Behold this star spinneth

round that star, and this other star with a tail goeth
and cometh in so many years! Let it go! He
from whose hand it came will guide and direct it.
But thou wilt say unto me, Stand aside, oh man,
for I am more learned than thou art, and have seen
more things. If thou thinkest that thou art in this
respect better than I am, thou art welcome. I
praise God that I seek not that which I require not.
Thou art learned in the things I care not for ; and
as for that which thou hast seen, I defile it. Will
much knowledge create thee a double belly, or wilt
thou seek paradise with thine eyes?' Such,
omitting the references to the Creator, would
probably have been the reply of Cheops to his
visitors, had they only had astronomical facts to
present him with. Or, in the plenitude of his
kingly power, he might have more decisively
rejected their teaching by removing their heads.

But the shepherd-astronomers had knowledge
more attractive to offer than a mere series of
astronomical discoveries. Their ancestors had

> Watched from the centres of their sleeping flocks
> Those radiant Mercuries, that seemed to move
> Carrying through æther in perpetual round
> Decrees and resolutions of the gods ;

and though the visitors of King Cheops had themselves rejected the Sabaistic polytheism of their

kinsmen, they had not rejected the doctrine that
the stars in their courses affect the fortunes of
men. We know that among the Jews, probably
the direct descendants of the shepherd-chiefs who
visited Cheops, and certainly close kinsmen of
theirs, and akin to them also in their monotheism,
the belief in astrology was never regarded as a
superstition. In fact, we can trace very clearly in
the books relating to this people, that they believed
confidently in the influences of the heavenly bodies.
Doubtless the visitors of King Cheops shared the
belief of their Chaldæan kinsmen that astrology
is a true science, 'founded' indeed (as Bacon ex-
presses their views) 'not in reason and physical
contemplations, but in the direct experience and
observation of past ages.' Josephus records the
Jewish tradition (though not as a tradition but as
a fact) that 'our first father, Adam, was instructed
in astrology by divine inspiration,' and that Seth
so excelled in the science, that, 'foreseeing the
Flood and the destruction of the world thereby, he
engraved the fundamental principles of his art
(astrology) in hieroglyphical emblems, for the
benefit of after ages, on two pillars of brick and
stone.' He says, farther on, that the Patriarch
Abraham, ' having learned the art in Chaldæa, when
he journeyed into Egypt taught the Egyptians the

sciences of arithmetic and astrology.' Indeed,
the stranger called Philitis by Herodotus may, for
aught that appears, have been Abraham himself;
for it is generally agreed that the word Philitis
indicated the race and country of the visitors,
regarded by the Egyptians as of Philistine descent
and arriving from Palestine. However, I am in
no way concerned to show that the shepherd-astronomers who induced Cheops to build the Great
Pyramid were even contemporaries of Abraham
and Melchizedek. What seems sufficiently obvious
is all that I care to maintain—namely, that these
shepherd-astronomers were of Chaldæan birth and
training, and therefore astrologers, though, unlike
their Chaldæan kinsmen, they rejected Sabaism or
star-worship, and taught the belief in one only
Deity.

Now, if these visitors were astrologers, who
persuaded Cheops, and were honestly convinced
themselves, that they could predict the events of
any man's life by the Chaldæan method of casting
nativities, we can readily understand many circumstances connected with the pyramids which have
hitherto seemed inexplicable. The pyramid built
by a king would no longer be regarded as having
reference to his death and burial, but to his birth

and life, though after his death it might receive his body. Each king would require to have his own nativity-pyramid, built with due symbolical reference to the special celestial influences affecting his fortunes. Every portion of the work would have to be carried out under special conditions, determined according to the mysterious influences ascribed to the different planets and their varying positions—

> Now high, now low, then hid,
> Progressive, retrograde, or standing still.

If the work had been intended only to afford the means of predicting the king's future, the labour would have been regarded by the monarch as well bestowed. But astrology involved much more than the mere prediction of future events. Astrologers claimed the power of ruling the planets—that is, of course, not of ruling the motions of those bodies, but of providing against evil influences or strengthening good influences which they supposed the celestial orbs to exert in particular aspects. Thus we can understand that while the mere basement layers of the pyramid would have served for the process of casting the royal nativity, with due mystic observances, the further progress of building the pyramid would supply the necessary means and indications for ruling the planets most potent in their influence upon the royal career.

Remembering the mysterious influence which astrologers ascribed to special numbers, figures, positions, and so forth, the care with which the Great Pyramid was so proportioned as to indicate particular astronomical and mathematical relations is at once explained. The four sides of the square base were carefully placed with reference to the cardinal points, precisely like the four sides of the ordinary square scheme of nativity.[1]   The eastern

---

[1] The language of the modern Zadkiels and Raphaels, though meaningless and absurd in itself, yet, as assuredly derived from the astrology of the oldest times, may here be quoted.   (It certainly was not invented to give support to the theory I am at present advocating.)   Thus runs the jargon of the tribe : 'In order to illustrate plainly to the reader what astrologers mean by the "houses of heaven," it is proper for him to bear in mind the four cardinal points.   The eastern, facing the rising sun, has at its centre the first grand angle or first house, termed the Horoscope or ascendant. The northern, opposite the region where the sun is at midnight, or the *cusp* of the lower heaven or nadir, is the Imum Cœli, and has at its centre the fourth house.   The western, facing the setting sun, has at its centre the third grand angle or seventh house or descendant.   And lastly, the southern, facing the noonday sun, has at its centre the astrologer's tenth house, or Mid-heaven, the most powerful angle, or house of honour.'   'And although,' proceeds the modern astrologer, 'we cannot in the ethereal blue discern these lines or terminating divisions, both reason and experience assure us that they certainly exist ; therefore the astrologer has certain grounds for the choice of his four angular houses' (out of twelve in all), 'which, resembling the palpable demonstration they afford, are in the astral science esteemed the most powerful of the whole.'— Raphael's *Manual of Astrology*.

side faced the Ascendant, the southern faced the
Mid-heaven, the western faced the Descendant,
and the northern faced the Imum Cœli. Again,
we can understand that the architects would have
made a circuit of the base correspond in length
with the number of days in the year—a relation
which, according to Prof. P. Smyth, is fulfilled in
this manner, that the four sides contain one hundred times as many pyramid inches as there are
days in the year. The pyramid inch, again, is
itself mystically connected with astronomical relations, for its length is equal to the five hundred
millionth part of the earth's diameter, to a degree
of exactness corresponding well with what we
might expect Chaldæan astronomers to attain.
Prof. Smyth, indeed, believes that it was exactly
equal to that proportion of the earth's polar diameter—a view which would correspond with his
theory that the architects of the Great Pyramid
were assisted by divine inspiration ; but what is
certainly known about the sacred cubit, which contained twenty-five of these inches, corresponds
better with the diameter which the Chaldæan
astronomers, if they worked very carefully, would
have deduced from observations made in their
own country, on the supposition which they would
naturally have made that the earth is a perfect

globe, not compressed at the poles. It is not, indeed, at all certain that the sacred cubit bore any reference to the earth's dimensions; but this seems tolerably well made out—that the sacred cubit was about twenty-five inches in length, and that the circuit of the pyramid's base contained a hundred inches for every day of the year. Relations such as these are precisely what we might expect to find in buildings having an astrological significance. Similarly, it would correspond well with the mysticism of astrology that the pyramid should be so proportioned as to make the height be the radius of a circle whose circumference would equal the circuit of the pyramid's base. Again, that long slant tunnel, leading downwards from the pyramid's northern face, would at once find a meaning in this astrological theory. The slant tunnel pointed to the pole-star of Cheops's time when due north below the true pole of the heavens. This circumstance had no observational utility. It could afford no indication of time, because a pole-star moves very slowly, and the pole-star of Cheops's day must have been in view through that tunnel for more than an hour at a time. But, apart from the mystical significance which an astrologer would attribute to such a relation, it may be shown that this slant tunnel is precisely what the astrologer would require in order to get the horoscope correctly.

Another consideration remains to be mentioned which, while strengthening the astrological theory of the pyramids, may bring us even nearer to the true aim of those who planned and built these structures.

It is known that the Chaldæans from the earliest times pursued the study of alchemy in connection with astrol, not hoping to discover the philosopher's ston by chemical investigations alone, but by carry out such investigations under special celest influence. The hope of achieving this disco by which he wo at once have had the means of acquiring illimitable wealth, would of itself account for the fact that Cheops expended so much labour and material in the erection of the Great Pyramid, seeing that, of necessity, success in the search for the philosopher's stone would be a main feature of his fortunes, and would therefore be astrologically indicated in his nativity-pyramid, or perhaps even be secured by following mystical observances proper for ruling his planets.

The elixir of life may also have been among the objects which the builders of the pyramids hoped to discover.

It may be noticed, as a somewhat significant circumstance, that, in the account given by Ibn Abd Alkokm of the contents of the various pyramids, those assigned to the Great Pyramid relate entirely to astrology and associated mysteries. It is, of course, clear that Abd Alkokm drew largely on his imagination. Yet it seems probable that there was also some basis of tradition for his ideas. And certainly one would suppose that, as he assigned a treasurer to the East pyramid ('a statue of black agate, his eyes open and shining, sitting on a throne with a lance'), he would have credited the building with treasure also, had not some tradition taught otherwise. But he says that King Saurid placed in the East pyramid, not treasures, but 'divers celestial spheres and stars, and what they severally operate in their aspects, and the perfumes which are to be used to them, and the books which treat of these matters.'[1]

[1] Arabian writers give the following account of Egyptian progress in astrology and the mystical arts : Nacrawasch, the progenitor of Misraim, was the first Egyptian prince, and the first of the magicians who excelled in astrology and enchantment. Retiring into Egypt with his family of eighty persons, he built Essous, the most ancient city of Egypt, and commenced the first dynasty of Misraimitish princes, who excelled as cabalists, diviners, and in the mystic arts generally. The most celebrated of the race were Nacrasch, who first represented by images the twelve signs of the zodiac ; Gharnak, who openly described the arts before kept secret ; Hersall, who first worshipped idols ; Sehlouk, who worshipped the

But, after all, it must be admitted that the strongest evidence in favour of the astrological theory of the pyramids is to be found in the circumstance that all other theories seem untenable. The pyramids were undoubtedly erected for some purpose which was regarded by their builders as most important. This purpose certainly related to the personal fortunes of the kingly builders. It was worth an enormous outlay of money, labour, and material. This purpose was such, furthermore, that each king required to have his own pyramid. It was in some way associated with astronomy, for the pyramids are built with most accurate reference to celestial aspects. It also had its mathematical and mystical bearings, seeing that the pyramids exhibit mathematical and symbolical peculiarities not belonging to their essentially structural requirements. And lastly, the erection of the pyramids was in some way connected with the arrival of certain learned persons from Palestine, and presumably of Chaldæan origin. All these circumstances accord well with the theory I have advanced ; while only some of

sun ; Saurid (King Saurid of Ibn Abd Alkokm's account), who erected the first pyramids and invented the magic mirror ; and Pharaoh, the last king of the dynasty, whose name was afterwards taken as a kingly title, as Cæsar later became a general imperial title.

them, and these not the most characteristic, accord with any of the other theories. Moreover, no fact known respecting the pyramids or their builders is inconsistent with the astrological theory. On the whole, then, if it cannot be regarded as demonstrated (in its general bearing, of course, for we cannot expect any theory about the pyramids to be established in minute details), the astrological theory may fairly be described as having a greater degree of probability in its favour than any hitherto advanced.

CHAPTER II.

THE RELIGION OF THE GREAT PYRAMID.

DURING the last few years a new sect has appeared which, though as yet small in numbers, is full of zeal and fervour. The faith professed by this sect may be called the religion of the Great Pyramid, the chief article of their creed being the doctrine that that remarkable edifice was built for the purpose of revealing—in the fulness of time, now nearly accomplished — certain noteworthy truths to the human race. The founder of the pyramid religion is described by one of the present leaders of the sect as 'the late worthy John Taylor, of Gower Street, London;' but hitherto the chief prophets of the new faith have been in this country Professor Smyth, Astronomer Royal for Scotland, and in France the Abbé Moigno. I propose to examine here some of the facts most confidently urged by pyramidalists in support of their views.

But it will be well first to indicate briefly the

doctrines of the new faith. They may be thus presented :—

The Great Pyramid was erected, it would seem, under the instructions of a certain Semitic king, probably no other than Melchizedek. By supernatural means, the architects were instructed to place the pyramid in latitude 30° north ; to select for its figure that of a square pyramid, carefully oriented ; to employ for their unit of length the sacred cubit corresponding to the 20,000,000th part of the earth's polar axis ; and to make the side of the square base equal to just so many of these sacred cubits as there are days and parts of a day in a year. They were further, by supernatural help, enabled to square the circle, and symbolised their victory over this problem by making the pyramid's height bear to the perimeter of the base the ratio which the radius of a circle bears to the circumference. Moreover, the great processional period, in which the earth's axis gyrates like that of some mighty top around the perpendicular to the ecliptic, was communicated to the builders with a degree of accuracy far exceeding that of the best modern determinations, and they were instructed to symbolise that relation in the dimensions of the pyramid's base. A value of the sun's distance more accurate by far than modern astronomers have

obtained (even since the last transit of Venus) wa/
imparted to them, and they embodied that dimension in the height of the pyramid. Other results
which modern science has achieved, but which by
merely human means the architects of the pyramid could not have obtained, were also supernaturally communicated to them ; so that the true mean
density of the earth, her true shape, the configuration of land and water, the mean temperature of
the earth's surface, and so forth, were either symbolised in the Great Pyramid's position, or in the
shape and dimensions of its exterior and interior.
In the pyramid also were preserved the true,
because supernaturally communicated, standards of
length, area, capacity, weight, density, heat, time,
and money. The pyramid also indicated, by certain
features of its interior structure, that when it was
built the holy influences of the Pleiades were
exerted from a most effective position—the meridian through the points where the ecliptic and
equator intersect. And as the pyramid thus significantly refers to the past, so also it indicates the
future history of the earth, especially in showing
when and where the millennium is to begin.
Lastly, the apex or crowning stone of the pyramid
was no other than the antitype of that stone of
stumbling and rock of offence, rejected by builders

who knew not its true use, until it was finally placed as the chief stone of the corner. Whence naturally, 'whosoever shall fall upon it'—that is, upon the pyramid religion—'shall be broken ; but on whomsoever it shall fall it will grind him to powder.'

If we examine the relations actually presented by the Great Pyramid—its geographical position, dimensions, shape, and internal structure—without hampering ourselves with the tenets of the new faith on the one hand, or on the other with any serious anxiety to disprove them, we shall find much to suggest that the builders of the pyramid were ingenious mathematicians, who had made some progress in astronomy, though not so much as they had made in the mastery of mechanical and scientific difficulties.

The first point to be noticed is the geographical position of the Great Pyramid, so far, at least, as this position affects the aspect of the heavens, viewed from the pyramid as from an observatory. Little importance, I conceive, can be attached to purely geographical relations in considering the pyramid's position. Professor Smyth notes that the pyramid is peculiarly placed with respect to the mouth of the Nile, standing ' at the southern apex of the Delta-land of Egypt.' This region being shaped like a fan, the pyramid, set at the part corresponding to the handle, was, he considers, 'that monument pure and undefiled in its religion through an idolatrous land, alluded to by Isaiah; the monument which was both " an altar to the Lord in the midst of the land of Egypt, and a pillar at the border thereof," and destined withal to become a witness in the latter days, and before the consummation of all things, to the same Lord, and to what He hath purposed upon mankind.' Still more fanciful are some other notes upon the pyramid's geographical position: as (i.) that there is more land along the meridian of the pyramid than on any other all the world round ; (ii.) that there is more land in the latitude of the pyramid than in any other; and (iii.) that the pyramid territory of Lower Egypt is at the centre of the dry land habitable by man all the world over.

It does not seem to be noticed by those who call our attention to these points that such coincidences prove too much. It might be regarded as not a mere accident that the Great Pyramid stands at the centre of the arc of shore-line along which lie the outlets of the Nile ; or it might be regarded as not a mere coincidence that the Great Pyramid stands at the central point of all the habitable land-surface of the globe ; or again, any one of the other

relations above mentioned might be regarded as
something more than a mere coincidence. But if,
instead of taking only one or other of these four
relations, we take all four of them, or even any two
of them, together, we must regard peculiarities of
the earth's configuration as the result of special
design which certainly have not hitherto been so
regarded by geographers. For instance, if it was
by special design that the pyramid was placed at
the centre of the Nile delta, and also by special
design that the pyramid was placed at the centre
of the land-surface of the earth, if these two relations are each so exactly fulfilled as to render the
idea of mere accidental coincidence inadmissible,
then it follows, of necessity, that it is through no
merely accidental coincidence that the centre of
the Nile delta lies at the centre of the land-surface
of the earth ; in other words, the shore-line along
which lie the mouths of the Nile has been
designedly curved so as to have its centre so
placed. And so of the other relations. The very
fact that the four conditions *can* be fulfilled simultaneously is evidence that a coincidence of the sort
may result from mere accident.[1] Indeed, the

[1] Of course it may be argued that nothing in the world is the
result of *mere* accident, and some may assert that even matters
which are commonly regarded as entirely casual have been specially
designed. It would not be easy to draw the precise line dividing

peculiarity of geographical position which really seems to have been in the thoughts of the pyramid architects, introduces yet a fifth condition which, by accident could be fulfilled along with the four others :—

It would seem that the builders of the pyramid were anxious to place it in latitude 30°, as closely as their means of observation permitted. Let us consider what ·result they achieved, and the evidence thus afforded respecting their skill and scientific attainments. In our own time, of course, the astronomer has no difficulty in determining with great exactness the position of any given latitude-parallel. But at the time when the Great Pyramid was built it must have been a matter of very serious difficulty to determine the position of any required latitude-parallel with a great degree of exactitude. The most obvious way of dealing with the difficulty would have been by observing the length of shadows thrown by upright posts at noon in spring and autumn. In latitude 30° north, the sun at noon in spring (or, to speak precisely, on the day of the vernal equinox) is just twice as far from the horizon as he is from the point vertically overhead ;

events which all men would regard as to all intents and purposes accidental from those which some men would regard as results of special providence. But common sense draws a sufficient distinction, at least for our present purpose.

and if a pointed post were set exactly upright at true noon (supposed to occur at the moment of the vernal or autumnal equinox), the shadow of the post would be exactly half as long as a line drawn from the top of the pole to the end of the shadow. But observations based on this principle would have presented many difficulties to the architects of the pyramid. The sun not being a point of light, but a globe, the shadow of a pointed rod does not end in a well-defined point. The moment of true noon, which is not the same as ordinary or civil noon, never does agree exactly with the time of the vernal or autumnal equinox, and may be removed from it by any interval of time not exceeding twelve hours. And there are many other circumstances which would lead astronomers like those who doubtless presided over the scientific preparations for building the Great Pyramid, to prefer a means of determining the latitude depending on another principle. The stellar heavens would afford practically unchanging indications for their purpose. The stars being all carried round the pole of the heavens, as if they were fixed points in the interior of a hollow revolving sphere, it becomes possible to determine the position of the pole of the star sphere, even though no bright conspicuous star actually occupies that point. Any bright star close by the pole is seen to revolve in a very small circle, whose centre is the pole itself. Such a star is our present so-called pole-star ; and, though in the days when the Great Pyramid was built, that star was not near the pole, another, and probably a brighter star, lay near enough to the pole [1] to serve as a pole-star, and to indicate by its circling motion the position of the actual pole of the heavens. This was at that time, and for many subsequent centuries, the leading star of the great constellation called the Dragon.

The pole of the heavens, we know, varies in position according to the latitude of the observer. At the north pole it is exactly overhead ; at the

[1] This star, called *Thuban* from the Arabian *al-Thúban*, the Dragon, is now not very bright, being rated at barely above the fourth magnitude, but it was formerly the brightest star of the constellation, as its name indicates. Bayer also assigned to it the first letter of the Greek alphabet ; though this is not absolutely decisive evidence that so late as his day it retained its superiority over the second magnitude stars to which Bayer assigned the second and third Greek letters. In the year 2790 B.C., or thereabouts, the star was at its nearest to the true north pole of the heavens, the diameter of the little circle in which it then moved being considerably less than one-fourth the apparent diameter of the moon. At that time the star must have seemed to all ordinary observation an absolutely fixed centre, round which all the other stars revolved. At the time when the pyramid was built this star was about sixty times farther removed from the true pole, revolving in a circle whose apparent diameter was about seven times as great as the moon's. Yet it would still be regarded as a very useful pole-star, especially as there are very few conspicuous stars in its neighbourhood.

equator the poles of the heavens are both on the horizon: and, as the observer travels from the equator towards the north or south pole of the earth, the corresponding pole of the heavens rises higher and higher above the horizon. In latitude 30° north, or one-third of the way from the equator to the pole, the pole of the heavens is raised one-third of the way from the horizon to the point vertically overhead ; and when this is the case the observer knows that he is in latitude 30°. The builders of the Great Pyramid, with the almost constantly clear skies of Egypt, may reasonably be supposed to have adopted this means of determining the true position of that thirtieth parallel on which they appear to have designed to place the great building they were about to erect.

It so happens that we have the means of forming an opinion on the question whether they used one method or the other ; whether they employed the sun or the stars to guide them to the geographical position they required. In fact, were it not for this circumstance, I should not have thought it worth while to discuss the qualities of either method. It will presently be seen that the discussion bears importantly on the opinion we are to form of the skill and attainments of the pyramid architects.

E 2

Every celestial object is raised above its true
position by the refractive power of our atmosphere,
being most raised when nearest the horizon and least
when nearest the point vertically overhead. This
effect is so marked on bodies close to the horizon
that if the astronomers of the pyramid times had
observed the sun, moon, and stars attentively when
so placed, they could not have failed to discover
the peculiarity. Probably, however, though they
noted the time of rising and setting of the celestial
bodies, they only made instrumental observations
upon them when these bodies were high in the
heavens. If so they remained ignorant of the
refractive powers of the air.[1] Now, if they had
determined the position of the thirtieth parallel of
latitude by observations of the noonday sun (in
spring or autumn), then since, owing to refraction,
they would have judged the sun to be higher than
he really was, it follows that they would have
supposed the latitude of any station from which
they observed to be lower than it really was. For
the lower the latitude the higher is the noonday
sun at any given season. Thus, when really in
latitude 30° they would have supposed themselves

---

[1] Even that skilful astronomer Hipparchus, who may be justly
called the father of observational astronomy, overlooked this
peculiarity, which Ptolemy would seem to have been the first
to recognise.

in a latitude lower than 30°, and would have
travelled a little farther north to find the proper
place, as they would have supposed, for erecting
the Great Pyramid. On the other hand, if they
determined the place from observations of the
movements of stars near the pole of the heavens,
they would make an error of a precisely opposite
nature. For, the higher the latitude the higher is
the pole of the heavens; and refraction, therefore,
which apparently raises the pole of the heavens,
gives to a station the appearance of being in a
higher latitude than it really is, so that the observer
would consider he was in latitude 30° north when
in reality somewhat south of that latitude. We
have only then to inquire whether the Great Pyramid was set north or south of latitude 30°, to
ascertain whether the pyramid architects observed
the noonday sun or circumpolar stars to determine
their latitude; always assuming (as we reasonably
may) that those architects did propose to set the
pyramid in that particular latitude, and that they
were able to make very accurate observations of
the apparent positions of the celestial bodies, but
that they were not acquainted with the refractive
effects of the atmosphere. The answer comes in
no doubtful terms. The centre of the Great Pyramid's base lies about one mile and a third *south* of

the thirtieth parallel of latitude ; and from this position the pole of the heavens, as raised by refraction, would appear to be very near indeed to the required position. In fact, if the pyramid had been set about half a mile still farther south the pole would have *seemed* just right.

Of course, such an explanation as I have here suggested appears altogether heretical to the pyra-midalists. According to them the pyramid archi-tects knew perfectly well where the true thirtieth parallel lay, and knew also all that modern science has discovered about refraction ; but set the pyra-mid south of the true parallel and north of the position where refraction would just have made the apparent elevation of the pole correct, simply in order that the pyramid might correspond as nearly as possible to each of two conditions, whereof both could not be fulfilled at once. The pyramid would indeed, they say, have been set even more closely midway between the true and the apparent parallels of 30° north, but that the Jeezeh hill on which it is set does not afford a rock foundation any farther north. ' So very close,' says Professor Smyth, ' was the great pyramid placed to the northern brink of its hill, that the edges of the cliff might have broken off under the terrible pressure had not the builders banked up there, most firmly, the immense mounds of rubbish which came from their work, and which Strabo looked so particularly for 1,800 years ago, but could not find.   Here they were, however, and still are, utilised in enabling the Great Pyramid to stand on the very utmost verge of its commanding hill, within the limits of the *two* required latitudes, as well as over the centre of the land's physical and radial formation, and at the same time on the sure and proverbially wise foundation of rock.'

The next circumstance to be noted in the position of the Great Pyramid (as of all the pyramids) is that the sides are carefully oriented.   This, like the approximation to a particular latitude, must be regarded as an astronomical rather than a geographical relation.   The accuracy with which the orientation has been effected will serve to show how far the builders had mastered the methods of astronomical observation by which orientation was to be secured.   The problem was not so simple as might be supposed by those who are not acquainted with the way in which the cardinal points are correctly determined.   By solar observations, or rather by the observations of shadows cast by vertical shafts before and after noon, the direction of the meridian, or north and south line, can theoretically be ascertained.   But probably in this case, as in determining the latitude, the builders took the stars for their guide. The pole of the heavens would mark the true north ; and equally the pole-star, when below or above the pole, would give the true north, but, of course, most conveniently when below the pole. Nor is it difficult to see how the builders would make use of the pole-star for this purpose. From the middle of the northern side of the intended base they would bore a slant passage tending always from the position of the pole-star at its lower meridional passage, that star at each successive return to that position serving to direct their progress ; while its small range east and west of the pole, would enable them most accurately to determine the star's true mid-point below the pole ; that is, the true north. When they had thus obtained a slant tunnel pointing truly to the meridian, and had carried it down to a point nearly below the middle of the proposed square base, they could, from the middle of the base, bore vertically downwards, until by rough calculation they were near the lower end of the slant tunnel ; or both tunnels could be made at the same time. Then a subter-ranean chamber would be opened out from the slant tunnel. The vertical boring, which need not be wider than necessary to allow a plumb-line to be suspended down it, would enable the architects to determine the point vertically below the point of suspension. The slant tunnel would give the direction of the true north, either from that point or from a point at some known small distance east or west of that point.[1] Thus, a line from some ascertained point near the mouth of the vertical boring to the mouth of the slant tunnel would lie due north and south, and serve as the required guide for the orientation of the pyramid's base. If this base extended beyond the opening of the slant tunnel, then, by continuing this tunnelling through the base tiers of the pyramid, the means would be obtained of correcting the orientation.

This, I say, would be the course naturally suggested to astronomical architects who had determined the latitude in the manner described above. It may even be described as the only very accurate method available before the telescope had been invented. So that if the accuracy of the orientation appears to be greater than could be obtained by the shadow method, the natural

---

[1] It would only be by a lucky accident, of course, that the direction of the slant tunnel's axis and that of the vertical from the selected central point would lie in the same vertical plane. The object of the tunnelling would, in fact, be to determine how far apart the vertical planes through these points lay, and the odds would be great against the result proving to be zero.

inference, even in the absence of corroborative evidence, would be that the stellar method, and no other, had been employed. Now, in 1779, Nouet, by refined observations, found the error of orientation measured by less than 20 minutes of arc, corresponding roughly to a displacement of the corners by about $37\frac{1}{2}$ inches from their true position, as supposed to be determined from the centre; or to a displacement of a southern corner by 53 inches on an east and west line from a point due south of the corresponding northern corner. This error, for a base length of 9,140 inches, would not be serious, being only one inch in about five yards (when estimated in the second way). Yet the result is not quite worthy of the praise given to it by Professor Smyth. He himself, however, by much more exact observations, with an excellent altazimuth, reduced the alleged error from 20 minutes to only $4\frac{1}{2}$, or to 9-40ths of its formerly supposed value. This made the total displacement of a southern corner from the true meridian through the corresponding northern corner, almost exactly one foot, or one inch in about twenty-one yards—a degree of accuracy rendering it practically certain that some stellar method was used in orienting the base.

Now there *is* a slanting tunnel occupying precisely the position of the tunnel which should, according to this view, have been formed in order accurately to orient the pyramid's base, assuming that the time of the building of the pyramid corresponded with one of the epochs when the star Alpha Draconis was distant 3° 42′ from the pole of the heavens. In other words, there is a slant tunnel directed northwards and upwards from a point deep down below the middle of the pyramid's base, and inclined 26° 17′ to the horizon, the elevation of Alpha Draconis at its lower culmination when 3° 42′ from the pole. The last epoch when the star was thus placed was *circiter* 2160 B.C.; the epoch next before that was 3440 B.C. Between these two we should have to choose, on the hypothesis that the slant tunnel was really directed to that star when the foundations of the pyramid were laid. For the next epoch before the earlier of the two named was about 28000 B.C., and the pyramid's date cannot have been more remote than 4000 B.C.

The slant tunnel, while admirably fulfilling the requirements suggested, seems altogether unsuited for any other. Its transverse height (that is, its width in a direction perpendicular to its upper and lower faces) did not amount to quite four feet; its breadth was not quite three feet and a half. It

was, therefore, not well fitted for an entrance passage to the subterranean chamber immediately
under the apex of the pyramid (with which
chamber it communicates in the manner suggested
by the above theory). It could not have been
intended to be used for observing meridian transits
of the stars in order to determine sidereal time;
for close circumpolar stars, by reason of their slow
motion, are the least suited of all for such a
purpose. As Professor Smyth says, in arguing
against this suggested use of the star, 'no observer
in his senses, in any existing observatory, when
seeking to obtain the time, would observe the
transit of a circumpolar star for anything else than
*to get the direction of the meridian to adjust his
instrument by.*' (The italics are his.) It is precisely
such a purpose (the adjustment, however, not of
an instrument, but of the entire structure of the
pyramid itself), that I have suggested for this
remarkable passage — this 'cream-white, stone-
lined, long tube,' where it traverses the masonry of
the pyramid, and below that dug through the solid
rock to a distance of more than 350 feet.

Let us next consider the dimensions of the
square base thus carefully placed in latitude 30°
north, to the best of the builders' power, with sides
carefully oriented.

It seems highly probable that, whatever special purpose the pyramid was intended to fulfil, a subordinate idea of the builders would have been to represent symbolically, in the proportions of the building, such mathematical and astronomical relations as they were acquainted with. From what we know by tradition of the men of the remote time when the pyramid was built, and what we can infer from the ideas of those who inherited, however remotely, the modes of thought of the earliest astronomers and mathematicians, we can well believe that they would look with superstitious reverence on special figures, proportions, numbers, and so forth. Apart from this, they may have had a quasi-scientific desire to make a lasting record of their discoveries, and of the collected knowledge of their time.

It seems altogether possible, then, that the smaller unit of measurement used by the builders of the Great Pyramid was intended, as Professor Smyth thinks, to be equal to the 500,000,000th part of the earth's diameter, determined from their geodetical observations. It was perfectly within the power of mechanicians and mathematicians so experienced as they undoubtedly were—the pyramid attests so much—to measure with considerable accuracy the length of a degree of latitude. They could not possibly (always setting aside the theory of divine inspiration) have known anything about the compression of the earth's globe, and therefore could not have intended, as Professor Smyth supposes, to have had the 500,000,000th part of the earth's polar axis, as distinguished from any other, for their unit of length. But if they made observations in or near latitude 30° north on the supposition that the earth is a globe, their probable error would exceed the difference even between the earth's polar and equatorial diameters. Both differences are largely exceeded by the range of difference among the estimates of the actual length of the sacred cubit, supposed to have contained twenty-five of these smaller units. And again, the length of the pyramid base-side, on which Smyth bases his own estimate of the sacred cubit, has been variously estimated, the largest measure being 9,168 inches, and the lowest 9,100 inches. The fundamental theory of the pyramidalists, that the sacred cubit was exactly one 20,000,000th part of the earth's polar diameter, and that the side of the base contained as many cubits and parts of a cubit as there are days and parts of a day in the tropical year (or year of seasons), requires that the length of the side should be 9,140 inches, lying between the limits indicated, but still so widely removed from either that it would appear very unsafe to base a theory on the supposition that the exact length is or was 9,140 inches. If the measures 9,168 inches and 9,110 inches were inferior, and several excellent measures made by practised observers ranged around the length 9,140 inches, the case would be different. But the best recent measures gave respectively 9,110 and 9,130 inches; and Smyth exclaims against the unfairness of Sir H. James in taking 9,120 as 'therefore the [probable] true length of the side of the great pyramid when perfect,' calling this ' a dishonourable shelving of the honourable older observers with their larger results.' The only other measures, besides these two, are two by Colonel Howard Vyse and by the French *savants*, giving respectively 9,168 and 9,163·44 inches. The pyramidalists consider 9,140 inches a fair mean value from these four. The natural inference, however, is, that the pyramid base is not now in a condition to be satisfactorily measured ; and assuredly no such reliance can be placed on the mean value 9,140 inches that, on the strength of it, we should believe what otherwise would be utterly incredible, viz. that the builders of the Great Pyramid knew 'both the size and shape of the earth exactly.' ' Humanly, or by human science, finding it out in that age was, of course, utterly impossible,' says Professor Smyth. But he is so confident of the average value derived from widely conflicting base measures as to assume that this value, not being humanly discoverable, was of necessity 'attributable to God and to His divine inspiration.' We may agree, in fine, with Smyth, that the builders of the pyramid knew the earth to be a globe ; that they took for their measure of length the sacred cubit, which, by their earth measures, they made very fairly approximate to the 20,000,000th part of the earth's mean diameter; but there seems no reason whatever for supposing (even if the supposition were not antecedently of its very nature inadmissible) that they knew anything about the compression of the earth, or that they had measured a degree of latitude in their own place with very wonderful accuracy.[1]

[1] It may, perhaps, occur to the reader to inquire what diameter of the earth, supposed to be a perfect sphere, would be derived from a degree of latitude measured with absolute accuracy near latitude 30°. A degree of latitude measured in polar regions would indicate a diameter greater even than the equatorial ; one measured in equatorial regions would indicate a diameter less even than the polar. Near latitude 30° the measurement of a degree of latitude would indicate a diameter very nearly equal to the true polar diameter of the earth. In fact, if it could be proved that the builders of the pyramid used for their unit of length an exact subdivision of the polar diameter, the inference would be that, while the coincidence itself was merely accidental, their measurement of a degree of latitude in their own country had been singularly accurate. By an approximate calculation I find that, taking the earth's compression at $1 \div 300$, the

But here a very singular coincidence may be noticed, or rather is forced upon our notice by the pyramidalists, who strangely enough recognise in it fresh evidence of design, while the unbeliever finds in it proof that coincidences are no sure evidence of design. The side of the pyramid containing 365¼ times the sacred cubit of 25 pyramid inches, it follows that the diagonal of the base contains 12,912 such inches, and the two diagonals together contain 25,824 pyramid inches, or almost exactly as many inches as there are years in the great precessional period. 'No one whatever amongst men,' says Professor Smyth after recording various estimates of the precessional period, 'from his own or school knowledge, knew anything about such a phenomenon, until Hipparchus, some 1,900 years after the Great Pyramid's foundation, had a glimpse of the fact ; and yet it had been ruling the heavens for ages, and was recorded in Ghizeh's ancient structure.' To minds not moved to most energetic forgetfulness by the spirit of faith, it would appear that when a square base had

diameter of the earth, estimated from the accurate measurement of a degree of latitude in the neighbourhood of the Great Pyramid, would have made the sacred cubit—taken at one 20,000,000th of the diameter—equal to 24·98 British inches ; a closer approximation than Professor Smyth's to the estimated mean probable value of the sacred cubit.

F

been decided upon, and its dimensions fixed, with reference to the earth's diameter and the year, the diagonals of the square base were determined also; and, if it so chanced that they corresponded with some other perfectly independent relation, the fact was not to be credited to the architects. Moreover it is manifest that the closeness of such a coincidence suggests grave doubts how far other coincidences can be relied upon as evidence of design. It seems, for instance, altogether likely that the architects of the pyramid took the sacred cubit equal to one 20,000,000th part of the earth's diameter for their chief unit of length, and intentionally assigned to the side of the pyramid's square base a length of just so many cubits as there are days in the year; and the closeness of the coincidence between the measured length and that indicated by this theory strengthens the idea that this was the builders' purpose. But when we find that an even closer coincidence immediately presents itself, which manifestly is a coincidence *only*, the force of the evidence before derived from mere coincidence is *pro tanto* shaken. For consider what this new coincidence really means. Its nature may be thus indicated :—Take the number of days in the year, multiply that number by 50, and increase the result in the same degree that the diagonal of a square exceeds the side—then the resulting number represents very approximately the number of years in the great precessional period. The error, according to the best modern estimates, is about one-575th part of the true period. This is, of course, a merely accidental coincidence, for there is no connection whatever in nature between the earth's period of rotation, the shape of a square, and the earth's period of gyration. Yet this merely accidental coincidence is very much closer than the other supposed to be designed could be proved to be. It is clear, then, that mere coincidence is a very unsafe evidence of design.

Of course the pyramidalists find a ready reply to such reasoning. They argue that, in the first place, it may have been by express design that the period of the earth's rotation was made to bear this particular relation to the period of gyration in the mighty precessional movement; which is much as though one should say that by express design the height of Monte Rosa contains as many feet as there are miles in the 6,000th part of the sun's distance.[1] Then, they urge, the architects were

---

[1] It is, however, almost impossible to mark any limits to what may be regarded as evidence of design by a coincidence-hunter. I quote the following from the late Professor De Morgan's *Budget of Paradoxes*. Having mentioned that 7 occurs less frequently than

not bound to have a square base for the pyramid ; they might have had an oblong or a triangular base, and so forth—all which accords very ill with the enthusiastic language in which the selection of a square base had on other accounts been applauded.

Next let us consider the height of the pyramid. According to the best modern measurements, it would seem that the height when the pyramid terminated above in a pointed apex, must have been about 486 feet. And from the comparison of the best estimates of the base side with the best estimates of the height, it seems very likely indeed that the intention of the builders was to make the height bear to the perimeter of the base the same ratio which the radius of a circle bears to the circumference. Remembering the range

any other digit in the number expressing the ratio of circumference to diameter of a circle, he proceeds : ' A correspondent of my friend Piazzi Smyth notices that 3 is the number of most frequency, and that $3\frac{1}{7}$ is the nearest approximation to it in simple digits. Professor Smyth, whose work on Egypt is paradox of a very high order, backed by a great quantity of useful labour, the results of which will be made available by those who do not receive the paradoxes, is inclined to see confirmation for some of his theory in these phenomena.' In passing, I may mention as the most singular of these accidental digit relations which I have yet noticed, that in the first 110 digits of the square root of 2, the number 7 occurs more than twice as often as either 5 or 9, which each occur eight times, 1 and 2 occurring each nine times, and 7 occurring no less than eighteen times.

of difference in the base measures, it might be supposed that the exactness of the approximation to
this ratio could not be determined very satisfactorily. But as certain casing stones have been
discovered which indicate with considerable exactness the slope of the original plane-surfaces of the
pyramid, the ratio of the height to the side of the
base may be regarded as much more satisfactorily
determined than the actual value of either dimension. Of course the pyramidalists claim a degree
of precision indicating a most accurate knowledge
of the ratio between the diameter and the circumference of a circle ; and the angle of the only
casing stone measured being diversely estimated
at 51° 50′ and 51° 52¼′, they consider 50° 51′ 14·3″
the true value, and infer that the builders regarded
the ratio as 3·14159 to 1. The real fact is, that
the modern estimates of the dimensions of the
casing stones (which, by the way, ought to agree
better if these stones are as well made as stated)
indicate the values 3·1439228 and 3·1396740 for
the ratio ; and all we can say is, that the ratio
really used lay *probably* between these limits,
though it may have been outside either. Now the
approximation of either is not remarkably close.
It requires no mathematical knowledge at all to
determine the circumference of a circle much more

exactly. 'I thought it very strange,' wrote a circle-squarer once to De Morgan ('Budget of Paradoxes,' p. 389), 'that so many great scholars in all ages should have failed in finding the true ratio, and have been determined to try myself.' 'I have been informed,' proceeds De Morgan, 'that this trial makes the diameter to the circumference as 64 to 201, giving the ratio equal to 3·1410625 exactly. The result was obtained by the discoverer in three weeks after he first heard of the existence of the difficulty. This quadrator has since published a little slip and entered it at Stationers' Hall. He says he has done it by actual measurement; and I hear from a private source that he uses a disc of twelve inches diameter, which he rolls upon a straight rail.' The 'rolling is a very creditable one; it is as much below the mark as Archimedes was above it. Its performer is a joiner who evidently knows well what he is about when he measures; he is not wrong by 1 in 3,000.' Such skilful mechanicians as the builders of the pyramid could have obtained a closer approximation still by mere measurement. Besides, as they were manifestly mathematicians, such an approximation as was obtained by Archimedes must have been well within their power; and that approximation lies within the limits above indicated. Professor Smyth remarks that the ratio was 'a quantity which men in general, and all human science too, did not begin to trouble themselves about until long, long ages, languages, and nations had passed away after the building of the Great Pyramid; and after the sealing up, too, of that grand primeval and prehistoric monument of the patriarchal age of the earth according to Scripture.' I do not know where the Scripture records the sealing up of the Great Pyramid; but it is all but certain that during the very time when the pyramid was being built astronomical observations were in progress which, for their interpretation, involved of necessity a continual reference to the ratio in question. No one who considers the wonderful accuracy with which, nearly two thousand years before the Christian era, the Chaldæans had determined the famous cycle of the Saros, can doubt that they must have observed the heavenly bodies for several centuries before they could have achieved such a success; and the study of the motions of the celestial bodies compels 'men to trouble themselves' about the famous ratio of the circumference to the diameter.

We now come upon a new relation (contained in the dimensions of the pyramid as thus determined) which, by a strange coincidence, causes the height of the pyramid to appear to symbolise the distance of the sun There were 5,813 pyramid inches, or 5,819 British inches, in the height of the pyramid according to the relations already indicated. Now, in the sun's distance, according to an estimate recently adopted and freely used,[1] there are 91,400,000 miles, or 5,791 thousand millions of inches—that is, there are approximately as many thousand millions of inches in the sun's distance as there are inches in the height of the pyramid. If we take the relation as exact we should infer for the sun's distance 5,819 thousand millions of inches, or 91,840,000 miles—an immense improvement on the estimate which for so many years occupied a place of honour in our books of astronomy. Besides, there is strong reason for believing that, when the results of recent observations are worked out, the estimated sun distance will be much nearer this pyramid value than even to the value 91,400,000 recently adopted. This result, which one would have thought so damaging to faith in the evidence from coincidence—nay, quite fatal after the other case in which a close coincidence had appeared by merest

---

[1] I have substituted this value in the article 'Astronomy,' of the *British Encyclopædia*, for the estimate formerly used, viz. 95,233,055 miles. But there is good reason for believing that actual distance is nearly 92,000,000 miles.

accident—is regarded by the pyramidalists as a perfect triumph for their faith.

They connect it with another coincidence, viz. that, assuming the height determined in the way already indicated, then it so happens that the height bears to half a diagonal of the base the ratio 9 to 10. Seeing that the perimeter of the base symbolises the annual motion of the earth round the sun, while the height represents the radius of a circle with that perimeter, it follows that the height should symbolise the sun's distance. 'That line, further,' says Professor Smyth (speaking on behalf of Mr. W. Petrie, the discoverer of this relation), 'must represent' this radius 'in the proportion of 1 to 1,000,000,000' (or *ten* raised to power *nine*), 'because amongst other reasons 10 to 9 is practically the shape of the Great Pyramid.' For, this building 'has such an angle at the corners, that for every ten units its structure advances inwards on the diagonal of the base, it practically rises upwards, or points to sunshine' (*sic*) 'by *nine*. Nine, too, out of the ten characteristic parts (viz. five angles and five sides) being the number of those parts which the sun shines on in such a shaped pyramid, in such a latitude near the equator, out of a high sky, or, as the Peruvians say, when the sun sets on the pyramid with all its rays.' The coincidence itself on which this perverse reasoning rests is a singular one—singular, that is, as showing how close an accidental coincidence may run. It amounts to this, that if the number of days in the year be multiplied by 100, and a circle be drawn with a circumference containing 100 times as many inches as there are days in the year, the radius of the circle will be very nearly one-1,000,000,000th part of the sun's distance. Remembering that the pyramid inch is assumed to be one-500,000,000th part of the earth's diameter, we shall not be far from the truth in saying that, as a matter of fact, the earth by her orbital motion traverses each day a distance equal to two hundred times her own diameter. But of course this relation is altogether accidental. It has no real cause in nature.[1]

Such relations show that mere numerical coin-

[1] It may be matched by other coincidences as remarkable and as little the result of the operation of any natural law. Take, for instance, the following strange relation, introducing the dimensions of the sun himself, nowhere, so far as I have yet seen, introduced among pyramid relations, even by pyramidalists : 'If the plane of the ecliptic were a true surface, and the sun were to commence rolling along that surface towards the part of the earth's orbit where she is at her mean distance, while the earth commenced rolling upon the sun (round one of his great circles), each globe turning round in the same time—then, by the time the earth had rolled its way once round the sun, the sun would have almost exactly reached the earth's orbit. This is only another way of saying that the sun's diameter exceeds the earth's in almost exactly the same degree that the sun's distance exceeds the sun's diameter.'

cidences, however close, have little weight as evidence, except where they occur in series. Even
then they require to be very cautiously regarded,
seeing that the history of science records many
instances where the apparent law of a series has
been found to be falsified when the theory has
been extended. Of course this reason is not quoted
in order to throw doubt on the supposition that the
height of the pyramid was intended to symbolise
the sun's distance. That supposition is simply inadmissible if the hypothesis, according to which the
height was already independently determined in
another way, is admitted. Either hypothesis
might be admitted were we not certain that the
sun's distance could not possibly have been known
to the builders of the pyramid ; or both hypotheses
may be rejected ; but to admit both is out of the
question.

Considering the multitude of dimensions of
length, surface, capacity, and position, the great
number of shapes, and the variety of material
existing within the pyramid, and considering,
further, the enormous number of relations (presented by modern science) from among which to
choose, can it be wondered at if fresh coincidences
are being continually recognised ? If a dimension
will not serve in one way, use can be found for it in

another ; for instance, if some measure of length does not correspond closely with any known dimension of the earth or of the solar system (an unlikely supposition), then it can be understood to typify an interval of time. If, even after trying all possible changes of that kind, no coincidence shows itself (which is all but impossible), then all that is needed to secure a coincidence is that the dimensions should be manipulated a little.

Let a single instance suffice to show how the pyramidalists (with perfect honesty of purpose) hunt down a coincidence. The slant tunnel already described has a transverse height, once no doubt uniform, now giving various measures from 47·14 pyramid inches to 47·32 inches, so that the vertical height from the known inclination of the tunnel would be estimated at somewhere between 52 64 inches and 52·85. Neither dimension corresponds very obviously with any measured distance in the earth or solar system. Nor when we try periods, areas, &c., does any very satisfactory coincidence present itself. But the difficulty is easily turned into a new proof of design. Putting all the observations together (says Professor Smyth), ‘I deduced 47·24 pyramid inches to be the transverse height of the entrance passage ; and computing from thence with the observed angle of inclination the vertical height, that came out 52·76 of the same inches. But the sum of those two heights, or the height taken up and down, equals 100 inches, which length, as elsewhere shown, is the general pyramid linear representation of a day of twenty-four hours. And the mean of the two heights, or the height taken one way only, and impartially to the middle point between them, equals fifty inches ; which quantity is, therefore, the general pyramid linear representation of only half a day. In which case, let us ask what the entrance passage has to do with half rather than a whole day ? '

On relations such as these—which, if really intended by the architect, would imply an utterly fatuous habit of concealing elaborately what he desired to symbolise—the pyramidalists base their belief that ' a Mighty Intelligence did both think out the plans for it, and compel unwilling and ignorant idolaters, in a primal age of the world, to work mightily both for the future glory of the one true God of Revelation, and to establish lasting prophetic testimony touching a further development, still to take place, of the absolutely Divine Christian dispensation.'

CHAPTER III.

THE PROBLEM OF THE PYRAMIDS.

So far as conditions of the soil, surrounding country, and so forth, are concerned, few positions could surpass that selected for the Great Pyramid and its companions. The pyramids of Ghizeh (fig. 1) are situated on a platform of rock, about 150 feet above the level of the desert. The largest of them, the pyramid of Cheops, stands on an elevation free all around, insomuch that less sand has gathered round it than would otherwise have been the case. How admirably suited these pyramids are for observing-stations is shown by the way in which they are themselves seen from a distance. It has been remarked by every one who has seen the pyramids that the sense of sight is deceived in the attempt to appreciate their distance and magnitude. 'Though removed several leagues from the spectator, they appear to be close at hand; and it is not until he has travelled some miles in a direct line towards them, that he becomes sensible of their vast bulk and also of the pure atmosphere through which they are viewed.'

In all the Egyptian pyramids, there is evidence of an astronomical plan.   In the Great Pyramid we find evidence that such a plan was carried out with

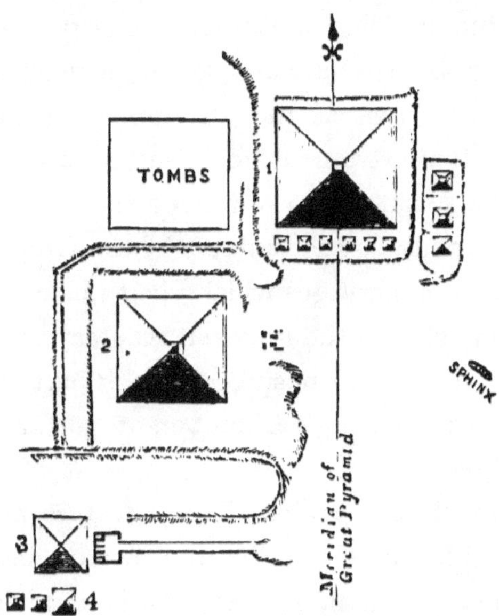

FIG. 1.   PLAN OF THE PYRAMIDS OF GHIZEH.
1. Pyramid of Cheops, or Great Pyramid.
2. Pyramid of Chephren, or second pyramid.
3. Pyramid of Mycerinus, or third pyramid.
4. Pyramid of Asychis, or fourth pyramid.

great skill, and with an attention to points of detail which shows that, for some reason or other, the edifice was required to be most carefully built in a special astronomical position.   It matters little at this stage of the inquiry whether we suppose the pyramid was erected for astronomical observation or not. It was certainly constructed in accordance with astronomical observations of great accuracy, and conducted with great skill. Moreover, it is obvious that to obtain such accuracy, the building was made to serve, while it was being built, the purpose of an astronomical observatory. Just as the astronomer in our own time uses the instrument he is setting up to adjust and make exact the position of the masonry on which it stands, so the builders of the Great Pyramid used the passages which they made within it to determine, with the greatest accuracy attainable by them, the proper position of each part of it, up to the so-called King's Chamber, at least, and probably higher.

So much is certain. Every feature thus far discovered in the Great Pyramid corresponds with this theory, and some features can be explained on no other.

With regard to their astronomical position, it seems clear that the builders intended to place the Great Pyramid precisely in latitude 30°, or, in other words, in that latitude where the true pole of the heavens is one-third of the way from the horizon to the point overhead (the zenith), and where the noon sun at true spring or autumn (when the sun rises almost exactly in the east, and sets almost exactly in the west) is two-thirds of the way from the horizon to the point overhead. In an observatory set exactly in this position, some of the calculations or geometrical constructions (as the case may be) involved in astronomical problems are considerably simplified. The first problem in Euclid, for example, by which a triangle of three equal sides is made, affords the means of drawing the proper angle at which the mid-day sun in spring or autumn is raised above the horizon, and at which the pole of the heavens is removed from the point overhead. Relations depending on this angle are also more readily calculated, for the very same reason, in fact, that the angle itself is more readily drawn. And though the builders of the Great Pyramid must have been advanced far beyond the stage at which any difficulty in dealing directly with other angles would be involved, yet they would perceive the great advantage of having one among the angles entering into their problems thus conveniently chosen. In our time, when by the use of logarithmic and other tables, all calculations are greatly simplified, and when also astronomers have learned to recognise that no possible choice of latitude would simplify their labours (unless an observatory could be set up at the North Pole itself, which would be in other respects inconvenient), matters of this sort are no longer worth considering, but to the mathematicians who planned the Great Pyramid they would have possessed extreme importance.

To set the centre of the pyramid's future base in latitude 30°, two methods could be used—the shadow method, and the pole-star method. If at noon, at the season when the sun rose due east and set due west, an upright A C were found to throw a shadow C D, so proportioned to A C that A C D would be one-half of an equal-sided triangle, then, theoretically, the point where this upright was placed would be in latitude 30°. As a matter of fact it would not be, because the air, by bending the sun's rays, throws the sun apparently somewhat above his true position. Apart from this, at the time of true spring or autumn, the sun does not seem to rise due east, or set due west, for he is raised above the horizon by atmospheric refraction, before he has really reached it in the morning, and he remains raised above it after he has really passed below—understanding the word 'really' to relate to his actual geometrical direction. Thus, at true spring and autumn, the sun rises to the north of east and sets slightly to the north of west.

The atmospheric refraction is indeed so marked, as
respects these parts of the sun's apparent course,
that it must have been quickly recognised. Probably, however, it would be regarded as a peculiarity only affecting the sun when close to the
horizon, and would be (correctly) associated with
his apparent change of shape when so situated.
Astronomers would be prevented in this way from
using the sun's horizontal position
at any season to guide them with
respect to the cardinal points, but
they would still consider the sun,
when raised high above the horizon, as a suitable astronomical
index (so to speak), and would have no idea
that even at a height of sixty degrees above the
horizon, or seen as in direction D A, fig. 2, he is seen
appreciably above his true position.

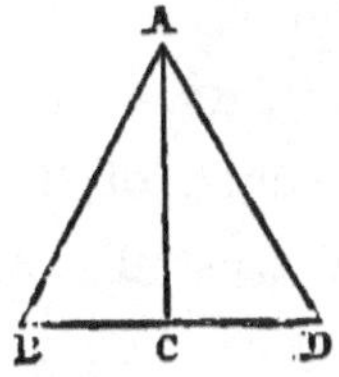

Fig. 2.

Adopting this method—the shadow method—to
fix the latitude of the pyramid's base, they would
conceive the sun was sixty degrees above the horizon at noon, at true spring or autumn, when in
reality he was somewhat below that elevation.
Or, in other words, they would conceive they were
in latitude 30° north, when in reality they were
farther north (the mid-day sun at any season
sinking lower and lower as we travel farther and

farther north). The actual amount by which, supposing their observations exact, they would thus set this station north of its proper position, would depend on the refractive qualities of the air in Egypt. But although there is some slight difference in this respect between Egypt and Greenwich, it is but small; and we can determine from the Greenwich refraction tables, within a very slight limit of error, the amount by which the architects of the Great Pyramid would have set the centre of the base north of latitude 30°, if they had trusted solely to the shadow method. The distance would have been as nearly as possible 1,125 yards, or say three furlongs.

Now, if they followed the other method, observing the stars around the pole, in order to determine the elevation of the true pole of the heavens, they would be in a similar way exposed to error arising from the effects of atmospheric refraction. They would proceed probably somewhat in this wise:—Using any kind of direction-lines, they would take the altitude of their polar star (1) when passing immediately under the pole, and (2) when passing immediately above the pole. The mean of the altitudes thus obtained would be the altitude of the true pole of the heavens. Now, atmospheric refraction affects the stars in the same way that it affects the sun, and the nearer a star is to the horizon, the more it is raised by atmospheric refraction. The pole-star in both its positions— that is, when passing below the pole, and when passing above that point—is raised by refraction, rather more when below than when above ; but the estimated position of the pole itself, raised by about the mean of these two effects, is in fact raised almost exactly as much as it would be if it were itself directly observed (that is, if a star occupied the pole itself, instead of merely circling close round the pole). We may then simplify matters by leaving out of consideration at present all questions of the actual pole-star in the time of the pyramid builders, and simply considering how far they would have set the pyramid's base in error, if they had determined their latitude by observing a star occupying the position of the true pole of the heavens.

They would have endeavoured to determine where the pole appears to be raised exactly thirty degrees above the horizon. But the effect of re-fraction being to raise every celestial object above its true position, they would have supposed the pole to be raised thirty degrees, when in reality it was less raised than this. In other words, they would have supposed they were in latitude 30°, when, in reality, they were in some lower latitude, for the pole of the heavens rises higher and higher above the horizon as we pass to higher and higher latitudes. Thus they would set their station somewhat to the south of latitude 30°, instead of to the north, as when they were supposed to have used the shadow method. Here again we can find how far they would set it south of that latitude. Using the Greenwich refraction table (which is the same as Bessel's), we find that they would have made a much greater error than when using the other method, simply because they would be observing a body at an elevation of about thirty degrees only, whereas in taking the sun's mid-day altitude in spring or autumn, they would be observing a body at twice as great an elevation. The error would be, in fact, in this case, about 1 mile 1,512 yards.

It seems not at all unlikely that astronomers, so skilful and ingenious as the builders of the pyramid manifestly were, would have employed both methods. In that case they would certainly have obtained widely discrepant results, rough as their means and methods must unquestionably have been, compared with modern instruments and methods. The exact determination from the shadow plan would have set them 1,125 yards to the north of the true latitude; while the exact determination from the pole-star method would have set them 1 mile 1,512 yards south of the true latitude. Whether they would thus have been led to detect the effect of atmospheric refraction on celestial bodies high above the horizon may be open to question. But certainly they would have recognised the action of some cause or other, rendering one or other method, or both methods, unsatisfactory. If so, and we can scarcely doubt that this would actually happen (for certainly they would recognise the theoretical justice of both methods, and we can hardly imagine that having two available methods, they would limit their operations to one method only), they would scarcely see any better way of proceeding than to take a position intermediate between the two which they had thus obtained. Such a position would lie almost exactly 1,072 yards south of true latitude 30° north.

Whether the architects of the pyramid of Cheops really proceeded in this way or not, it is certain that they obtained a result corresponding so well with this that if we assume they really did intend to set the base of the pyramid in latitude 30°, we find it difficult to persuade ourselves that they did not follow some such course as I have just indicated—the coincidence is so close

considering the nature of the observations involved.
According to Professor Piazzi Smyth, whose observational labours in relation to the Great Pyramid are
worthy of all praise, the centre of the base of this
pyramid lies about 1 mile 568 yards south of the
thirtieth parallel of latitude. This is 944 yards
north of the position they would have deduced
from the pole-star method; 1 mile 1,693 yards
south of the position they would have deduced
from the shadow method; and 1,256 yards south
of the mean position between the two last named.
The position of the base seems to prove beyond
all possibility of question that the shadow method
was not the method on which sole or chief reliance
was placed, though this method must have been
known to the builders of the pyramid. It does
not, however, prove that the star method was the
only method followed. A distance of 944 yards
is so small in a matter of this sort that we might
fairly enough assume that the position of the base
was determined by the pole-star method. If, however, we supposed the builders of the pyramid to
have been exceedingly skilful in applying the
methods available to them, we might not unreasonably conclude from the position of the pyramid's
base that they used both the shadow method and
the pole-star method, but that, recognising the

superiority of the latter, they gave greater weight to the result obtained by employing this method. Supposing, for instance, they applied the pole-star method three times as often as the shadow method, and took the mean of all the results thus obtained, then the deduced position would lie three times as far from the northern position obtained by the shadow method as from the southern position obtained by the pole-star method. In this case their result, if correctly deduced, would have been only about 156 yards north of the actual present position of the centre of the base.

It is impossible, however, to place the least reliance on any calculation like that made in the last few lines. By *à posteriori* reasoning such as this one can prove almost anything about the pyramids. For observe, though presented as *à priori* reasoning, it is in reality not so, being based on the observed fact, that the true position lies more than three times as far from the northerly limit as from the southern one. Now, if in any other way, not open to exception, we knew that the builders of the pyramid used both the sun method and the star method, with perfect observational accuracy, but without knowledge of the laws of atmospheric refraction, we could infer from the observed position the precise relative weights they attached to the two methods.   But it is altogether unsafe, or, to speak plainly, it is in the logical sense a perfectly vicious manner of reasoning, to ascertain first such relative weights on an assumption of this kind, and, having so found them, to assert that the relation thus detected is a probable one in itself, and that since, when assumed, it accounts precisely for the observed position of the pyramid, therefore the pyramid was posited in that way and no other.   It has been by unsound reasoning of this kind that nine-tenths of the absurdities have been established on which Mr. Taylor and Professor Smyth and their followers have established what may be called the pyramid religion.

All we can fairly assume as probable from the evidence, in so far as that evidence bears on the results of *à priori* considerations, is that the builders of the Great Pyramid preferred the pole-star method to the shadow method, as a means of determining the true position of latitude 30° north. They seem to have applied this method with great skill, considering the means at their disposal, if we suppose that they took no account whatever of the influence of refraction.   If they took refraction into account at all, they considerably underrated its influence.

Piazzi Smyth's idea that they knew the *precise*

position of the thirtieth parallel of latitude, and also the *precise* position of the parallel, where, owing to refraction, the pole-star would appear to be thirty degrees above the horizon, and deliberately set the base of the pyramid between these limits (not exactly or nearly exactly half way, but somewhere between them), cannot be entertained for a moment by any one not prepared to regard the whole history of the construction of the pyramid as supernatural. My argument, let me note in passing, is not intended for persons who take this particular view of the pyramid, a view on which reasoning could not very well be brought to bear.

If the star method had been used to determine the position of the parallel of 30° north latitude, we may be certain it would be used also to orient the building. Probably, indeed, the very structures (temporary, of course) by which the final observations for the latitude had been made, would remain available also for the orientation. These structures would consist of uprights so placed that the line of sight along their extremities (or along a tube perhaps borne aloft by them in a slanting position) pointed to the pole-star when immediately below or immediately above the pole. Altogether the more convenient direction of the two would be that towards the pole-star when below the pole. The extremities of these uprights, or the axis of the upraised tube, would lie in a north-and-south line considerably inclined to the horizon, because the pole itself being thirty degrees above the horizon, the pole-star, whatever star this might be, would be high above the horizon even when exactly under the pole. No star far from the pole would serve to determine the meridian line of the pyramid's base, or rather the meridian line corresponding to the position of the underground passage directed towards the pole-star when immediately under the pole.

A line at right angles to the meridian line thus obtained would lie due east and west, and the true position of the east-and-west line would probably be better indicated in this way than by direct observation of the sun or stars. If direct observation were made at all, it would be made not on the sun in the horizon near the time of spring and autumn, for the sun's position is then largely affected by refraction. The sun might be observed for this purpose during the summer months, at moments when calculation showed that he should be due east or west, or crossing what is technically termed the *prime vertical*. Possibly the so-called azimuth trenches on the east side of the Great

Pyramid may have been in some way associated with observations of this sort, as the middle trench is directed considerably to the north of the east point, and not far from the direction in which the sun would rise when about thirty degrees (a favourite angle with the pyramid architects) past the vernal equinox. But I lay no stress on this point. The meridian line obtained from the underground passage would have given the builders so ready a means of determining accurately the east-and-west lines for the north-and-south edges of the pyramid's base, that any other observations for this purpose can hardly have been more than subsidiary. They could in the first place set up a pointed upright, as A B in fig. 3, at the middle of the northern edge of the base, and another shorter one, C D, so that at one of the epochs, it would not matter which, an eye placed as at E would see the points C and E in the same straight line as the pole-star S. Then the line D B would lie north and south.

This would only be a first rough approximation, however. The builders would require a much more satisfactory north-and-south line than D B. At this stage of proceedings, what could be more perfect as a method of obtaining the true bearing of the pole than to dig a tubular hole into the solid rock, along which tube the pole-star at its lower culmination should be visible? Perfect stability would be thus ensured for this fundamental direction-line. It would be easy to obtain the direction with great accuracy, even though at first starting the borings were not quite correctly made. And the farther the boring was continued downwards towards the south, the greater the accuracy of the direction-line thus obtained. Of course there could be no question whatever in such underground boring of the advantage of taking the lower passage of the pole-star, not the upper. For a line directly from the star at its upper passage would slant downwards at an angle of more than thirty degrees from the horizon, while a line directly from the star at its lower passage would slant downwards at an angle of less than thirty degrees; and the smaller this angle the less would be the length and the less the depth of the boring required for any given horizontal range.

Besides perfect stability, a boring through the solid rock would present another most important advantage over any other method of orienting the base of the pyramid. In the case of an inclined direction-line above the level of the horizontal base, there would be the difficulty of determining the precise position of points under the raised line ; for manifest difficulties would arise in letting fall plumb-lines from various points along the optical axis of a raised tubing. But nothing could be simpler than the plan by which the horizontal line corresponding to the underground tube would be determined.

To obtain this, they would bore a slant passage in the solid rock, as D G, which should point

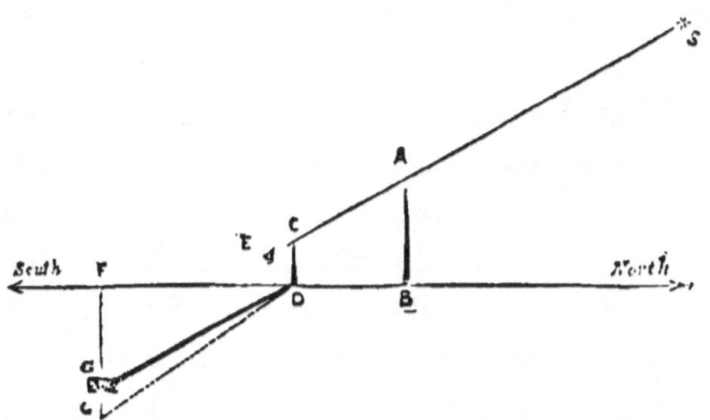

FIG. 3. SHOWING HOW THE BUILDERS OF THE PYRAMID PROBABLY
OBTAINED THEIR BASE.

directly to the pole-star *s* when due north, starting their boring by reference to the rough north-and-south line D B, but guiding it as they went on by noticing whether the pole-star, when due north, remained visible along the passage. But they would now have to make a selection between its passage above the pole and its passage below the pole. In using the uprights D and B, they could take either the upper or the lower passage ; but the underground boring could have but one direction, and they must choose whichever of the two passages of the star they preferred. As already remarked they would take the lower passage, not only as the more convenient passage for observation, but because the length of their boring D G would be less, for a given horizontal range F D, if the lower passage of the star *s* were taken, than it would be for the upper passage, when its direction would be as D G'.

When they had bored far enough down to have a sufficient horizontal range F D (the longer this range, of course, the truer the north-and-south direction), they would still have to ascertain the true position of F, the point vertically above G. For this purpose they would get F first as truly as they could from the line D B prolonged, and would bore down from F vertically (guiding the boring, of course, with a plumb-line) until they reached the space opened out at G. The boring F G might be of very small diameter. Noting where the plumb-line let down from F to G reached the floor of the space G, they would ascertain how far F lay to the east or to the west of its proper position over the *centre* of the floor of this space. Correcting the position of F accordingly, they would have F D the true north-and-south line.

This method could give results of considerable accuracy ; and it is the only method, in fact, which could do so. When, therefore, we find that the base of the pyramid *is* oriented with singular accuracy, and secondly that just such a boring as D G exists beneath the base of the pyramid, *running three hundred and fifty feet through the solid rock on which the pyramid is built*, we cannot well refuse to believe that the slant passage was bored for this purpose, which it was so well fitted to subserve, and which *has* been so well subserved in some way.

In all the pyramids of Ghizeh, indeed, there is such a tunnelling as we might expect on almost any theory of the relation of the smaller pyramids to the great one. But the slant tunnel under the great pyramid is constructed with far greater skill and care than have been bestowed on the tunnels under the other pyramids. Its length underground amounts to more than 350 feet, so that, viewed from the bottom, the mouth, about four feet across from top to bottom on the square, would give a sky range of rather less than one-third of a degree, or about one-fourth more than the moon's apparent diameter. But of course there was nothing to prevent the observers who used this tube from greatly narrowing these limits by using diaphragms, one covering up all the mouth of the tube, except a small opening near the centre, and another correspondingly occupying the lower part of the tube from which the observation was made.

It seems satisfactorily made out that the object of the slant tunnel, which runs 350 feet through the rock on which the pyramid is built, was to observe the Pole-star of the period at its lower culmination, to obtain thence the true direction of the north point. The slow motion of a star very near the pole would cause any error in time, when this observation was made, to be of very little importance, though we can understand that even such observations as these would remind the builders of the pyramid of the absolute necessity of good time-measurements and time-observations in astronomical research.

If this opinion is adopted, and for my own part I cannot see how it can well be questioned, we cannot possibly accept the opinion that the slant tunnel was bored for another purpose solely, or even chiefly, unless it can be shown that that other purpose in the first place was essential to the plans of the builders, in the second place could be subserved in no other way so well, and in the third place was manifestly subserved in this way to the knowledge of those who made the slant borings.

Finding this point clearly made out, we can fairly use the observed direction of the inclined passage to determine what was the position of the Pole-star at the time when the foundations of the great pyramid were laid, and even what that Pole-star may have been. On this point there has never been much doubt, though considerable doubt exists as to the exact epoch when the star occupied the position in question. According to the observations made by Professor Smyth, the entrance passage has a slope of about 26° 27′, which would have corresponded, when refraction is taken into account, to the elevation of the star observed through the passage, at an angle of about 26° 29′ above the horizon. The true latitude of the pyramid being 29° 58′ 51″, corresponding to an elevation of the true pole of the heavens by about 30° $\frac{1}{2}$′ above the horizon, it follows that if Professor Smyth obtained the true angle for the entrance passage, the Pole-star must have been about 3° 31$\frac{1}{2}$′ from the pole. Smyth himself considers that we ought to infer the angle for the entrance passage from that of other internal passages, presently to be mentioned, which he thinks were manifestly intended to be at the same angle of inclination, though directed southwards instead of northwards. Assuming this to be the case though

for my own part I cannot see why we should do so
(most certainly we have no *à priori* reason for so
doing), we should have 26° 18′ as about the required
angle of inclination, whence we should get about
3° 42′ for the distance of the Pole-star of the pyramid's time from the true pole of the heavens.   The
difference may seem of very slight importance, and
I note that Professor Smyth passes it over as if it
really were unimportant; but in reality it corresponds to somewhat large time-differences.

In the year 2170 B.C., and again (last before
that) in the year 3350 B.C., and also for several
years on either side of those dates, a certain bright
star *did* look down that boring, or, more precisely,
could be seen by any one who looked up that boring, when the star was just below the pole in its circuit round that point.   The star was a very important one among the old constellations, though it has
since considerably faded in lustre, being no other
than the star Alpha of the constellation the Dragon,
which formerly was the polar constellation.   For
hundreds of years before and after the dates 3350
and 2170 B.C., and during the entire interval between
those dates, no other star would at all have suited
the purposes of the builders of the pyramid ; so that
we may be tolerably sure this was the star they
employed.   Therefore the boring, when first made

must have been directed towards this star. We conclude, then, with considerable confidence, that it was somewhere about one of the two dates 3350 B.C., and 2170 B.C., that the erection of the great pyramid was begun. And from the researches of Egyptologists it has become all but certain that the *earlier* of these dates is very near the correct epoch. But though the boring thus serves the purpose of dating the pyramid, it seems altogether unlikely that the builders of the pyramid intended to record the pyramid's age in this way. They could have done that, if they had wanted to, at once far more easily and far more exactly, by carving a suitable record in one of the inner chambers of the building. But nothing yet known about the pyramid suggests that its builder wanted to tell future ages anything whatever. So far from this, the pyramid was carefully planned to reveal nothing. Only when men had first destroyed the casing, next had found their way into the descending passage, and then had, in the roughest and least skilful manner conceivable (even so, too, by an accident), discovered the great ascending gallery, were any of the secrets of this mighty tomb revealed—for a tomb and nothing else it has been ever since Cheops died. To assert that all these events lay within the view of the architect who *seemed* so carefully to endeavour to render them impossible, is to ask that men should set their reasoning faculties on one side when the pyramid is in question. And lastly, we have not a particle of evidence to show that the builders of the pyramid had any idea that the date of the building *would* be indicated by the position of the great slant passages. They may have noticed that the Pole-star was slowly changing its position with respect to the true pole of the heavens; and they may even have recognised the rate and direction in which the Pole-star was thus moving. But it is utterly unlikely that they could have detected the fact that the pole of the heavens circles round the pole of the ecliptic in the mighty precessional period of 25,920 years;[1] and unless they knew this, they

[1] If the architect of the great pyramid knew anything about the great precessional period, then—unless such knowledge was miraculously communicated—the astronomers of the pyramid's time must have had evidence which could only have been obtained during many hundreds of years of exact observation, following of course on a long period during which comparatively imperfect astronomical methods were employed. Their astronomy must therefore have had its origin long before the date commonly assigned to the Flood. In passing I may remark that in a paper on the pyramid by Abbé Moigno, that worthy but somewhat credulous ecclesiastic makes a remark which seems to show that the stability and perfection of the great pyramid, and therefore the architectural skill acquired by the Egyptians in the year 2170 B.C. (a date he accepts), proves in some unexplained way the comparative youth of the human race. To most men it would seem that the more perfect men's work at any given date, the longer must have been the preceding interval during which men were acquiring the skill thus displayed. On the con-

would not know that the position of the slant passage would tell future generations aught about the pyramid's date. On all these accounts (1) because the builders probably did not care at all about our knowing anything on the subject, (2) because if they did they would not have adopted so clumsy a method, and (3) because there is no reason for believing, but every reason for doubting, that they knew the passage *would* tell future ages the date of the pyramid's erection, we must regard as utterly improbable, if not utterly untenable, the proposition that the builders had any such purpose in view in constructing the slant passage.

I am therefore somewhat surprised to find Sir E. Beckett, who does not accept the wild ideas of the pyramid religionists, nevertheless dwelling, not on the manifest value of the slant passages to builders desiring to orient such an edifice as the great pyramid, but on the idea that those builders may have wanted to record a date for the benefit of future ages. After quoting a remark from Mr. Wackerbarth's amusing review of Smyth's book, to the effect that the hypothesis about the slant

trary, the pyramids, says Abbé Moigno, 'give the most solemn contradiction to those who would of set purpose throw back the origin of man to an indefinite remoteness.' It would have been well if he had explained how the pyramids do this.

passage is liable to the objection that, the mouth of the passage being walled up, it is not easy to conceive how a star could be observed through it, Beckett says, 'Certainly not, after it was closed; but what has that to do with the question whether the builders thought fit to indicate the date to any-one who might in after ages find the passage, by reference to the celestial dial, in which the pole of the earth travels round the pole of the ecliptic in 25,827 years, like the hand of a clock round the dial?' But in reality there is no more extravagant supposition among all those ideas of the pyramid-alists (which Beckett justly regards as among the wildest illustration of 'the province of the imagination in science ') than the notion that this motion of the pole of the earth was known to the builders of the pyramid, or that, knowing it, they adopted so preposterous a method of indicating the date of their labours.

Let us return to the purposes which seem to have been actually present in the minds of the pyramid builders.

Having duly laid down the north-and-south line F D, in fig. 5, and being thus ready to cut out from the nearly level face of the solid rock the corner sockets of the square base, they would have to choose what size they would give the base. This would be a question depending partly on the nature of the ground at their disposal, partly on the expense to which King Cheops was prepared to go. The question of expense probably did not influence him much ; but it requires only a brief inspection of the region at his disposal (in the required latitude, and on a firm rock basis) to see that the nature of the ground set definite limits to the base of the building he proposed to erect. As Piazzi Smyth remarks, it is set close to the very verge of the elevated plateau, even dangerously near its edge. Assuming the centre of the base determined by the latitude observations outside, the limit of the size of the base was determined at once. And apart from that, the hill country directly to the south of the great pyramid would not have permitted any considerable extension in that direction, while on the east and west of its present position the plateau does not extend so far north as in the longitude actually occupied by the pyramid.

These considerations probably had quite as much to do with the selection of the dimensions of the base as any that have been hitherto insisted upon. Sir E. Beckett says, after showing that the actual size of the base was in other respects a convenient one (in its numerical relation to previous measures), the great pyramid 'must be some size,'

but 'why Cheops wanted his pyramid to be about'
its actual size he does not profess to know.   Yet, if
the latitude of the centre of the base were really
determined very carefully, it is clear that the
nearest, and in this case the northern, verge of the
rock plateau would limit the size of the base ; and
we may say that the size selected was the largest
which was available, subject to the conditions
respecting latitude.   True, the latitude is not correctly determined ; but we may fairly assume it
was meant to be, and that the actual centre of the
base was supposed by the builders to lie exactly in
latitude 30 degrees north.

However, we may admit that the dimensions
adopted were such as the builders considered convenient also.   I fear Sir E. Beckett's explanation
on this point, simple and commonplace though it is,
is preferable to Professor Smyth's.   If, by the way,
the latter were right, not only in his views, but in
the importance he attaches to them, it would be no
mere *façon de parler* to say 'I fear ;' for a rather
unpleasant fate awaits all who 'shorten the cubit' as
Sir E. Beckett does.   'I will not attempt,' says
Professor Smyth, 'to say what the ancient Egyptians would have thought' of certain 'whose car-
riages,' it seems, 'try to stop the way of great
pyramid research,' 'for I am horrified to remember

the Pharaonic pictures of human souls sent back from heaven to earth, in the bodies of pigs, for far lighter offences than shortening the national cubit.' Sir E. Beckett has sought to shorten the pyramid cubit, which with Smyth is 'the sacred, Hebrew earth-commensurable, anti-Canite cubit,' a far heavier offence probably than merely 'shortening the national cubit.' But after all, it is unfortunately too true, that if the shorter cubit which Beckett holds to have been used by the pyramid builders was not so used, the pyramid does its best to suggest that it was ; and if Beckett and those who follow him (as I do in this respect) are wrong, the pyramid and not they must be blamed. For, apart from the trifling detail that the Hebrew cubit of 25 inches is entirely imaginary, 'neither this cubit, nor any multiple of it, is to be found in a single one of all Mr. Smyth's multitude of measurements, except two evidently accidental multiples of it in the diagonals of two of the four corner sockets in the rock ; which are not even square, and could never have been seen again after the pyramid was built, if the superstructure had not been broken up and stolen, which was probably the last thing that Cheops or his architect expected.' But of the other cubit, 'the pyramid and the famous marble " Coffer," in the king's chamber (which was doubtless also Cheops's coffin until his body was "resurrectionised " by the thieves who first broke into the pyramid), do contain clear indications.' The cubit referred to is the working cubit of 20¾ inches, or about a fiftieth of an inch less. For a person of average height, it is equal to about the distance from the elbow to the tip of the middle finger, *plus* a hand's-breadth, the former distance being the natural cubit (for a person of such height). The natural cubit is as nearly as possible half-a-yard, and most probably our yard measure is derived from this shorter cubit. The working cubit may be regarded as a long half-yard, the double working cubit or working Egyptian yard measure, so to speak, being 41½ inches long.

The length of the base-circuit of the great pyramid may be most easily remembered by noticing that it contains as many working cubits as our mile contains yards, viz., 1,760 ; giving 440 cubits as the length of each of the four sides of the base. If Lincoln's Inn Fields were enlarged to a square having its sides equal to the greatest sides of the present Fields, the area of this, the largest 'square ' in London, would be almost exactly equal to that of the pyramid's base—or about 13½ acres. The front of Chelsea Hospital has almost the same length as a side of the pyramid's base, so also has the frontage of the British Museum, including the houses on either side to Charlotte Street and Montague Street. The average breadth of the Thames between Chelsea and London Bridge, or, in other words, the average span of the metropolitan bridges, is also not very different from the length of each side of the great pyramid's base. The length measures about 761 feet, or nearly 254 yards. Each side is in fact a furlong of 220 double cubits or Egyptian yards.

The height of the pyramid is equal to seven-elevenths of the side of the base, or to 280 cubits, or about 484 feet. This is about 16 feet higher than the top of Strasburg Cathedral, 24 feet higher than St. Peter's at Rome, and is about 130 feet higher than our St. Paul's.

These are all the dimensions of the pyramid's exterior I here propose to mention. Sir E. Beckett gives a number of others, some of considerable interest, but of course all derivable from the fact that the pyramid has a square base 440 cubits in the side, and has a height of 280 cubits. I may notice, however, in passing, that I quite agree with him in thinking that the special mathematical relation which the pyramid builders intended to embody in the building was this, that the area of each of the four faces should be equal to a square having its sides equal to the height of the pyramid. Herodotus tells us that this was the condition which the builders adopted ; and this condition is fulfilled at least as closely as any of the other more or less fanciful relations which have been recognised by Taylor and his followers.

Having their base properly oriented, and being about to erect the building itself, the architects would certainly not have closed the mouth of the slant tunnel pointing northwards, but would have carried the passage onwards through the basement layers of the edifice, until these had reached the height corresponding to the place where the prolongation of the passage would meet the slanting north face of the building. I incline to think that at this place they would not be content to allow the north face to remain in steps, but would fit in casing stones (not necessarily those which would eventually form the slant surface of the pyramid, but more probably slanted so as to be perpendicular to the axis of the ascending passage). They would probably cut a square aperture through such slant stones corresponding to the size of the passage elsewhere, so as to make the four surfaces of the passage perfectly plane from its greatest depth below the base of the pyramid to its aperture, close to the surface to be formed eventually by the casing stones of the pyramid itself.

Now, in this part of his work, the astronomical architect could scarcely fail to take into account the circumstance that the inclined passage, however convenient as bearing upon a bright star near the pole when that star was due north, was, nevertheless, not coincident in direction with the true polar axis of the celestial sphere. I cannot but think he would in some way mark the position of their true polar axis. And the natural way of marking it would be to indicate where the passage of his Pole-star *above* the pole ceased to be visible through the slant tube. In other words he would mark where a line from the middle of the lowest face of the inclined passage to the middle of the upper edge of the mouth was inclined by twice the angle 3° 42′ to the axis of the passage. To an eye placed on the optical axis of the passage, at this distance from the mouth the middle of the upper edge of the mouth would (*quam proximè*) show the place of the true pole of the heavens. It certainly is a singular coincidence that at the part of the tube where this condition would be fulfilled, there is a peculiarity in the construction of the entrance passage, which has been indeed

otherwise explained, but I shall leave the reader to
determine whether the other explanation is altogether a likely one. The feature is described by
Smyth as 'a most singular portion of the passage
—viz. a place where two adjacent wall-joints, similar, too, on either side of the passage, were *vertical*
or nearly so; while every other wall-joint, both
above and below, was *rectangular* to the length of
the passage, and, therefore, largely *inclined* to the
vertical.' Now I take the mean of Smyth's determinations of the transverse height of the entrance
passage as 47·23 inches (the extreme values are
47·14 and 47·32), and I find that, from a point on
the floor of the entrance passage, this transverse
height would subtend an angle of 7° 24' (the range
of Alpha Draconis in altitude when on the meridian) at a distance 363·65 inches from the transverse mouth of the passage. Taking this distance
from Smyth's scale in Plate xvii. of his work on
the pyramid ('Our Inheritance in the Great Pyramid'), I find that, if measured along the base of
the entrance passage from the lowest edge of the
vertical stone, it falls exactly upon the spot where
he has marked in the probable outline of the un-
cased pyramid, while, if measured from the upper
edge of the same stone, it falls just about as far
within the outline of the cased pyramid as we

should expect the outer edge of a sloped end stone to the tunnel to have lain.

It may be said that from the floor of the entrance passage no star could have been seen, because no eye could be placed there. But the builders of the pyramid cannot reasonably be supposed to have been ignorant of the simple properties of plane mirrors, and by simply placing a thin piece of polished metal upon the floor at this spot, and noting where they could see the star and the upper edge of the tunnel's mouth in contact by reflection in this mirror, they could determine precisely where the star could be seen touching that edge, by an eye placed (were that possible) precisely in the plane of the floor.

I have said there is another explanation of this peculiarity in the entrance passage, but I should rather have said there is another explanation of a line marked on the stone next below the vertical one. I should imagine this line, which is nothing more than a mark such ' as might be ruled with a blunt steel instrument, but by a master hand for power, evenness, straightness, and still more for rectangularity to the passage axis,' was a mere sign to show where the upright stone was to come. But Professor Smyth, who gives no explanation of the upright stone itself, except that it seems, from its upright position, to have had 'something representative of setting up, or preparation for the erecting of a building,' believes that the mark is as many inches from the mouth of the tunnel as there were years between the dispersal of man and the building of the pyramid ; that thence downwards to the place where an ascending passage begins, marks in like manner the number of years which were to follow before the exodus ; thence along the ascending passage to the beginning of the great gallery the number of years from the exodus to the coming of Christ ; and thence along the floor of the grand gallery to its end, the interval between the first coming of Christ and the second coming, or the end of the world, which it appears was to have taken place in the year 1881. It is true not one of these intervals accords with the dates given by those who are considered the best authorities in Biblical matters,—but so much the worse for the dates.

To return to the pyramid.

But what special purpose had the architect in view, as he planned the addition of layer after layer of the pyramidal structure ? So far as the mere orienting of the faces of the pyramid was concerned, he had achieved his purpose so soon as he had obtained, by means of the inclined passage, the true direction of the north and south lines. But assuming that his purpose was to provide in some way for astronomical observation, a square base with sides facing the cardinal points would not be of much use. It would clearly give horizontal direction-lines, north and south, east and west, north-east and south-west, and north-west and south-east. For if observers were set at the four corners, A, B, C, D, as in fig. 4, with suitable uprights, where dots are shown at these corners, a line of sight from D's upright to A's would be directed towards the south, from the same upright to B's would be directed towards the south-west, and from the same to C's would be directed towards the west. Lines of sight from the other three uprights to each of the remaining ones would give the other directions named, or eight directions in all round the horizon.

The only possible way in which the pyramid could have been oriented so accurately as it has been, was by stellar observations. Of all observations for *that* purpose, those made on the pole-star of the time would have been the most effective. If there is a star which the astronomer observes less than another when using his observatory for that

chief of all purposes to which a great public observatory, at any rate, can be applied, it is the pole-
star, simply because that star moves so slowly
round its small circle. But for determining the
direction of the true north point (and also for determining latitude) the pole-star is invaluable. No
astronomer who thinks over the problem at all, can
fail to see that the builder of the Great Pyramid
would have been driven by the requirements of his
case to make just such a slant descending passage
as that which opens out (now that the casing-
stones have been removed) on the northern side of
the pyramid, not far above its base. It is equally
certain that such a descending passage would have
been directed to the position of the pole-star when
it was due north and at its lowest. The position
of the pole-star when exactly above the pole would
have been just as well suited for determining the
direction of the true north, but the slant passage
would have had to run deeper down into the solid
rock to give the same degree of accuracy, and the
extra labour would have been wasted.

When, after marking the position of the base,
the question of obtaining the true level came to be
considered, only one method effective enough to
give the required accuracy would have been available—viz. the use of water, flooding the squared

space cut out in the solid rock. A difficult and costly task, doubtless, in itself, but a mere nothing considered with reference to the labour and cost to which the builders were prepared to go. For this purpose, the descending passage would have to be temporarily plugged ; and as soon as the water-level had been marked at several stations on each side of the base, the plug could be removed, and the water run off into the pit which had been excavated underneath. A depth of a few inches of water all over the base would have sufficed for this purpose, but more probably a mere channel all round the base was prepared.

After thus orienting the base by aid of the pole-star, and levelling it by using a property of liquids which was, of course, well known to them, the architects would place layer after layer, carrying towards the north the passage for observing the pole-star, so that as each layer was placed, the work of orienting, and possibly of levelling, might be repeated, and an ever-increasing exactitude secured.

But they would know that ere long the direct pole-star observations would fail them ; for the passage would presently reach the northern face of the pyramid. By again using a well-known property of liquids, however, combined with a well-known property of light rays, they would continue the process of orienting to a much greater height. (When I say well-known, I mean well-known to them : they were manifestly skilful engineers and architects, and as surely as they were well acquainted with the properties of matter, so surely must they have been acquainted with the mathematical relations on which the simpler optical laws depend. Possibly they knew laws more recondite ; but the simpler laws they certainly knew.) Now, the plan which would quickly suggest itself to any one knowing these laws, would be to make use of the reflected rays from a star when the direct rays could no longer be employed. We know that when a ray from a luminous object is reflected at a plane surface, the reflected ray and the incident ray make equal angles with a line perpendicular to the surface at the point of incidence, and are also both in the same plane with that perpendicular. Now, what the pyramid architects wanted was to have a constant means of determining the direction of north and south—in other words, a constant knowledge of the position of what modern astronomers call the plane of the meridian. They had this so long as they could observe the pole-star when due north, through a passage opening out within the square layer they were adding to the pyramid. When, as their work continued, this passage opened out in the part of the sloping side already completed, they could still determine the meridian plane if they carried up a passage through the masonry in such a direction as to contain the rays from the pole-star after reflection at a horizontal surface, such as that of still water. For a perpendicular to the surface of still water is directed to the zenith, and the direct and reflected rays from the star (due north) lie, therefore, in the meridian plane which passes through the north and south points and through the zenith.

Now this is precisely what the pyramid builders seem to have done, as is shown in fig. 5, the dimensions of which are taken from Smyth's book, ' Our Inheritance in the Great Pyramid.' A E is the long slant passage, which for convenience we may call the descending passage, D C is an ascending passage of exactly the same character, which, therefore, we might have presumed was intended for a similar purpose, even if the consideration of the natural course which intelligent builders would have pursued had not led us to expect to find precisely such an ascending passage here. But it may be asked how the reflected rays from the star were obtained? Nothing could have been simpler. The very same process which had been applied in levelling would

be all that would be needed here. If the descending passage were for a time (a day, or even an hour

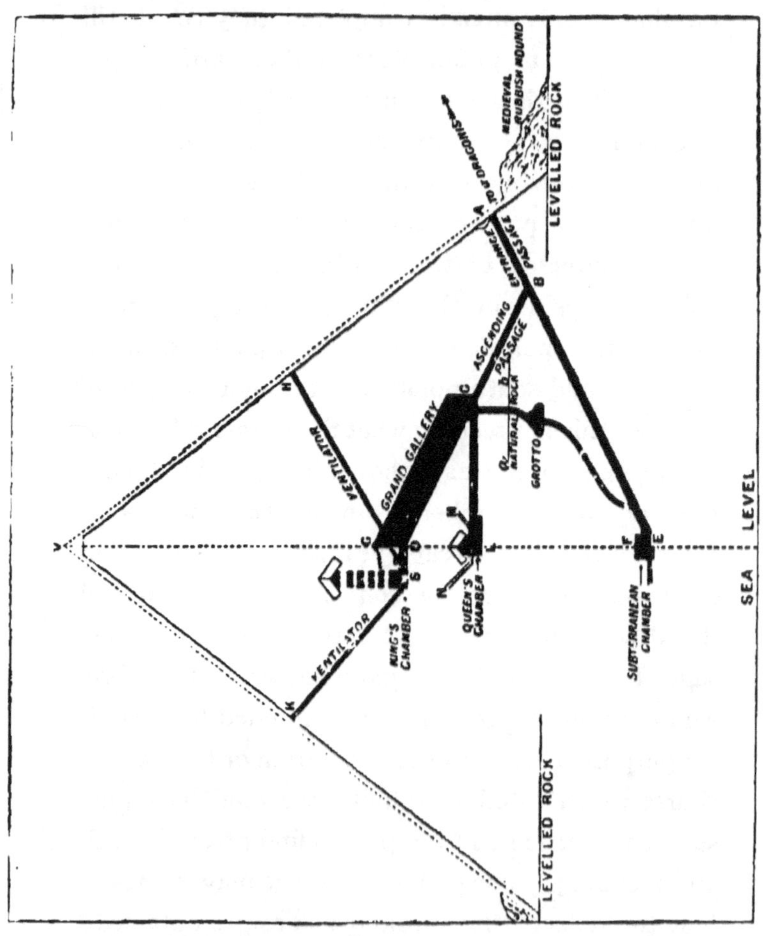

Fig. 5.

would suffice) plugged at B, and water poured in so
as to partially fill the angle thus formed at B, the

surface of that water would reflect the rays of Alpha Draconis up the ascending passage B C. The direction for the south line thus indicated could be marked, and then the plug left to slide down to the subterranean chamber. Once a year (supposing one layer of stones added each year, as Lepsius surmises) would have sufficed for this operation.

Not only do we thus find a natural and perfect explanation of the circumstance (hitherto unexplained) that the ascending passage is inclined at the same angle to the horizon as the descending passage, but precisely as we might expect from a true theory, we find that other points of difficulty have here their explanation.[1] It is obvious that at B the casing-stones of the descending passage would have to be very closely set and carefully cemented, so that the water used, year after year, in obtaining

---

[1] Most pyramidalists content themselves by assuming, as Sir E. Beckett puts it, ' that the same angle would probably be used for both sets of passages, *as there was no reason for varying it,*' which is not exactly an explanation of the relation. Mr. Wackerbarth has suggested that the passages were so adjusted for the purpose of managing a system of balance cars united by ropes from one passage to another ; but this explanation is open, as Beckett points out, to the fatal objection that the passages meet at their lowest point, not at their highest, so that it would be rather a puzzle ' to work out the mechanical idea.' The reflection explanation is not only open to no such objections, but involves precisely such an application of optical laws as we should expect from men as ingenious as the pyramid builders certainly were.

the reflected rays, might not percolate through and do mischief. Now, just here, we find the stones of the descending passage arranged with greater precision and made of better material. 'Why,' says Smyth—who notices everything, but seems always to insist on some forced explanation—'why did the builders change the rectangular joint at that point, and execute such unusual angle as they chose in place of it, in a better material of stone than elsewhere, and yet with so little desire to call general attention to it, that they made the joints fine and close to that degree that they escaped the attention of all men until 1865 A.D. ?' 'The answer came from the diagonal joints themselves, in discovering that the stone between them was opposite to the butt end of the portcullis of the first ascending passage, or to the hole whence the prismatic stone of concealment through 3,000 years, had dropped out almost before Al Manoun's eyes. Here, therefore, was a secret sign in the pavement of the entrance passage, appreciable only to a careful eye and a measurement by angle, but made in such hard material that it was evidently intended to last to the end of human time with the Great Pyramid, and has done so thus far.' In other words the stones were thus carefully fitted that they might be a sign to Professor Piazzi Smyth and the pyramidalists in 1865, just as the descending and ascending passages were all to be signs. It may show great want of taste to say that all these features indicate the builders' plan, and were in no sort intended for the benefit of remote generations of men belonging to an alien race; but it seems a long way more natural.

At any rate, it is certain that men having no knowledge of the telescope, and no means of securing accuracy of direction as our astronomers do by *magnifying*, would have adopted precisely such plans as thus far seem most clearly indicated in the pyramid structure, making long passages in solid materials, and where necessary, changing the lines of sight by simple reflection. When we consider that this would be their natural course, and that even minute details of structure (some hitherto unexplained) correspond with the theory that they adopted this course, the conclusion seems fair that the theory is a sound one.[1] Of course, it cannot be

---

[1] Albeit, I cannot but think that this ascending passage must also have been so directed as to show some bright star when due south. For if the passage had only given the meridian plane, but without permitting the astronomer to observe the southing of any fixed star, it would have subserved only one-half its purposes as a meridional instrument. It is to be remembered that, supposing the ascending passage to have its position determined in the way I have described, there would be nothing to prevent its being also made to show any fixed star nearly at the same elevation. For it could

acceptable to pyramidalists, who prefer to believe that the labours of the pyramid builders were

readily be enlarged in a vertical direction, the floor remaining un-altered. Since it is not enlarged until the great gallery is reached (at a distance of nearly 127 feet from the place where the ascent begins), it follows, or is at least rendered highly probable, that some bright star was in view through that ascending passage. Now, taking the date 2170 B.C., which Professor Smyth assigns to the beginning of the Great Pyramid, or even taking any date (as we fairly may), within a century or so on either side of that date, we find no bright star which would have been visible when due south, through the ascending passage. I have calculated the position of that circle among the stars along which lay all the points passing 26° 18′ above the horizon when due south, in the latitude of Ghizeh, 2170 years before the Christian era; and it does not pass near a single conspicuous star. There is only one fourth magnitude star which it actually approaches—namely, Epsilon Ceti; and one fifth magnitude star, Beta of the Southern Crown. When we remember that Egyptologists almost without exception assert that the date of the building of the pyramid must have been more than a thousand years earlier than 2170 B.C., and that Bunsen has assigned to Menes the date 3620 B.C., while the date 3300 B.C. has been assigned to Cheops or Suphis on apparently good authority, we are led to inquire whether the other epoch when Alpha Draconis was at about the right distance from the pole of the heavens may not have been the true era of the commencement of the Great Pyramid. Now, the year 3300 B.C., though a little late, would accord fairly well with the time when Alpha Draconis was at the proper distance $3\frac{3}{7}°$ from the pole of the heavens. If the inclination of the entrance passage is 26° 27′, as Professor Smyth made it, the exact date for this would be 3390 B.C.; if 26° 40′, as others made it before his measurements, the date would be about 3320 B.C., which would suit well with the date 3300 B.C., since a century either way would only carry the star about a third of a degree towards or from the pole. Now, when we inquire whether in the year 3300 B.C. any bright star would have been visible, at southing, through the ascending passage, we find that a very bright star indeed, an orb otherwise directed by architects knowing all that is now known in science, and more ; but we are, at least, saved from the incongruity of assuming that these wondrously-gifted architects were idiotic enough to adopt the blundering plan assigned to them—hiding away for preservation their sacred symbolisms and prophetic teachings, in a building so constructed that its interior could only be reached by being forcibly broken into, and would as a matter of fact be never properly measured until it had lost in great part the perfection of form on which its value for the supposed purpose depended.

This will appear still more clearly when we consider the Great Gallery, which to the astronomer is the most obviously astronomical part of the building, but to the pyramidalist is a sort of ' Zadkiel's Almanac ' in stone.

All the features thus far have been such as we should expect to find in a massive structure such as this, intended—for whatever reason—to be very carefully oriented. They are such, in fact, as could not but exist in a building oriented so successfully as the Great Pyramid unequestionably is, unless

remarkable as the nearest of all the stars, the brilliant Alpha Centauri, shone as it crossed the meridian right down that ascending tube. It is so bright that, viewed through that tube, it must have been visible to the naked eye, even when southing in full daylight.

some utterly incredible chance had enabled the builders, by an imperfect method, to hit accidentally on so perfect an orientation. Even then, in passing from the ground level to higher levels, they must inevitably have lost the perfection of their orientation, unless they had had such means of keeping their work correct as we find they had. This being so, the chances being practically infinite against their first obtaining, and afterwards retaining, such accuracy of orientation, without long, slant passages, such as we find within the pyramid, we are logically justified in saying it is *certain* that the passages were used in that way, and were intended originally to subserve that purpose.

The case is somewhat altered when we reach the point C, where the ascending passage ceases to be of the same small square section as the descending one. Up to this point its purpose is obvious. But so far as *mere* orientation was concerned, there seems no reason why it should not have retained the same section to a higher level. It is true that the nearer it approached to the central line, L F,[1] the less effective its direct value ; but certainly this

---

[1] This line is not vertically below the vertex, V, but central, in the sense of being the vertical line where the horizontal north and south line from the ascending and descending passages crosses the east and west plane through the vertex.

value would not be increased by increasing the size of the passage, whether in a vertical or a horizontal direction ; and from and after the point C it is increased in both directions.

Now, we are certain that the builders of the pyramid wanted to orient it very carefully, simply because we find that they did so. We do not know *why* they did. But it seems antecedently unlikely that *all* they wanted was to get the pyramid perfectly four-square to the cardinal points. The natural idea is, that being, as we see by their work they were, astronomers of great skill, they had an astronomical purpose of some sort. They had thus far been working with manifest reference to the meridional plane, just as an astronomer of our own time would ; and it looks very much, even from what we have already seen, as though they had considered this plane for the same reason that the modern astronomer considers it — viz. because this is the plane in which all the heavenly bodies culminate, or attain the middle and highest point of their passage from the eastern to the western horizon. They might have had only a fancy for exact orientation, though one can hardly tell why they should. Still, men of different races have taken strange fancies, and, unlikely though it seems, this might have been such an one, just as the building of colossal tombs seems to have been.

At the point C, however, all doubt ceases. The astronomical nature of the builders' purpose becomes here as clear and certain as already the astronomical nature of their methods has been. For from here upwards the small ascending passage is changed to one of great height, so as to command a long vertical space of the heavens, precisely as a modern astronomer sets his transit circle to sweep the vertical meridian. The floor, however, of the ascending passage, and even its sides, are carried on unchanged in direction, right up to D, where the central vertical (see preceding note) meets the ascending gallery. So that from B to D, except where the horizontal passage C L to the so-called Queen's Chamber is carried off, the floor of ascending passage and gallery formed a perfectly uniform slant plane.

And here let us pause to inquire—seeing that the astronomical purpose of the passage is made manifest—what shape an astronomer, who was also an architect, would give to the great ascending slit, as it were, through which the transits of the heavenly bodies were to be watched. As an astronomer, he would like it to be very high and relatively narrow; but as an architect, he would see that the vertical section could not have such a shape as A B C D in fig. 6; for then, not only would the side walls, A C, B D, be unstable, but the observer would not be comfortbl situated. Yet, as an astronomer, he would know that such a shape as is shown in fig. 7 would be unsuitable. To mention only one case out of many, supposing he wanted not only to observe a transit of a heavenly body along such a course as $p_1 p_2$, or $q_1 q_2$ (which, during the short time the body was visible would be practically a horizontal line), but also by observations on successive nights to determine the course of a heavenly body on the star sphere along a path as $P_1 P_2$, which might be inclined: then, the slant of the walls would entirely defeat his purpose. He would require, as an astronomer, that the walls should be absolutely vertical (note the difference between the paths $p_1 p_2$, $q_1 q_2$, $P_1 P_2$, in fig. 6, and the similarly-lettered paths in fig. 7), while as an architect he would know that they must be closer at the top than at the bottom of a passage so lofty as the Great Ascending Gallery. Fig. 8, giving the actual shape of the vertical section of the Great Gallery, shows how the astronomical architects of the Great Pyramid combined both qualities. Every part of the walls is abso

K

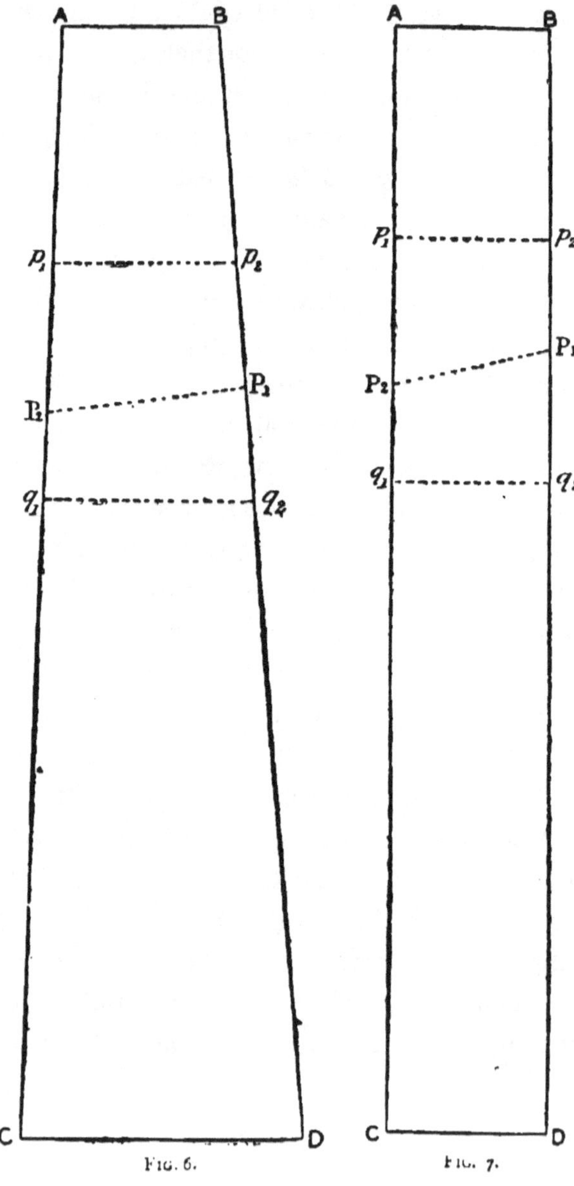

FIG. 6.　　　FIG. 7.

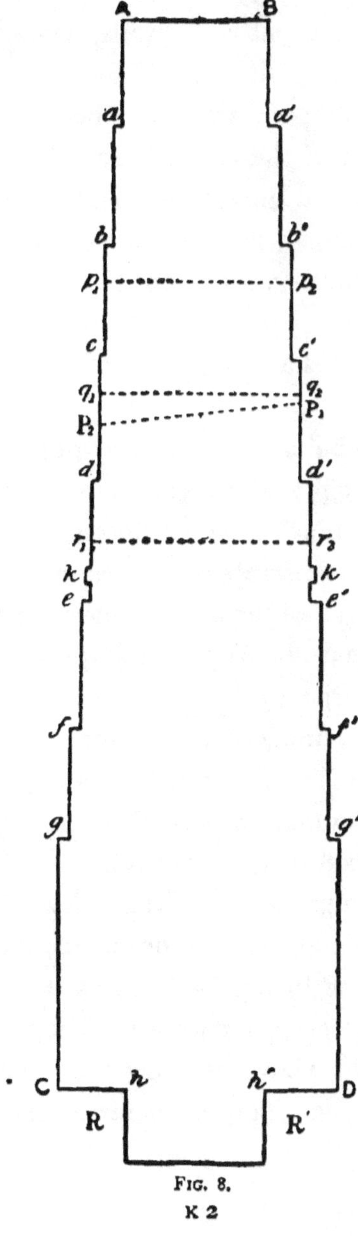

Fig. 8.

K 2

lutely vertical, and yet the walls, regarded as wholes, are aslant.

If we had not seen from the beginning the astronomical plan of the Great Pyramid, and that such a plan indicated an astronomical purpose, we should find, I take it, in this double character of the Ascending Gallery, proof positive that it was intended for astronomical observations. Only an astronomer would have set the architect such a problem.

But it may be said, How are observers to be stationed along a slant gallery such as this, with smooth and much-inclined floor? Is not the idea that such an unstable place was intended for exact astronomical observation almost as absurd as the notion that the top of the pyramid was meant for that purpose?

Certainly, if a modern astronomer were planning a slant gallery for transit work he would arrange for comfortable observation (the only observation which can be trustworthy).

Now the ramps, as Professor Piazzi Smyth calls them—the long slant stone banks, shown in section at R and R' in fig. 8—seem as if they had some reference to such a purpose. They are at a convenient height above the level of the slant floor, insomuch that Smyth pictures his Arabs leaning on them, stepping on to them, and so forth. But they would not serve of themselves to make observations easy. The observer has to be set in the middle of the gallery (at whatever point of its length he may be), and he ought to be comfortably seated. I think, if I were planning for his comfort (which means fitness to make good observations), I should have seats set across from ramp to ramp. They must be movable, of course : and if there were not something along the ramps' upper surface to hold them, they would slide down, carrying the observer most uncomfortably with them. I should, therefore, have holes cut out along the tops of the ramps at convenient distances; the holes on one side being exactly opposite those on the other. A set of cross benches should then be made, with projections corresponding to these holes. Then a bench could be set wherever it was wanted, or several at a time, so that different observers might watch the same transit across different parts of the field of view, as along p_1 p_2, q_1 q_2, and r_1 r_2. For some observations, indeed, such holes would serve yet another purpose. By means of them, screens could be set up by which to diminish the field of view and make the observations more exact. Or on such screens, images of the sun (showing the sun spots, be it remarked) could be thrown through a small opening on a screen, covering for the time the mouth of the gallery. For such observations the holes would be convenient; for the seats they would be absolutely essential.

Now no traces of the seats themselves, with their projections, cushions, &c., &c., have been found, or were likely to be found. But holes in the ramps are there still; twenty-eight of them there were originally in each ramp, though now only twenty-six remain, owing to the destruction of a ramp-stone. They are situated just as they should be to subserve the purposes I have mentioned— that is, at equal distances (of about $5\frac{1}{2}$ feet), and each hole on the east side of the gallery is exactly opposite the corresponding hole on the left side.

Regarded as a sort of architectural transit instrument, the Great Gallery would, of course, have to be carried up to a certain height, and there open out on the level to which the pyramid had then attained, the sides and top being carried up until the southernmost end of the gallery was completed with a vertical section like that shown in fig. 10 (facing p. 138). This would be the 'object end' of the great observing-tube. The observer might be anywhere along the tube, according to the position of the object whose transit was to be observed.

Now notice that the most important object of transit observations is to determine the time at which the objects observed cross the meridian. Either the observer has to determine at what time this happens, or, by noting when it happens, to ascertain the time ; in one case, knowing the time, he learns the position of the celestial object in what is called right ascension (which may be called its position measured around the celestial sphere in the direction of its rotation); in the other, knowing the position of the object in right ascension, he learns the time. But whether the observer is doing one or the other of these things, he must have a time-indicator of some sort. Our modern astronomer has his clock, beating seconds with emphatic thuds, and he notes the particular thuds at or near which the star crosses the so-called wires in the field of view (really magnified spider lines). We may be tolerably certain that the observer in the Grand Gallery had no such horological instrument. But he *must* have had a time-indicator of some sort (and a good one, we may notice in passing), or the care shown in the construction of the gallery would have been in great part wasted.

Now, whence could his time-sounds have been conveyed to him but from the upper end of the gallery ? A time-measure of some sort—probably a clepsydra, or water-clock—must have been set there, and persons appointed to mark the passage of time in some way, and to note also the instants when the observer or observers in the Great Gallery signalled the beginning or end of transit across the gallery's field of view. These time-indicating persons, with their instruments, would have occupied the space where now are the floors of the so-called Antechamber and King's Chamber—then, of course, not walled in (or the walls would have obstructed the view along the gallery). These persons themselves would not obstruct the view, unless they came too near the mouth of the gallery. Or they might be close to the mouth of the gallery at its sides, without obstructing the view.

But now, notice that if the place they thus occupied—the future King's Chamber (perhaps, as the region in or near which all the observations of the heavenly host in culmination had been made) —were in the centre of the square top of the pyramid as thus far built, they would be very much in the way of other observers, who ought to be stationed at certain special points on this horizontal top, to observe certain important horizontal lines, viz. the lines directed to the cardinal points and to points midway between these. An observer who had this task assigned him should occupy the very centre of the square top of the, as yet, incomplete pyramid, so that the middle point of each side would mark a cardinal point, while the angles of the square would mark the mid-cardinal points. Also this central point ought not only to command direction-lines to the angles and bisections of the sides, but to be commanded, without obstruction, by direction-lines from these points.

Thus the upper end of the Great Ascending Gallery should not be exactly at the centre, but somewhat either to the west or to the east of the centre of the great square summit of the incomplete pyramid.

Let us see how this matter was actually arranged :—

Fig. 9 shows the incomplete pyramid, as supposed to be viewed from above. The four sockets, *s.w.*, *n.w.*, *n.e.*, and *s.e.*, were supposed, until quite recently, to mark the exact position of the four base angles of the pyramid. It turns out, however, that they are rather below the level of the real basal plane of the structure, which is, therefore, somewhat smaller than had been supposed.

Fig. 9 is, however, chiefly intended to show the nature of the square platform, which formed the top of the pyramidal frustum when the level of the floor of the gallery of the King's Chamber had just been reached. We have a horizontal section of the pyramid, in fact, taken through the floor of the King's Chamber and Antechamber—that is, through S D, in the figure on p. 120. The bottle-shaped black space, near *O*, gives the section of the slanting gallery, beginning on the southern side at its widest part, reaching a narrower part somewhat to the north of *O*, and thereafter narrowing towards the north, till the section of the uppermost or narrowest part is reached. The dotted lines show where the Grand Gallery and the narrow ascending passage (ascending for one passing towards the King's Chamber) pass downwards into the structure of the pyramid : at *e* is the place where descending and ascending passages meet. The position, also, of the entrance-hole, forced in by Al Mamoun, at about the level of the angle *c*, is indicated.

At *O* is the centre of the square surface, which then formed the top of the structure. If posts were placed at the angles *n.w.*, *s.w.*, *s.e.*, *s.w.*, and also at *n.*, *e.*, *s.*, and *w.*, an observer stationed at *O* would have the cardinal and the mid-cardinal points exactly indicated. Now the point *O* is about eight and a-half paces from the middle of the southern opening of the Grand Gallery ; so that, if there were an assistant observer at *o*, he could communicate time signals readily both to the observers in

9. Horizontal Section of the Great P

9. Horizontal Section of the Great P

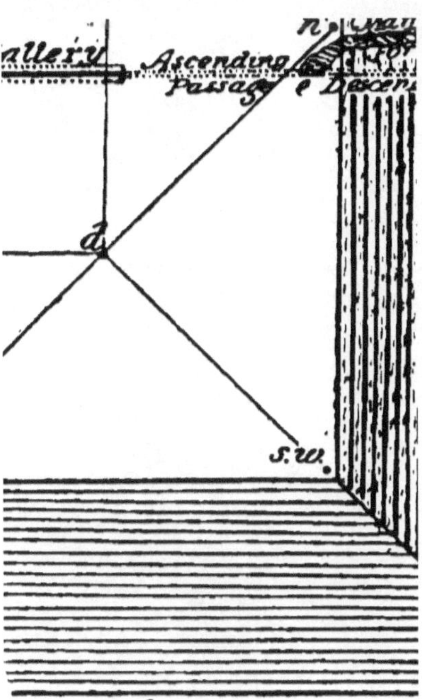

irough floor of King's Chamber.

the gallery and to the observer at *O*. All such observations as the easting, southing, westing, and northing of heavenly bodies would belong to the observer at *O*, uprights of suitable height being erected at *n., e., s.,* and *w.* He could also observe when heavenly bodies passed the mid-cardinal directions, *n.w., s.w., s.e.,* and *s.w.* It will be noticed that if we suppose the Grand Gallery completed, which would carry it to a height of about 28 feet above the level of the floor at *o*, the slant of the gallery would yet be such that the observer at *O*, supposing him to observe by means of an instrument raised a few feet above the level of the floor, would be perfectly well able to look along the horizontal direction-line from *O* to *s.w.* (Most of his observations would, of course, be directed to points above the horizon.)

But I think if I were planning such observations on the square surface *e., s., w., n.,* I should wish to have several observers at work in thus taking azimuths (directions referred to the cardinal points) and altitudes, just as several transit observers were manifestly provided for in the construction of the Grand Gallery.

I should set an observer at *n.*, to observe in directions *n.-n.w., n.-w., n.-s.* (that is, *n.O.*), *n.-e.*, and *n-s.w.* ; another at *w.*, another at *e.*, and another at *s.*, to observe in the corresponding directions belonging to their stations. Observers at *n.w.*, *s.w.*, *s.e.*, and *s.w.* could also do excellent work. In fact, between them they could take the horizontal cardinal and mid-cardinal directions better than the observer stationed at *O*, though his would be the best station for general work with the astrolabe.

Yet again, for observing heavenly bodies at considerable altitudes, stations nearer to the uprights at *s.w.*, *w.*, *n.w.*, &c., would be useful. Where else could they be so well placed as at the points *a*, *b*, *c*, *d*, where the lines *w.s.*, *w.n.*, *e.s.*, and *e.n.* intersect the diagonals of the square surface of the pyramidal structure? Note, also, that these observing stations would be at convenient distances from each other. The sides of this square surface would be roughly about 175 paces long, so that such a distance as *a.w.*, or *a.O* would only be about 62 yards (the length of the Grand Gallery being about 52 yards).

Thus there would be thirteen observers of azimuthal directions and altitudes, whose work would be combined with that of at least seven transit observers along different parts of the length of the Great Gallery with its seven transit widths (as shown by its section, fig. 8, p. 131). Twenty observers in all (the transit workers provided with the great

FIG. 16.—Vertical Section through the Grand Gallery.

fixed transit instruments in the gallery itself, the others armed perhaps with astrolabes, armillary spheres for reference, direction-tubes, or ring-carry-ing rods) would be able to make observations only inferior in accuracy to those made in our own time with telescopic adjuncts.

Fig. 10 is intended to show something of the structure of the interior of the Great Gallery. The stones outside are supposed to be seen in section, only one-fourth of the gallery being given. For correct perspective, six or seven more layers of stone should have been shown below the lowest in the picture. But this would have given to the illustration an inconvenient shape. It will be seen that a section of the southern sky, very convenient for observation, would be seen from the interior of the Grand Gallery. The central vertical through this section would (as seen from the middle of any of the cross seats) be the true meridian. But the moment of transit might be equally well observed by taking the moments when a star was first seen (from the middle of a cross seat) on the eastern edge of the vertical sky space, and when the star disappeared : the instant midway between these would be the true time of transit. By combining the observations made by several 'watchmen of the night,' stationed in different parts of the Grand

Gallery, a very close approximation to true sidereal time could be obtained.

I apprehend, however, that astronomers who had shown themselves so ingenious in other respects, would not have omitted to note the advantage of suitably-adjusted screens for special transit observations ; and it seems to me likely that the long grooves shown in section at k and k' (fig. 8, p. 131) might have been used in connection with such a purpose, and not *merely* (though that was probably one of the objects they were intended to subserve) to carry a horizontal sliding cross-bar, by means of which the altitude of a celestial body at the moment of transit could be more readily determined. We must not forget that transit observers have to determine what is called the declination of a star (its distance from the equator), as well as what is called the right ascension, or distance measured parallel to the equator from a certain assigned point on that circle. For this purpose the horizontal lines $a\,a'$, $b\,b'$, &c. (fig. 8), would be useful, but not sufficient. I incline to think that the method used to obtain accuracy in observations for determining declination involved a very practical use of the grooves $k\,k'$. Possibly a horizontal bar ran from k to k', carrying vertical rods, across which, at suitable distances, horizontal lines were drawn (or, better still, horizontal rods could be slid to any required height). The horizontal bar could be slid to any convenient position, the vertical rods adjusted, and at the time of transit the horizontal rods could be shifted to such a height as just to touch a star when seen by an observer in the gallery at the moment of mid-transit.

If a telescopist in our own time will try to plan out a method of determining the declinations and right ascensions of stars (say, for the purpose of forming a trustworthy star chart or catalogue), without using a telescope, by using such an observing place as the Great Gallery, he will see how much might be done, so far as equatorial and zodiacal stars were concerned ; and they are altogether the most important, even now, and were still more so in the days when the stars in their courses were supposed to rule the fates of men and nations.

How far the structure of the Grand Gallery corresponds with the requirements of this theory can be judged from the following description given by Professor Greaves in 1638 :—' It is,' he says, ' a very stately piece of work, and not inferior, either in respect of the curiosity of art or richness of materials, to the most sumptuous and magnificent buildings ;' and a little further on he says: ' This

gallery, or corridor, or whatever else I may call it,
is built of white and polished marble (limestone),
the which is very evenly cut in spacious squares or
tables. Of such materials as is the pavement,
such is the roof and such are the side walls that
flank it; the coagmentation or knitting of the
joints is so close, that they are scarcely discernible
to a curious eye; and that which adds grace to
the whole structure, though it makes the passage
the more slippery and difficult, is the acclivity or
rising of the ascent. The height of this gallery is
26 feet' (Professor Smyth's careful measurements
show the true height to be more nearly 28 feet),
'the breadth of 6·870 feet, of which 3·435 feet are
to be allowed for the way in the midst, which is
set and bounded on both sides with two banks
(like benches) of sleek and polished stone; each
of these hath 1·717 of a foot in breadth, and as
much in depth.' These measurements are not
strictly exact. Smyth made the breadth of the
gallery above the banks or ramps, as he calls them,
6 feet 10½ inches; the space between the ramps,
3 feet 6 inches; the ramps nearly about 1 foot
8$\frac{1}{14}$ inches broad, and nearly 1 foot 9 inches high,
measured transversely; that is, at right angles to
the ascending floor.

The diversity of width which I have indicated

as a desirable feature in a meridional gallery, is a
marked feature of the actual gallery. 'In the
casting and ranging of the marbles' (limestone),
'in both the side walls, there is one piece of architecture,' says Greaves, 'in my judgment, very
graceful, and that is that all the courses or stones,
which are but seven (so great are these stones), do
set and flag over one another about three inches;
the bottom of the uppermost course overlapping
the top of the next, and so in order, the rest as
they descend.' The faces of these stones are
exactly vertical; and as the width of the gallery
diminishes upwards by about six inches for each
successive course, it follows that the width at the
top is about $3\frac{1}{2}$ feet less than the width, 6 feet
$10\frac{1}{5}$ inches, at the bottom, or agrees in fact with
the width of the space between the benches or
ramps. Thus the shadow of the vertical edges of
the gallery at solar noon just reached to the edges
of the ramps, the shadow of the next lower vertical
edges falling three inches from the edges higher
up the ramps, those of the next vertical edges
six inches from these edges, still higher up, and so
forth. The true hour of the sun's southing could
thus be most accurately determined by seven sets
of observers placed in different parts of the gallery, and near midsummer, when the range of the

L

shadows would be so far shortened, that a smaller number of observers only could follow the shadows' motions; but in some respects, the observations in this part of the year could be more readily and exactly made than in winter, when the shadow-spaces of various width would range along the entire length of the gallery.

Similar remarks would apply to the moon, which could also be directly observed. The planets and stars of course could only be observed directly.

The Grand Gallery could be used for the observation of any celestial body southing higher than 26°18′ above the horizon; but not very effectively for objects passing near the zenith. The Pleiades could be well observed. They southed about $63\frac{3}{4}°$ above the horizon in the year 2140 B.C., or thereabouts, when they were on the equinoctial colure.[1] But if I am right in taking the year

[1] This date is sometimes given earlier, but when account is taken of the proper motion of these stars we get about the date above mentioned. I cannot understand how Dr. Ball, Astronomer Royal for Ireland, has obtained the date 2248 B.C., unless he has taken the proper motion of Alcyone the wrong way. The proper motion of this star during the last 4,000 years has been such as to increase the star's distance from the equinoctial colure; and therefore, of course, the actual interval of time since the star was on the colure is less than it would be calculated to be if the proper motion were neglected.

3300 B.C., when Alpha Centauri shone down the smaller ascending passage in southing, the Pleiades were about 58° only above the horizon when southing, and therefore even more favourably observable from the great meridional gallery.

In passing I may note that at this time, about 3300 years before our era, the equinoctial point (that is, the point where the sun passes north of the equator, and the year begins according to the old manner of reckoning) was midway between the horns of the Bull. So that then, and then alone, a poet might truly speak of spring as the time—

> Candidus auratis aperit quum cornibus annum
> Taurus,

as Virgil incorrectly did (repeating doubtless some old tradition) at a later time. Even Professor Smyth notices the necessity that the Pyramid Gallery should correspond in some degree with such a date. 'For,' says he, 'there have been traditions for long, whence arising I know not, that the seven overlappings of the Grand Gallery, so impressively described by Professor Greaves, had something to do with the Pleiades, those proverbially seven stars of the primeval world,' only that he considers the pyramid related to *memorial,* not observing astronomy ' of an earlier date than Virgil.' The Pleiades also were not regarded as belonging to Taurus, but as forming an independent star group.

We have seen that the Great Pyramid is so perfectly oriented as to show that astronomical observations of great accuracy were made by its architects. No astronomer can doubt this, for the simple reason that every astronomer knows the exceeding difficulty of the task which the architects solved so satisfactorily, and that nothing short of the most careful observation would have enabled the builders to secure anything like the accuracy which, as a matter of fact, they did secure. Many, not acquainted with the nature of the problem, imagine that all the builders had to do was to use some of those methods of taking shadows, as, for instance, at solar noon (which has to be first determined, be it noticed), or before and after noon, noting when shadows are equal (which is not an exact method, and requires considerable care even to give what it *can* give—imperfect orientation), and so forth. But to give the accuracy which the builders obtained, not only in the orientation, but in getting the pyramid very close to latitude 30° (which was evidently what they wanted), only very exact observations would serve.

Indeed, if a modern astronomer, knowing nothing about the pyramid, were asked how the thing could be done without telescopic aid, he would be apt to say that no greater accuracy than (for instance) Tycho Brahe obtained with his great quadrant at Uranienburg could have been secured. Now, the orientation of the Great Pyramid approaches much closer to exactness than the best observations by Tycho Brahe with that justly-celebrated instrument.[1]

[1] In the first place, many seem quite unaware of the difficulty of orienting a building like the Great Pyramid with the degree of accuracy with which that building actually has been oriented. One gravely asks whether (as Narrien long since suggested) a plumb-line, so hung as to be brought into line with the pole-star, would not have served as well as the great descending passage. Observe how all the real difficulties of the problem are overlooked in this ingenious solution. We want to get a long line—a line at least 200 yards long—in a north and south position. We must fix its two ends ; and as the pole-star is not available as a point along the line, we set our plumb-line at the northern end of the line, and our observing tube or hole, or whatever it may be (only it is not a telescope, for we are Egyptians of the time of Cheops, and have none), at the other. The pole-star being at an altitude of $26\frac{1}{2}$ degrees, the plumb-line should be nearly 100 yards long, to be seen (near the top), coincident with the pole-star, from a station 200 yards away. That is a tolerably long plumb-line. Then its upper part (thus to be seen *without telescopic aid at night*) would be about 260 yards away. The observer's eyesight would have to be tolerably keen.

I am also asked whether a dishful of water would not serve quite as well as a great mass of water, at the corner where the descending and ascending passages meet, to give the reflected rays from a star. It would, and so would a thimbleful—just as a thread of cotton would serve as well as a half-inch rope for the plumb-line

Seeing this, and observing that the ascending

just considered.   But just in proportion as the water surface was diminished would the difficulty of seeing a star by reflected rays be increased.   The builders had, doubtless, good reason for making the descending passage about four feet wide and as many high.   It at any rate enabled them to see the pole-star readily, just as the wide 'field' of a comet-finder enables the astronomer to bring a celestial object very easily into view.   Whatever reason they had for thus securing a tolerably large field of view, they would have precisely the same reason for retaining it undiminished when they used the reflected instead of the direct rays in observing a star. Now for this purpose nothing short of the whole breadth of the descending and ascending passages would suffice—in other words, no dishful or thimbleful of water would have served their purpose.

Then it is asked why the descending passage should be repeated in the other pyramids when the orientation had already been secured in the Great Pyramid—manifestly in ignorance of the fact that it would be far more difficult to take the orientation for one pyramid from another, than to do it independently.   It is also asked whether the slant descending passages were not obviously meant for the sliding down of the king's sarcophagus.   Sliding the sarcophagus down that it might afterwards be hauled up the ascending passage ! or if not, what was the ascending passage for? and why was it of the same cross section as the descending passage?   If the sarcophagus alone had been in question, we may be certain that the pyramid engineers would never have arranged for sliding it down from the level of the entrance to the descending passage, to the place where the ascending passage begins, in order afterwards to raise it by the ascending passage.   If they meant to go down to the underground chamber they would not have raised it at all, but let it down from the level of the pyramid's base.   But to say truth, moving the sarcophagus was a mere nothing compared with the lifting of the great solid blocks which formed the pyramid's mass.   The engineers who moved these great solid blocks to their places would not have wanted slant passages at the right friction slope, and all the rest of it, by which to take the sarcophagus to its place ; nor would they have provided for unnecessary descents or ascents either, but have taken the sarcophagus from the outside to its proper level, and sent it along a level passage.

and descending passages are just such as the astronomer would make to secure such a result, we may accept, without doubt, the belief that they were made for that purpose.

Then we saw that the features of the Great Ascending Gallery were not such as would be essential, or even desirable, to increase or maintain the accuracy of the orientation, as layer after layer was added to the pyramid, but are precisely such as would be essential if the pyramid was meant to subserve (as one, at least, of its objects) the purpose of an observatory.

But persons unfamiliar with astronomy will say, This Great Ascending Gallery would only enable astronomers to observe stars when due south, or nearly so, and only those which, when due south, were within a certain distance above or below the point towards which the axis of the Great Gallery is directed. Were all the other stars left unobserved? And again, we know that the Egyptians, like all ancient astronomers, paid great attention to the rising and setting of the heavenly bodies, and especially to what was called the heliacal rising and setting of the stars. In what way would the Great Gallery help them here?

Now, with regard to the first point, we note that the chief instrument of exact observation in modern observatories, the one which, as it were, governs all the others, has precisely this quality— it is *always* directed to the meridian, and has, indeed, a very much narrower range of view on either side of the meridian than the Great Gallery had. And though it is indeed free to range over the whole arc of the meridian from the south horizon point through the point overhead to the north horizon point, it is mainly employed over about that range north and south of the celestial equator which was commanded by the Great Gallery. The visitor at Greenwich sees the great equatorial, and imagines that to be the chief observing instrument. The comparatively unobtrusive transit circle seems far less important. But the time observations, which are far and away the most important observations made at Greenwich, are all made, or at least all regulated, by the transit observations. So are the observations for determining the positions of stars.

When the equatorial is used to make a time or position observation, it is used as a differential instrument; it is employed to determine how far east or west a star may be (theoretically, how much it differs in right ascension measured by time) from another; and again, to show how far north or south a star may be (theoretically, how much it differs in declination) from another, whose right ascension and declination have already been determined by repeated observations with the transit circle. Similarly, the altitude and azimuth instrument is used in direct subordination to the transit circle.

The astronomers who observed from the Great Pyramid doubtless made many more observations off the meridian than on it. They made multitudinous observations of the rising and setting of stars, and especially of their heliacal risings and settings (which last, however, though we hear so much of them, belonged *ex necessitate* to but a very rough class of observations). They no doubt often used astrolabes and similar instruments to determine the positions of stars, planets, comets, &c., when off the meridian, with reference to stars whose places were already determined by the use of their great meridional instrument. But all those observations were regulated by, and derived their value from, the work done in the Great Ascending Gallery. The modern astronomer sees that this was the only way in which exact observations of the heavenly bodies all over the star-sphere could possibly have been made ; and seeing the extreme care, the most marvellous pains, which the astronomers of the Great Pyramid took to secure good meridional work, the astronomer recognises in him a fellow-worker.   He says, with the poet :—

> I am as old as Egypt to myself,
> Brother to them that squared the Pyramids :
> By the same stars I watch.

And now consider what was this great observatory of ancient Egypt—the most perfect ever made till telescopic art revealed a way of exact observation without those massive structures.   A mighty mass, having a base larger than the square of Lincoln's Inn, rising by just fifty layers to a height of about 142 feet, and presenting towards the south the appearance shown in fig. 11, where the mouth of the Great Gallery is seen opening southwards, and the lines are shown which have been already indicated as 'observing directions' in the picture facing p. 138.   The pyramid observatory is shown in section in fig. 12.   It will be noticed that the successive layers are not of equal thickness.   There are just fifty between the base and plane of the floor of the King's Chamber.   The direction-lines for the mid-day sun at midsummer, midwinter, and the equinoxes are shown ; also the lines to the two stars, Alpha Draconis and Alpha Centauri, are given at the subpolar meridional passage of the former and the meridional passage

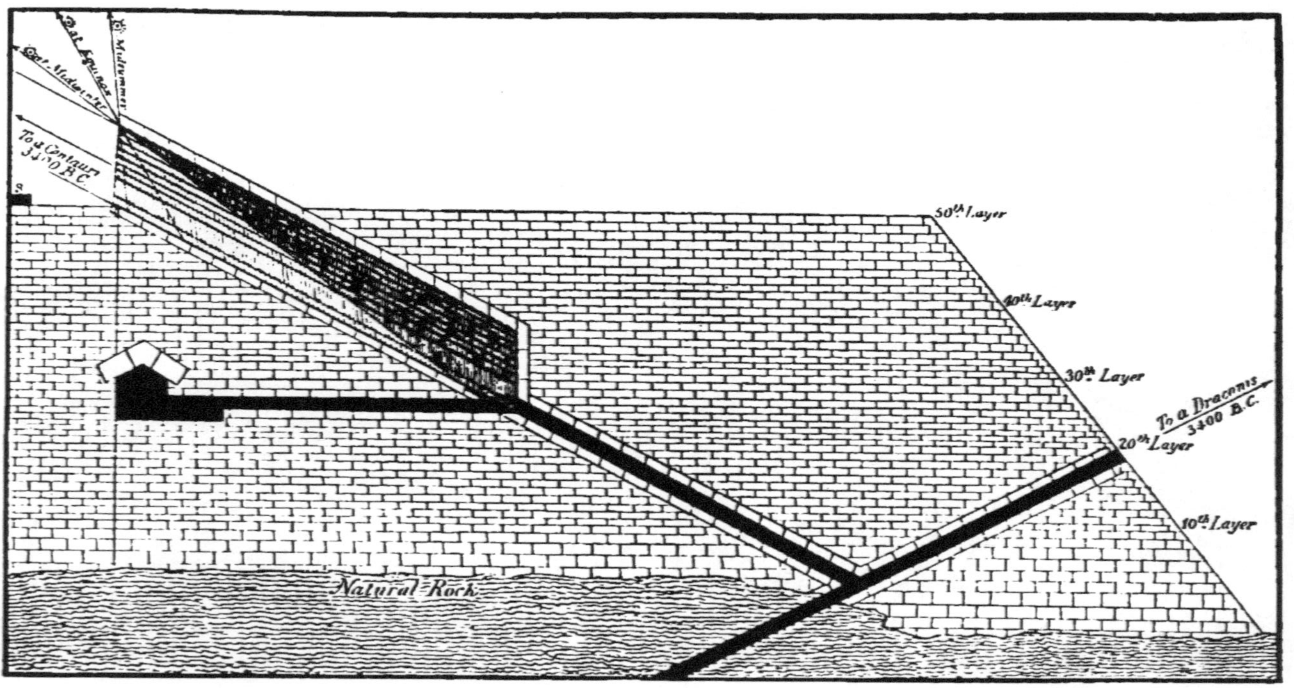

FIG. 12.—Vertical Section of the Great Pyramid, showing the Ascending and Descending Passages, Grand Gallery, and Queen's Chamber.

of the latter, at the date when the descending and ascending passages thus commanded both these stars. Within fifty years or so on either side of this date, the pyramid must, I should think, have been built. The later date when Alpha Draconis was at the right distance from the pole, 2170 B.C.,[1] is absolutely rejected by Egyptologists—not one being ready to admit that the date of the Pyramid King can have been anywhere near so late.

Thus far all has been tolerably plain sailing. Of the astronomical use and purpose (not quite the same thing, be it noticed) of the Great Gallery, there can be small room for doubt, when we find (1) every feature in all the passages and in the Great Gallery correspond with the requirements of the theory, and (2) many features explicable in no other way.

[1] Some may be disposed to reject a change which they may imagine displaces the Pleiades from the position which Professor Piazzi Smyth assigned to that interesting group at the date when he supposed the pyramid was bu lt. But there never was the least real significance in that position. If the mistaken idea entertained by many, and repeated by Flammarion, Haliburton, and others, that the Pleiades at their meridian shone down the Great Gallery at the very time when the pole-star of 2170 B.C. shone down the descending gallery, had been correct, there might have been some reason to be struck by the coincidence. But it should hardly be necessary to tell the reader, what every astronomer knows, that the Pleiades never did or could shine down the Great Gallery, and in the year 2170 B.C. were thirty-eight degrees (!) north of that position.

But here our difficulties begin. Astronomy no longer lends its aid when we ask why the builder of the Great Pyramid wanted to have an astronomical observatory as well as a tomb. To begin with, I suppose Egyptologists are quite clear that a main purpose of each pyramid was that it should serve for a tomb. And I suppose, further, that this being so, it was essential that each pyramid, including that one which we have been regarding hitherto only in its astronomical aspect, should be as nearly as possible completed before the death of its future occupant. There may be, for aught I know, some reason to believe that in the days of the pyramids an Egyptian king might be able in some way to assure himself of the *bona fides* of his successors, and that they would continue the work which he had begun and more than half completed. But it is very difficult to imagine that this really was the case. Human nature must in those days have resembled pretty closely human nature in our own time; and it seems as unlikely that a king could trust in his successors so far as to believe they would expend large sums of money and a great amount of labour in completing a work in which they had no direct or actual interest, as that, supposing he trusted them to this degree, their conduct after his death would have justified his confidence. Thus, when we find that the Great Pyramid was actually completed in the most careful and perfect manner, we have very strong reason for believing it to have been all but completed during the lifetime of the king, its builder—if it was indeed intended for his tomb. I must confess that the exclusively tombic theory of the Great Pyramid (at least) had always seemed to me utterly incredible, even before I advanced what seems to me the only reasonable interpretation of its erection. One may admit that the singular taste of the Egyptian kings for monstrous tombs was carried to a preposterous extent, but not to an extent quite so preposterous as the exclusively tombic theory would require. Of course, when we see that the details of the great edifice indicate unmistakably an astronomical object, which was regarded as of such importance as to justify the extremest care, our opinion is strengthened that the pyramid was not solely meant for a tomb. For this would bring in another absurdity, scarcely less than that involved in the exclusively tombic theory of structures so vast, if even they were non-astronomical—this, namely, that the Egyptian kings thought the celestial bodies and their movements so especially related to *them*, that their long home must be astronomically posited with a degree of care far surpassing that which has *ever* [1] been given to an astronomical observatory. Common sense compels us to believe that whether the Great Pyramid was meant for a tomb or not, its astronomical character was given to it for some purpose relating to the living king who had it built. (I suppose Egyptologists are absolutely certain that the Great Pyramid *was* built by one king, and, therefore, within a few decades of years.)

Now, it is not reasonable to suppose King Cheops' purpose was simply scientific. We may fairly take it for granted that the king who expended such vast sums and sacrificed so many lives to build for himself a tomb, was not a man taking a disinterested interest in science, or even ready to help the priests of his day to regulate religious ceremonials by astronomical observations conducted with reference only to general religious relations. To put the matter plainly, the builder of the Great Pyramid must have thought of himself first ; next, of his dynasty ; then, perhaps, of the priesthood (though always with reference to the bearing of religious ceremonies on the welfare of himself and his dynasty) ; lastly, of his people, as

---

[1] Even in our own time, though we get greater accuracy in our observations than Cheops obtained in his pyramid, we have not to give anything like the same degree of care to the work.

part of his wealth and power. For abstract science he cared not, as may be well assured, a single jot. I do not wish to suggest that Cheops was wickedly selfish. I have no doubt he was thoroughly persuaded that he was carrying out the purpose of his existence in expending much treasure and many lives on his own well-being (both before and after death). But there can be no doubt this *was* the real object of his expenditure of time, and wealth, and human life on the great structure which bears his name.

Now, our thoughts are at once turned by these considerations to that one sole line along which astronomy ever has been followed with the hope of material profit ; and we are led to remember that if there is one idea which has more strongly taken possession of the human race than any other, or one which more than any other is associated with the astronomy of ancient Egypt, it is the idea that the stars in their courses rule the fate of men and nations. We remember that even now, when science has shown the utter incorrectness of the ideas that underlie the ancient system of astrology, this system has its influence over millions. Even now the terms belonging to the system remain part of our language. Our very religion has all its times and seasons regulated in ways derived from the astrological system of old Egypt. Our Sunday is the old Chaldæan and Egyptian quarter-month rest day, and the Jewish Sabbath is this quarter-month rest day associated with the belief in the malefic influence of the planet (Saturn), which formerly ruled the last day of the week (still called Saturday or Saturn's-day).[1] The morning and

[1] A correspondent of *Knowledge* touched on the association which I mentioned as existing between the Jewish Sabbath (our Saturday) and Saturn ; labouring, manifestly, under the impression that the point at issue was the identity of the Roman god Saturn with the Scandinavian deity assigned to Saturday. But of course this is not the question at issue. It is not the god Saturn, but the planet Saturn, which is associated with Saturday. How any one can reconcile the clear statement of Dion Cassius with the belief that the days of the week were not associated with the planets until the twelfth century, passes my comprehension. Dion Cassius distinctly attributes the invention of the week to the Egyptians, and as he wrote a thousand years before the time named, there can be no question as to the greater antiquity of the week-day names. In the ancient Brahminical astronomy the days are associated with the same planets as among the Egyptians. See Mr. Colebrooke's papers in the *Asiatic Researches.* Among more familiar discussions of this matter may be cited Bailly's *Astronomie Indienne et Orientale*, and Bohlen's *Das Alte Indien.* Dion Cassius refers to the connection between musical intervals and the planets, showing that probably the old Egyptian lore which Pythagoras of Samos brought to Greece, included the association between the planets and the days of the week; that, in fact, all three subjects were connected—planets, musical intervals, and the days of the week. Longfellow thus poetically renders the views of Egyptian astrologers on these, with them, mystical matters :—

> ' Like the astrologers of eld,
> In that great vision I beheld
> Greater and deeper mysteries.
> I saw, with its celestial keys,

evening sacrifices of the Jews and their new moon festivals were manifestly astronomical in origin—in other words astrological (for astronomy was nothing except as astrology to the old Chaldæans and Egyptians). The Feast of the Passover, however later associated with other events, was derived from the old astrological observance of the passage of the sun (the Passing over of the Sun-God) across the equator, ascendingly; while the Feast of Tabernacles was in like manner ruled by the passage of the sun over the equator descendingly. Our calendar rules for Easter and other festivals would never, we may be well assured, have been made to depend on the moon, but for their original derivation from astronomical (that is astrological) ceremonial.[1]

> Its chords of air, its frets of fire,
> The Samian's great Æolian lyre,
> Rising through all its sevenfold bars,
> From earth unto the fixèd stars.
> And through the dewy atmosphere,
> Not only could I see but hear
> Its wondrous and harmonious strings
> In sweet vibration, sphere by sphere;
> From Dian's circle light and near,
> Onward to vaster, wider rings,
> Where, chanting through his beard of snows
> Majestic, mournful Saturn goes,
> And down the sunless realms of space
> Reverberates the thunder of his bass.'

[1] The Jewish people, when they left Egypt after their long

When we remember that the astronomy of the time of Cheops was essentially astrology, and astrology a most important part of religion, we begin to see how the erection of the mighty mass of masonry for astronomical purposes may be explained—or, rather, we see how, being certainly astronomical, it *must* be explained. Inasmuch as it is an astronomical building, erected in a time when astronomy was astrology, it was erected for astrological purposes. It was in this sense a sort of temple, erected, indeed, for the peculiar benefit of one man or of a single dynasty; but as he was a king in a time when being a king meant a great deal, what benefited him he doubtless regarded as a benefit also to his people: in whatever sense the Great Pyramid had a religious significance with regard to him, it had also a national religious significance.

It would have been worth Cheops' while to have this great astrological observatory erected, even if

sojourn there, had doubtless become thoroughly accustomed to the religious observances of the Egyptians (at any rate there is not the slightest reference even to the Sabbath before the sojourn in Egypt), and were disposed not only to retain these observances, but to associate with them the Egyptian superstitions. We know this, in fact, from the Bible record. Moses could not—no man ever could—turn a nation from observances once become part of their very life, but he could, and did, deprive them of their superstitious character.

by means of it he could learn only what was to happen, the times and seasons which were likely to be fortunate or unfortunate for him or his race, and so forth. But in his day, as in ours, astrology claimed not only to read but also to rule the stars Astrologers did not pretend that they could actually regulate the movements of the heavenly bodies, but they claimed that by careful observation and study they could show how the best advantage could be taken of the good dispositions of the stars, and their malefic influences be best avoided. They not only claimed this, but doubtless many of them believed it; and it is quite certain that those who were not astronomers (*i.e.* astrologers) were fully persuaded of the truth of the system which, even when the discovery of the true nature of the planets has entirely disproved it, retains still its hold upon the minds of the multitude.

There is, so far as I can see, no other theory of the Great Pyramid which even comes near to giving a common-sense interpretation of the combined astronomical and sepulchral character of this wonderful structure. If it is certain, on the one hand, that the building was built astronomically, and was meant for astronomical observation, it is equally certain that it was meant for a tomb, that it was closed in very soon after the king died for whom it was built, that, in fine, its astronomical value related to himself alone. As an astrological edifice, a gigantic horoscope for him and for him only, we can understand its purport, much though we may marvel at the vast expenditure of care, labour, and treasure at which it was erected. Granted full faith in astrology (and we know there was such faith), it was worth while to build even such a structure as the Great Pyramid ; just as, granted the ideas of Egyptians about burial, we can understand the erection of so mighty a mass for a tomb, and all save its special astronomical character. Of no other theory, I venture to say, than that which combines these two strange but most marked characteristics of the Egyptian mind, can this be said.

I could descant at great length on the value which the Great Pyramid, when in the condition represented in fig. 11 (frontispiece) and fig. 12, must have had for astronomical observation. I could show how much more exactly than by the use of any gnomon, the sun's annual course around the celestial sphere could be determined by observations made from the Great Gallery, by noting the shadow of the edges of the upper opening of the gallery on the sides, the floor, and the upper surfaces of the ramps. The moon's monthly path and its changes could have been dealt with in the same effective way. The geocentric paths, and thence the true paths, of the planets could be determined very accurately by combining the use of tubes or ring-carrying rods with the direction-lines determined from the gallery's sides, floor, &c. The place of every visible star along the Zodiac (astrologically the most important part of the stellar heavens) could be most accurately determined. Had the pyramid been left in that incomplete, but astronomically most perfect, form, the edifice might have remained for thousands of years the most important astronomical structure in the world. Nay, to this very day it would have retained its pre-eminence, provided, of course, that its advantages over other buildings had been duly supplemented by modern instrumental and optical improvements.

Unfortunately, the Great Pyramid was erected solely for selfish purposes. It was to be the tomb of Cheops, and whatever qualities it had for astronomical observation were to be devoted to his service only. The incalculable aid to the progress of astronomy which might have been obtained from this magnificent structure entered in no sort into its king-builder's plan. Centuries would have been required to reap even a tithe of the knowledge which might have been derived from pyramid observations, and such observations were limited to a few years—twenty, thirty, forty, or fifty at the outside.

Now, while I am fully conscious that the astrological theory of the Great Pyramid is open to most obvious, and, at the first sight, most overwhelming objections, I venture to say not only that these are completely met by what is certainly known about the pyramid, but that the astrological theory (combined, of course, with the tomb theory) is demonstrably the true explanation of all that had been mysterious in the Great Pyramid.

Take the chief points which have perplexed students of the pyramids generally, and of the Great Pyramid in particular.

1. Granting the most inordinate affection for large sepulchral abodes, how can we account for the amazing amount of labour, money, and time bestowed on the Great Pyramid?

The astrological theory at once supplies the answer. If the builder believed what we know was actually believed by all the Oriental nations respecting planetary and stellar influences, it was worth his while to expend that and more on the pyramid, to read the stars for his benefit, and to 'rule' stars and planets to his advantage.

2. If the pyramids were but vast tombs, why should they be astronomically oriented with extreme care—to assume for a moment that this is the only astronomical relation established certainly respecting them ?

Astrology answers this difficulty most satisfactorily. For astrological study of the heavens, the pyramid (in its incomplete or truncated condition) could not be too accurately oriented.

3. Granted that the Great Pyramid was for a time used as an astronomical observatory, and that its upper square platform was used for cardinal directions in the way shown in fig. 9, what connection is there between these direction-lines (the only ones which would naturally arise from the square form) and astrological relations ?

These lines remain to this very day in use among astrologers. The accompanying figure, taken from 'Raphael's Astrology' (Raphael being doubtless some Smith, or Blodgett, or Higginbotham), represents the ordinary horoscope, and its relations (now unmeaning) to a horizontal, carefully-oriented square plane surface, such as the top of the pyramid was, with just such direction-lines as would naturally be used on such a platform :—

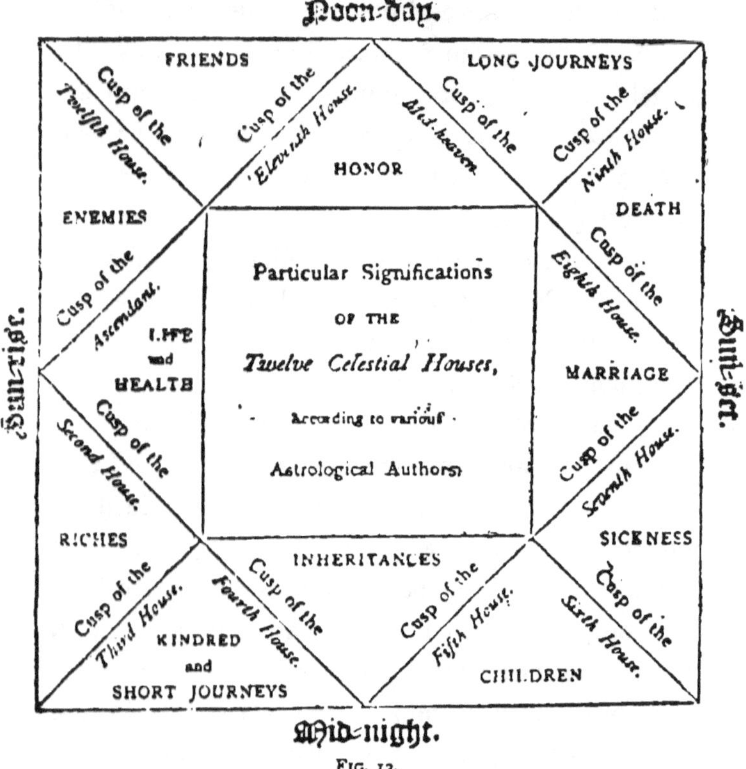

FIG. 13.

4. Why did each king want a tomb of his own? Why should not a larger family mausoleum, one in which all the expense and labour given to all the pyramids might have been combined, have been preferred?

It may be noted here, that, according to some

traditions, the second pyramid, though somewhat smaller than the first, and altogether inferior in design, was begun somewhat earlier. I would invite special attention to this point. It is one of those perplexing details which are always best worth examining when we want to obtain a true theory. The second pyramid was certainly built during the reign of the builder of the first or Great Pyramid. It must have been built, then, with his sanction, for his brother, Chephren, according to Herodotus ; Noun-shofo, or Suphis II., according to the Egyptian records. Enormous quantities of stone, of the same quality as the stone used for the Great Pyramid, were conveyed to the site of the second pyramid, during the very time when the resources of the nation were being largely taxed to get the materials for the Great Pyramid conveyed to the place appointed for that structure. It would appear, then, that there was some strong —in fact, some insuperable—objection to the building of one great pyramid, larger by far than either the first or second, for both the brothers. Yet nothing has ever been learned respecting the views of the Egyptians about tombs (save only what is learned from the pyramids themselves, if we assume that they were only built as tombs) which would suggest that each king wanted a monstrous pyramid sepulchre for himself. If we could doubt that Cheops valued his brother and his family very highly, we should find convincing proof of the fact, in the circumstance that he allowed enormous sums to be expended on his brother's pyramid, and a great quantity of labour to be devoted to its erection, at the time when his own was in progress at still greater expense, and at the cost of still greater labour. But if he thus highly esteemed his brother, and regarding him as the future ruler of Egypt, recognised in him the same almost sacred qualities which the people of Egypt taught their rulers to recognise in themselves, what was to prevent him from combining the moneys and the labours which were devoted to the two pyramids in the construction of a single larger pyramid, which could be made doubly secure, and more perfectly designed and executed? Is anything whatever known respecting either the Egyptians or any race of tomb-loving, or rather corpse-worshipping people, which would lead us to suppose that a number of costly separate tomb pyramids would have been preferred to a single, but far larger, pyramid-mausoleum, which should receive the bodies of all the members of the family, or at least of all those of the family who had ruled in turn over the land? If we could imagine for a moment that Cheops would have objected to such an arrangement, is it not clear that when he died his successors would have taken possession of his pyramid, removing his body perhaps, or not allowing it to be interred there, *if* the sole or even the chief purpose for which a pyramid was erected was that it might serve as a gigantic tomb?

We may indeed note, as a still more fatal objection to the theory that the chief purpose for which a pyramid was built was to serve as the builder's tomb, that it would have been little short of madness for Cheops to devote many years of his life, enormous sums of money, and the labour of myriads of his people, to the construction of a building which might and probably would be turned after his death to some purpose quite different from that for which he intended it. It is not to be supposed, and indeed history shows it certainly was not the case, that the dynasties which ruled over Egypt were more secure from attack than those which ruled elsewhere in the East during those days. Cheops cannot have placed such implicit reliance on his brother Chephren's good faith as to feel sure that, after his own death, Chephren would complete the pyramid, place Cheops' body in it, and close up the entrance so securely that none could find the way into the chamber where the body was laid. Cheops could not even be certain that Chephren would survive him, or that his own son, Mycerinus or Menkeres, would be able to carry out the purpose for which he (Cheops) had built the pyramid.

Apart, then, from that feature of the tomb theory which seems so strangely to have escaped notice—the utter wildness of the idea that even the most tomb-loving race would build 'tombs quite so monstrous as these—we see that there are the strongest possible objections against the credibility of the merely tombic theory (to use a word coined, I imagine, by Professor Piazzi Smyth, and more convenient perhaps than defensible). It seems clear on the face of things that the pyramids must have been intended to serve some useful purpose during the lifetime of the builder. It is clear also (all, indeed, save the believers in the religion of the Great Pyramid, will admit *this* point) that each pyramid served some purpose useful to the builder of the pyramid, and to him only. Cheops' pyramid was of no use to Chephren, Chephren's of no use to Mycerinus, and so forth. Otherwise we might be sure, even if we adopted for a moment the exclusively tombic theory, that though Chephren might have been so honest as not to borrow his brother's tomb when Cheops was departed, or Mycerinus so honest as not to despoil either his uncle or his father, yet among some of the builders of the pyramids such honesty would have been wanting. It is clear, however, from all the traditions which have reached us respecting the pyramids, that no anxiety was entertained by the builder of any pyramid on this score. Cheops seems to have been well assured that Chephren would respect his pyramid, and even (at great expense) complete it ; and so of all the rest. There must, then, have been some special reasons which rendered the pyramid of each king useless altogether to his successor.

Astrology at once supplies a reason. Dead kings of one family might sleep with advantage in a single tomb ; but each man's horoscope must be kept by itself. Even to this day, the astrological charlatan would not discuss one man's horoscope on the plan drawn out and used for another man's. Everything, according to ancient astrological superstition, would have become confused and indistinct. The ruling of the planets would have been imperfect and unsatisfactory, if King Cheops' horoscope platform had been used for Chephren, or Chephren's for Mycerinus. The religious solemnities which accompanied astrological observations in the days when the chief astrologers were high priests,

would have been rendered nugatory if those performed under suitable conditions for one person
were followed by others performed under different
conditions for another person.

5. How is it that the pyramid of Chephren
(Cheops' brother), though about as large, is quite
inferior to the pyramid of Cheops, the pyramid of
Mycerinus (Cheops' son) much smaller, and that
of Asychis (Cheops' grandson) very much smaller,
while to the younger sons and daughters of Cheops
very small pyramids, within the same enclosure as
the Great Pyramid, are assigned?

The astrological answer is obvious. Cheops
not only had full faith in astrology—as, indeed, all
men had in his day—but his faith was so lively
that he put it in practice in a very energetic way
for the benefit of himself and dynasty. Chephren
probaby had similar faith. For the two brothers,
separate pyramids, nearly equal in size, were
made, either at the command of Cheops alone, or
with such sanction from Chephren as his (probable)
separate authority required and justified. *At the
same time*, and because his fortunes were obviously
associated in the closest manner with those of his
father and uncle, Cheops (or Cheops and Chephren)
would have a pyramid made for Mycerinus, but on
a smaller scale. Probably, the astrology of those

days assigned the proper proportion in which the horoscope-platform for a son should be less than that for a father. It is noteworthy, at any rate, that the linear dimensions of the pyramid of Asychis are less than those of the pyramid of Mycerinus, in just the same degree that these are less than the linear dimensions of the pyramid of Cheops.

6. It is certain that if Mycerinus had built his own pyramid, he would have erected one larger, not smaller, than his father's, while Asychis would have made his pyramid larger yet; whereas, as a mere matter of fact, the pyramid of Asychis is utterly insignificant in size compared with the pyramid of Cheops. The sides of the bases of the four pyramids were roughly as follows:—The pyramid of Cheops, 760 feet; that of Chephren, 720 feet; that of Mycerinus, 330 feet; that of Asychis, 160 feet. The pyramid of Cheops exceeds that of Asychis much more than 150 times in volume. It is not in accordance with what we know of human nature to suppose that Asychis would have been content with so insignificant a version of his grandfather's pyramid. Rather than that, he would have had no pyramid at all, but invented some new sepulchral arrangement. Yet it adds enormously to the difficulties of the pyra-

mid problem to suppose that Cheops and Chephren arranged for the erection of all the pyramids,
or, at any rate, that the smaller pyramids were
raised to the horoscope-platform level during their
lifetime.

Here, however, the astrological theory, instead
of encountering, as all other theories do, a new
and serious difficulty, finds fresh support; for this
arrangement is precisely what we should expect
to find if the Great Pyramid was erected to its
observing platform for astrological observation and
the religious observances associated with them. It
is certain that with the ideas Cheops must have
had (on that theory) of the importance of astronomical observations to determine, and partly
govern, his future, he would not have left his sons
without their pyramidal horoscopes. Even if we
suppose he entertained such jealousy of his brother
Chephren, as Oriental (and some Occidental)
princes have been known to entertain of their near
kinsfolk and probable successors, that would be
but an additional reason for having his brother's
horoscope-pyramid erected on such a scale as the
astrologers and priests considered suitable in the
case of such near kinship. For by means of the
observations made by the astrological priesthood
from Chephren's horoscope-platform, Cheops could

learn, according to the astrological doctrines in which he believed, the future fortunes of his brother, and even be able to rule the planets in his own defence, where their configurations seemed favourable to Chephren and threatening to himself.

7. But it may be urged that, beyond the general statement that the pyramids were intended as the tombs of their respective builders, we learn too little from ancient writers to form any satisfactory idea of their object.

It so happens, however, that the only precise statement handed down to us respecting the use of the pyramids—not merely of the Great Pyramid, but of all the pyramids—accords with the astrological theory in every detail, and with no other theory in any degree. For we learn from Proclus that the pyramids of Egypt (which, according to Diodorus, had existed 3,600 years before his history was written, about 8 B.C.) terminated above in a platform, from which the priests made their celestial observations.

Observe how much is implied in this short statement :—

First, *all* the pyramids had a use independent of their final purpose as tombs; a use, therefore, during the lifetime of their future tenants, and presumably—one may say certainly—relating to the interests of those persons.

Secondly, this use was precisely such as we have been led to infer with all but absolute certainty, already, from the study of the Great Pyramid.

Thirdly, the astronomical observations were made by priests, and were therefore religious in character—a description which could only apply to astronomical observations made for astrological purposes. In all probability, the priests who made these observations professed a religion differing little from pure Sabaism, or the worship of the heavenly host. But it must be remembered that astrology was the natural offspring of Sabaism. Wherever we find an astronomical priesthood, there we find faith in astrology. But to say truth, where among ancient Oriental nations was such faith wanting? The Jews had less of it than other Oriental nations, but they were not free from it. As they had all their religious observances regulated by the heavenly bodies, so they recognised the influence of the 'stars in their courses.' If they believed the heavenly bodies to be for 'seasons' (of religious worship), and for 'days and years,' they believed them also to be for 'signs.' This also was the view of the ancient Chaldæans.

' It is evident,' says the late Mr. George Smith, ' from the opening of the inscriptions on the first tablet of the Chaldæan astrology and astronomy, that the functions of the stars were, according to the Babylonians, to act not only as regulators of the seasons and the year, but also to be used as signs, as in Genesis i. 14; for in those ages it was generally believed that the heavenly bodies gave, by their appearance and positions, signs of events which were coming on the earth.'

In fine, while there is no other theory of the pyramids generally, and of the Great Pyramid in particular, which has either positive or negative evidence in its form, the astrological theory is supported by all the known positive evidence; and strong though such support is, it derives yet greater strength from the utter failure of all other admissible theories to sustain the weight against them. There are difficulties in the astrological theory, no doubt, but they are difficulties arising from our inability to understand how men ever had such fulness of faith in astrology as to devote enormous sums and many years of labour to the pursuit of astrological researches, even for their own interests. Yet we know in other ways that astrology really was accepted in those days with the fulness of faith thus implied. While, however, the only serious difficulty in the astrological theory thus disappears when closely examined, the difficulties in the way of all other theories are so great, that, to all intents and purposes, they are not so much difficulties as impossibilities.

I do not say that there is nothing surprising in what is known, when the theory is admitted that the Great Pyramid was built by Suphis or Cheops in order that astronomical observations might be continued throughout his life, to determine his future, to ascertain what epochs were dangerous or propitious for him, and to note such unusual phenomena among the celestial bodies as seemed to bode him good or evil fortune. It does seem amazing, despite all we know of the fulness of faith reposed by men of old times in the fanciful doctrines of astrology, that any man, no matter how rich or powerful, should devote many years of his life, a large portion of his wealth, and the labours of many myriads of his subjects, to so chimerical a purpose. It *is* strange that a building erected for that purpose should not be capable of subserving a similar purpose for his successors on the throne of Egypt. Strange also that he should have been able to provide in some way for the completion of the building after his death, though that must have been a work of enormous labour, and very expensive, even though all the materials had been prepared during his own lifetime.

But I do assert with considerable confidence that no other theory has been yet suggested (and almost every imaginable theory has been advocated) which gives the slightest answer to these chief difficulties in the pyramid problem. The astrological theory, if accepted, gives indeed an answer which requires us to believe the kingly builder of the Great pyramid, and, in less degree, those who with him or after him built the others, to have been utterly selfish, tyrannical, and superstitious—or, in brief, utterly unwise. But unfortunately the study of human nature brings before us so many illustrations of the existence of such folly and superstition in as great or even greater degree, that we need not for such reasons reject the astrological theory. Of other theories it may be said that, while not one of them, except the wild theory which attributes the Great Pyramid to divinely instructed architects, presents the builders more favourably, every one of these theories leaves the most striking features of the Great Pyramid entirely unexplained.

Lastly, I would note that the pyramids when rightly viewed must be regarded, not as monuments which should excite our admiration, but as stupendous records of the length to which tyranny and selfishness, folly and superstition, lust of power and greed of wealth, will carry man. Regarded as works of skill, and as examples of what men may effect by combined and long-continued labour, they are indeed marvellous, and in a sense admirable. They will remain in all probability, and will be scarcely changed, when every other edifice at this day existing on the surface of the earth has either crumbled into dust or changed out of all knowledge. The museums and libraries, the churches and cathedrals, the observatories, the college buildings and other scholastic edifices of our time, are not for a moment to be compared with the Great Pyramid of Egypt in all that constitutes material importance, strength, or stability. But while the imperishable monuments of old Egypt are records of tyranny and selfishness, the less durable structures of our own age are, in the main, records of at least the desire to increase the knowledge, to advance the interests, and to ameliorate the condition of the human race. No good whatever has resulted to man from all the labour, misery, and expense involved in raising those mighty structures which seem fitted to endure while the world itself shall last. They are and ever have been splendidly worthless. On the other hand, the less costly works of our own time, while their very construction has involved good instead of misery to the lowlier classes, have increased the knowledge and the well-being of mankind. The goodly seed of the earth, though perishable itself, germinates, fructifies, and bears other seed, which will in turn bring forth yet other and perchance even better fruits ; so the efforts of man to work good to his fellow-man instead of evil, although they may lead to perishable material results, will yet germinate, and fructify, and bear seed, over an ever-widening field of time, even to untold generations.

APPENDICES.

APPENDIX A.

THE GREAT PYRAMID MEASURES, AND THE DIAMETERS AND DISTANCES OF THE SUN, EARTH, AND MOON.

BY JOSEPH BAXENDELL, F.R.A.S.

A FEW months ago the results of a partial discussion of the Great Pyramid measures, given by Professor C. Piazzi Smyth, in the fourth edition of his work entitled ' Our Inheritance in the Great Pyramid,' led me to believe that the data which had formed the basis of the design for the pyramid were the diameters and distances of the sun, earth, and moon, combined with the ratio (π) of the circumference of a circle to its diameter—a quantity which forms an important feature in the relations of the pyramid measures; and, also, that in order to reduce the results of the astronomical data to magnitudes suitable for the design and construction of the pyramid, a scale of one pyramid inch to a length, one-thousandth part greater than the present English mile, or 63,360 pyramid inches, had been used by the architect; but as I found that the values of the diameters and distances given in various astronomical works, especially those for the diameter and distance of the sun, would not yield results agreeing *exactly* with the pyramid measures, although they were generally remarkably close approximations, I was induced to undertake a more extended discussion and analysis of the measures, with a view to ascertain, if possible, the exact values which had been employed by the architect in his reductions, and it thus became necessary to attempt a solution of the following problem. Given approximate values of the diameters and distances of the sun, earth, and moon, to find the values which in simple combinations will give, with *strict exactness*, the various pyramid measures and numbers, the scale for the reductions being one pyramid inch for a pyramid mile of 63,360 pyramid inches. For some time I had considerable difficulty in forming the requisite number of suitable equations for the complete solution of this problem, but ultimately succeeded, and obtained the following values :—

	Pyramid Miles	English Miles
Diameter of the Sun . ⁻ .	855,938	856,793
Equatorial diameter of the Earth	7,917·7	7,925·6
Diameter of the Moon . .	2,157·2	2,159·3
Mean distance of the Sun . .	91,758,800	91,850,558
Mean distance of the Moon .	238,483	238,721

Let $S =$ distance of the sun ; $M =$ distance of the moon ; $s =$ diameter of the sun ; $e =$ equatorial diameter of the earth ; $m =$ diameter of the moon. Then the following equations, in which pyramid miles and inches are adopted, will show the relations between these numbers and the pyramid measures :—

$$\text{I.} \quad \frac{se}{m} = 1,000,000\pi.$$

It is probably owing to the remarkable relation in the magnitudes of the three bodies shown by this equation that the quantity π forms so prominent a feature in the relations of the pyramid measures.

2. $\sqrt{s\pi^2} = 9{,}131\cdot05 =$ length of one side of the base of the pyramid.

3. $\sqrt{s2\pi} = 5{,}813\cdot01 =$ height of the pyramid.

4. $\dfrac{s\pi^2 \ \sqrt{\pi}}{25{,}000} = 1{,}881\cdot59 =$ length of Grand Gallery

5. $\dfrac{2\sqrt{s\pi}\sqrt{\pi}}{25} = 412\cdot13 =$ length of King's Chamber.

6. $\dfrac{\sqrt{s\pi}\sqrt{\pi}}{1{,}000} = 5\cdot151{,}646 =$ the number which has been called the key number to the dimensions of the King's Chamber, and of the pyramid generally.

7. $S = \dfrac{25{,}000{,}000e}{m}.$

8. $M = \dfrac{em\pi}{3^2 5^2}.$

9. $M = \dfrac{sc^3}{9mS}.$

10. $\dfrac{2S}{5\cdot151{,}646M} = 149\cdot37 =$ height of ante-chamber.

11. $\dfrac{3\sqrt{SM/s\pi^3}}{250e} = 36{,}524\cdot22 =$ perimeter of base of the Pyramid.

12. $\dfrac{3\sqrt{SM/s\pi^3}}{500c\pi} = 5{,}813\cdot01 =$ height of the pyramid.

13. $\dfrac{cs\pi^4}{75\sqrt{SM}} = 1{,}881\cdot59 =$ length of Grand Gallery.

14. $\dfrac{80c\sqrt{s\pi^2}}{3\sqrt{SM}} = 412\cdot13 =$ length of the King's Chamber.

Among the equations I obtained during the investigation were several which gave a smaller value for the diameter of the sun ; and as I am not aware that any sensible difference has ever been observed between the polar and equatorial diameters, this result seemed adverse to the theory of a connection between the pyramid measures and the diameters of the three bodies, until it occurred to me that probably one diameter referred to the photosphere, and the other to the comparatively dark and solid or liquid body of the sun.   This latter diameter is 853,718 pyramid miles, or 2,220 miles less than that of the photosphere, and the following equations, in which it is represented by the Greek letter σ, will show its connection with the pyramid measures :—

15. $\dfrac{\sigma^2 \pi}{c^2} = 36{,}524\cdot20 =$ perimeter of base.

16. $\dfrac{\sigma^2}{2c^2} = 5{,}813\cdot01 =$ height of pyramid,

17. $\dfrac{\sigma^2}{100c^2} = 116\cdot26 =$ length of ante-chamber.

18. $\dfrac{\sigma^2 \sqrt{\pi}}{50c^2} = 412\cdot13.$

19. $\dfrac{\sigma^4 \pi \sqrt{\pi}}{400{,}000c^4} = 1{,}881\cdot59.$

20. $\left(\dfrac{\sigma^2 \sqrt[4]{\pi^3}}{c^2 2\sqrt{10^5}} \right)^2 = 1{,}881\cdot59.$

21. $\dfrac{\sigma^2 \sqrt{\pi}}{4{,}000c^2} = 5\cdot1{,}516.$

The length of the earth's polar axis is assumed by pyramidists to be 500,000,000 pyramid inches, or 7,891·41 pyramid miles of 63,360 pyramid inches to the mile, or 7,899·30 English miles, while the value derived by Col. Clarke, from an elaborate discussion of measurements of arcs of meridian, is 7,899·11 English miles—the difference being, therefore, less than two-tenths of a mile. I was, therefore, much surprised to find that the pyramid measures would not yield a less diameter for the earth than 7,892·54 pyramid miles, or more than a mile greater than the generally-accepted length of the polar diameter. The question therefore arose—Can this latter length be in error to the extent indicated, or is the value I have obtained connected in any way with some marked feature of the pyramid?   It seemed to be highly improbable, if not impossible, that the results of the calculations of Bessel, Airy, and Clarke could be in error to the extent of more than a small fraction of a mile ; and assuming, therefore, that the figure of the earth is truly spheroidal with major axis $= 7,717\cdot7$, and minor axis $= 7,891\cdot41$ pyramidal miles, I calculated the geocentric latitude in which a diameter will be 7,892·54 miles, and found it to be 78° 25′ 33″; and, deducting this from 90°, we have 11° 34′ 27″.   A glance at this result at once suggested that it was the polar distance of the pyramid pole-star, a Draconis, multiplied by the quantity π, and on dividing 11° 34′ 27″ by π, I obtained 3° 41′, which is a very close approximation to the calculated polar distance of a Draconis at the time of the building of the pyramid.   Now a section of the earth through the parallel of latitude marked out in so singular a manner has a diameter of 1,583·54 pyramid miles, or exactly one-fifth of the earth's equatorial diameter, and an area of 1,969,462 miles, or one twenty-fifth that of a section through the equator, which is 49,236,600 miles.   The occurrence of the pyramid numbers 5 and 25 in connection with the diameter thus indicated in so striking a manner gives a peculiar importance to it, and accordingly I have found that expressions in which it is a factor can be formed which give *exactly* the various pyramid measures. Thus, representing this diameter by the Greek letter η (eta), we have

22. $\quad \eta = \dfrac{S\sqrt{\pi}}{4,000 \times 5\text{·}151,646} = 7,892\text{·}54.$

23. $\quad \eta = \dfrac{Se^2}{\sigma^2}.$

24. $\quad \dfrac{S\sqrt{\pi}}{4,000\eta} = 5\text{·}151,646.$

25. $\quad \dfrac{S}{\eta} = 11,626\text{·}02 = 100$ times length of ante-chamber.

26. $\quad \dfrac{S^2\pi\sqrt{\pi}}{4,000\eta^2 5\text{·}151,646} = 36,524\text{·}22.$

27. $\quad \dfrac{\sqrt{2e\eta}}{100} = 111\text{·}795 =$ height of granite wainscot in ante-chamber.

28. $\quad \dfrac{450\sigma^2\eta}{5\text{·}151,646e^3m\pi} = 149\text{·}37.$

29. $\quad \dfrac{S^2\pi\sqrt{\pi}}{400,000\eta^2} = 1,881\text{·}59.$

30. $\quad \dfrac{S\pi 5\text{·}151,646}{100\eta} = 1,881\text{·}59.$

31. $\quad \dfrac{S\pi}{4\eta} = 9,131\text{·}05.$

32. $\quad \dfrac{S}{2\eta} = 5,813\text{·}01.$

It may be remarked that the diameter η is exactly one seven-thousandth part greater than the polar diameter, and that the parallels of latitude in which it occurs may be regarded as the limits of the habitable portion of the globe.

The results of my investigation having proved that a measure corresponding to our English mile, and containing 63,360 pyramid inches, was used by the architect of the pyramid, it became a matter of interest to ascertain, if possible, how it originated, and ultimately I arrived at the following formula :—

$$33. \quad 10 \sqrt{\frac{se}{m}} = 17,724 \text{'}5 \text{ miles,}$$

which is the circumference of a circle whose area is 25,000,000 miles, or equal to the area of a section of the earth through the parallel of latitude in which the length of a diameter is equal to the mean of all the earth's diameters (7,904'545 p. miles). This area, expressed in pyramid inches, is equal to a square, the side of which has a length of 316,800,000 inches, and this, divided by 5,000 = 63,360 inches.

My experience in the development of the theory which has yielded the results given in this paper has convinced me that there is no feature of the Great Pyramid, or relation of its various parts, which cannot be expressed in terms of the astronomical data I have used, and in some cases, as I have already shown, two, three, or more equations can be formed, each containing one or more factors not in the others, but giving precisely the same result. It is evident, therefore, that the builder possessed a far greater amount of mathematical and astronomical knowledge than it has hitherto been supposed could possibly have been acquired by the ordinary course of observation and scientific investigation in

the early age of the world when the pyramid was built;
and the fact that the values of the diameters and distances used by him are within the limits of the probable
errors of the means of the best astronomical determinations of recent times proves that, so far at least as these
values are concerned, modern science has made no real
advance upon the science known to the builder of the
Great Pyramid 4,000 years ago.

APPENDIX B.

EXCAVATIONS AT THE PYRAMIDS.[1]

GHIZEH PYRAMIDS. *Nov.* 26, 1881.

BY W. M. FLINDERS PETRIE.

DURING the past six weeks excavations have been
carried on by me here, under the authorisation of M.
Maspero, not for obtaining portable antiquities, but for
deciding questions of architecture and measurement.
Many points of interest have been uncovered for the first
time in modern history, though the work was not on a
large scale, and the number of excavators never exceeded
twenty. There have been over 280 holes sunk, varying
from a foot deep to shafts twenty feet deep and trenches
ninety feet long.

A brief notice of the work done may be worth giving

[1] From a letter to the *Academy.*

at once, without waiting for the complete publication of it, along with my survey of the pyramids (made during five months of last season), to which it is a necessary sequel, for fixing the exact fiducial points of the ancient

At the Great Pyramid, the entrance passage has been cleared enough to examine it throughout, and to enter the subterranean chamber freely. Some of the loose gravel in the 'grotto' of the well has been moved, showing that there is a natural vertical fissure filled with the gravel. The casing and pavement of the pyramid have been found *in situ*, at about the middle of the west, east, and south sides ; it was already exposed on the north side, on which alone it has been hitherto known. The outer edge of the rock-cut bed of the pavement has been cleared in parts of the sides, and at the north-east and south-west corners. The great basalt pavement has been cleared in parts, and the edge of the rock-cut bed of it has been traced along the north-east and south sides ; but its junction with the limestone pyramid paving (which is at the same level) could not be found, as both are destroyed at that part. The ends of the great trenches around the basalt pavement have been partly cleared. The bottom and sides of the east-north-east trench have been cleared in parts to show the form. No bottom was found under nine feet of sand in the north trench. The small north-north-east trench has been cleared in parts up to its inner end at the basalt paving, where it is much smaller, and forks into two. The various rock cuttings and trenches north-east of the pyramid have been cleared and surveyed, but refilled, as the road passes over them.

A piece of the casing of the pyramid, found near the base on the west side, has Greek inscriptions, apparently Pto . . . . Sōt . . . . (perhaps Ptolemy VIII., as the s is round); and Markos K . . . ., over which is hammered roughly . . . m a j . . . in Arabic. Nothing, besides a few fragments with single letters, had been previously discovered of the many inscriptions that existed on the casing.

At the second pyramid the corners have been all cleared. The site of the edge of the casing has been found in six places near the corners, and the casing itself uncovered at the south-west. The edge of the bed of the pavement has been found on the north and west sides. The peribolus walls of the pyramid have been cleared in many parts, showing that they are all carefully built, and not of 'heaped stone rubbish,' as had been hitherto supposed. Also, the so-called 'lines of stone rubbish' on the west side of the pyramid prove to be all built walls, forming a series of long galleries about sixty in number, each about 100 ft. long, 9 ft. wide, and 7 ft. high, with ends and thresholds of hewn limestone. They would suffice to house two or three thousand men, and I can only suppose that they were the workmen's barracks. Fragments of fine statues in diorite and alabaster were found here, like those in the temple of this pyramid. The great bank of chips on the south side of the cyclopean wall north of the pyramid proves to have retaining walls built in it to hold up the stuff. The peribolus wall on the south-south-east of the pyramid is of fine limestone, of good workmanship, like most of the tombs of the period. The enormous heaps of rubbish south of this wall were slightly cut, and found to consist of tipped out, stratified, clean chips of lime-stone, like the rubbish banks of the Great Pyramid, but inferior stone.

At the third pyramid, the granite casing has been un-covered at its base in five places near the corners. The peribolus walls have been cleared in many parts all round, and found, in every case, not to consist of heaped stones, but to have carefully-built vertical faces, like the second pyramid peribolus, but of inferior work ; and the wall on the south side is better built, and very wide.

The small pyramids have not been cleared for lack of time, as they are rather deeply buried ; but a part of the rock-cut bed of pavement of the northern one near the Great Pyramid was accidentally uncovered close to the edge of the bed of the basalt pavement.

Though I am obliged to suspend work here at pre-sent, yet I shall be very glad to receive any suggestions of points needing examination (addressed to Poste Restante, Cairo) ; and, if they are practicable, I may find an opportunity for further work two or three months hence.

When all the paper work of this survey is finished, we shall know the sizes and distances of the pyramids within a quarter of an inch ; and there will be fresh soil for the growth of theories, *as the Great Pyramid proves to be several feet smaller than hitherto supposed,* the sockets not defining the casing at the pavement level, though defining it, perhaps, at their own respective levels.

NOTE ON THE ABOVE.

With the discovery that the base of the pyramid is several feet shorter than had been supposed, a number of relations supposed to connect the Great Pyramid with astronomy go overboard at a single stroke. Still, the coincidences remain. Indeed, it only requires that the pyramid inch should be slightly altered for the relations to be all once more perfectly fulfilled. What will be done with the arguments showing the true pyramid inch to be almost exactly the same as the British inch, and the true cubit to be twenty-five of these inches, I do not know : but past experience shows that whatever the precise value of the pyramid inch, as deduced from these new measures, may prove to be, will be shown to be just the value which corresponds most perfectly with what may be called the pyramid religion. Let us see what is the nature of the coincidences on which pyramidalists lay so much stress.

We find that while the pyramid fulfils closely the relation which Herodotus says it was intended to fulfil, each slant face being equal in area to the square of the height, it also very nearly fulfils what Taylor tells us was the real purpose of the builder, the height being nearly equal to the radius of a circle having a circumference equal to the perimeter of the square base ; and again, it almost as closely fulfils another relation, in having the

slant at the edge very nearly as 9 vertically to 10 horizon-
tally.   Now, to the ignorant, it seems as though the close
approximation of the building's proportions to these three
relations proves demonstrably the mathematical skill of
the builders, if not their divine inspiration.   As a matter of fact, however, we see from the co-existence of
these three relations, any one of which might as well as
another be the real one which the builders had in view
(were it not certain, from what Herodotus tells us, that
the first only was their building rule), how easy it is to
find such relations if we only look carefully for them,
for two out of the three are certainly accidental.   So
that apart from the evidence of Herodotus, we should
be free to reject all three, on the sound plea that since
coincidence can so readily be detected, no reliance
can be placed upon any argument from mere coincidence.

Then, again, according to the measurements just
negatived, there were exactly as many cubits of 25
inches in each side as there are days in the year, or
36,524 inches in the circuit of the base.   One would
have said that if this were really proved, and if the height
were determined by any one of the three geometrical
rules just indicated, all the dimensions of the Great
Pyramid, as a whole, were determined once for all.   But
even in the early days of the pyramid religion, the
pyramidalists were not content with this.   They found
that the two diagonals of the square base together contained as many inches as there are years in the Great
Precessional Period, and that the height contained as

many inches as there are in the one thousand-millionth part of the sun's distance ; though, of course, if these relations really hold, they indicate coincidences, and very singular ones too, entirely outside of the pyramid. As thus :—Take one-fourth the number of days in the year, and double the square of this number ; the square root of the product equals half the number of years in the Great Precessional Period. And again, taken 100 times the number of days in the year, and reduce the number thus obtained in the same ratio that the radius is less than the circumference of a circle ; you will then have a number equal to the number of inches which there are in one thousand-millionth part of the sun's distance. These two relations exist quite independently of the pyramid, and, so seen, even pyramidalists must admit that they are but singular numerical coincidences. They have not a particle of real significance, any more than this one, which I make pyramidal (by a very transparent device) merely to show how easy it is to work such things :— Take the square base of the pyramid, and divide each side into as many parts as the pyramid has faces. Join the corresponding divisions of opposite sides of the base so that the base is divided into sixteen squares. In each of these squares, save one, place a number (after the manner of the abomination of desolation to which in our own post-pyramidal days hath been assigned the name of the ' Fifteen Puzzle ')—then it may be shown that the number of arrangements which can be made of these fifteen numbers in the aforesaid sixteen squares is equal to the number of miles separating our solar system

from that star which, according to the best Egyptolo-
gical investigations of the date of the Great Pyramid,
shone, at its meridional culmination, directly down
the Great Gallery and its prolongation the ascending
passage.

Then comes my ingenious and (outside the pyramid)
scientific friend, Mr. Baxendell, who, accepting the pyramid dimensions assigned by Professor Smyth, finds other
relations which they fulfil equally well, showing, of course,
other singular coincidences existing quite independently
of the pyramid. Nay, he finds several independent
coincidences for each dimension, failing, apparently,
to notice that the most remarkable feature of his paper
—the singular closeness of the numerical results—exists
(scarcely in diminished degree), if the pyramid be left
entirely out of the question. Take, for instance, what
I find many regard as singularly impressive, the six
different formulæ, by which he gets out 1881·59 as the
number of inches in the length of the Grand Gallery
(which I need hardly say is not known to anything
like this degree of exactitude). They are as follows :—

$$\frac{s\pi^2\pi\sqrt{\pi}}{25{,}000} = \frac{es\pi^4}{75\sqrt{SM}} = \frac{\sigma^4\pi\sqrt{\pi}}{400{,}000c^4} = \left(\frac{\sigma^2\,\sqrt[4]{\pi^3}}{c^2 2\sqrt{10^5}}\right)^2$$

$$= \frac{S^2\pi\sqrt{\pi}}{400{,}000\eta^2} = \frac{S\,\sigma\,\sqrt{\pi}}{400{,}000c^2\eta} = 1881{\cdot}59.$$

How terrible these formulæ appear, in conjunction
with the circumstance, that by taking dates for the Fall,
the Exodus, and the birth of Christ, not quite agreeing
with those approved by recognised theological authorities,

the length of the descending and ascending passages correspond so closely with the intervals between the first and second and the second and third of those events (years representing inches), as to compel us to believe that the Christian dispensation cannot last more years than there are inches in the Grand Gallery ! Now these formulæ, when analysed, are found to indicate a number of really curious coincidences between the numbers representing S, the sun's distance, M the moon's, s the sun's diameter, e the earth's (equatorial), σ the diameter of the sun's liquid body—quietly assumed, for we know nothing about it—η another terrestrial diameter, and π the ratio of the circumference to a diameter of a circle. If the pyramid had no existence, these curious coincidences would remain. The fact that they exist, and are in themselves so singular, shows simply how little value there is in the argument from mere coincidence. Given ten or twenty numbers taken at random from different columns of the 'Times' newspaper, or the dimensions of a house, or field, or a piece of furniture, or, in fine, taken from anywhere we like, it will be found that with a little patience, any number of coincidences may be found among the numbers themselves, or connecting them with any other set of numbers, with the dimensions of the solar system, with the volumes, diameters, densities, &c., of the planets, or, in fine, with whatsoever we please. One of the best proofs ever given of this is found in the multitude of relations, independent of the pyramid, which have turned up while pyramidalists have been endeavouring to connect the pyramid with the solar system. These coincidences are altogether more curious than any coincidence between the pyramid and astronomical numbers ; the former are as close and remarkable as they are real, the latter, which are only imaginary, have only been established by the process which schoolboys call 'fudging'—and now new measures have left the work to be done all over again.

THE ORIGIN OF THE WEEK.

It may be assumed, with Ideler, that the week has originated from the length of the synodic months . . . and that reference to the planetary series, together with planetary days and hours, belong to an entirely different period of advanced and speculative culture.— HUMBOLDT (*Cosmos*).

I PROPOSE in this essay to consider how the week probably had its origin, presenting, as occasion serves, such subsidiary evidence as can be derived from history or tradition. Usually this and kindred subjects have been dealt with *à posteriori*. Observances, festivals, chronological arrangements, and so forth, known or recorded to have been adopted by various nations, have been examined, and an inquiry made into their significance. The result has not been altogether satisfactory. Many interesting facts have been brought to light as research has proceeded, and several elaborate theories have been advanced on nearly every point of chronological research. Any one of these theories, examined alone, seems to be established almost beyond dispute by the number of facts seemingly attesting in its favour; but when we find that for another and yet another theory a similar array of facts can be adduced, we lose faith in all theories thus supported. At least those only retain their belief in a theory of the kind who have given so much care to its preparation that they have had no time to examine the evidence favouring other theories.

On the other hand, there is much to be said in favour of an *à priori* method of dealing with ancient chronological arrangements. We know certainly how the heavens appeared to men of old times; if occasion arise we can determine readily and certainly the exact aspect of the heavens at any given place and time; we know generally the conditions under which the first observations of the heavens must have been made; hence we can infer, not unsafely, what particular objects would have been first noted, or would have been early chosen as time-measures; what difficulties would have presented themselves as time proceeded; and how such difficulties would have been met.

The inquiry, let me remark at the outset, has an interest other than that depending on chronological relations. I know of none better suited to commend to our attention the movements of the

heavenly bodies, which, as Carlyle has remarked, I
think, though taking place all the time around us,
are not half-known to most of us. As civilisation
indeed progresses, the proportion of persons acquainted with the motions of the heavenly bodies
becomes less and less ; both because artificial
measures of time come more generally into use,
and because fewer persons in proportion are engaged out of doors at night under conditions
making the movements of the heavens worth
observing. Even the increased interest taken of
late in the study of astronomy has not tended, I
believe, to increase the number who have a familiar
acquaintance with the heavenly bodies and their
motions. So soon as a student of astronomy sets
up an observatory, indeed, he is more likely to
forget what he already knows about ordinary
celestial phenomena than to pay closer attention
to them. If he wants to observe a particular star
or planet, he does not turn to the heavens—one
may almost say indeed, strange though it sounds,
that the heavens are the last place he would think
of looking at; he simply sets the circles of his
telescope aright, knowing that the star or planet
he wants will then be in the field of view. The
telescope is as often as not turned to the object
before the door of the revolving dome has been

opened—that is, while no part of the sky is in view.

It is precisely because in old times matters must have been entirely different, and familiarity with astronomical facts much more important to persons not themselves engaged in the study of astronomy, that the method of inquiry which I propose now to pursue respecting the origin of the week is so full of promise. If we will but put ourselves mentally in the position of the shepherds and tillers of the soil in old times, we can tell precisely what they were likely to notice, in what order, and in what way.

In the first place, I think, it will appear that some division of the month analogous to the week must have been suggested as a measure of time long before the year. Commonly the year is taken as either the first and most obvious of all time-measures, or else as only second to the day. But in its astronomical aspect the year is not a very obvious division of time. I am not here speaking, be it understood, of the exact determination of the length of the year. That, of necessity, was a work requiring much time, and could only have been successfully achieved by astronomers of considerable skill. I am referring to the commonplace year, the ordinary progression of those celestial phenomena which mark the changes of the seasons. As Whewell well remarks of the year, the repetition of similar circumstances at equal intervals is less manifest in this case (than in that of the day), and, the intervals being much longer, some exertion of memory becomes requisite in order that the recurrence may be perceived. A child might easily be persuaded that successive years were of unequal length ; or, if the summer were cold, and the spring and autumn warm, might be made to believe, if all who spoke in its hearing agreed to support the delusion, that one year was two. Of course the recurrence of events characterising the natural year is far too obvious to have been overlooked even before men began to observe the heavenly bodies at all. The tiller of the soil must observe the right time to plant seeds of various kinds that they may receive the right proportion of the summer's heat; the herdsman could not but note the times when his flocks and herds brought forth their young. But no definite way of noting the progress of the year by the movements of the sun or stars[1] would probably have suggested itself until some time after the moon's motions had been

---

[1] There are many reasons for believing, as I may one day take an opportunity of showing, that the year was first measured by the stars, not by the sun.

used as means of measuring time. The lunar changes, on the other hand, are very striking and obvious; they can be readily watched, and they are marked by easily determinable stages. 'It appears more easy,' says Whewell, 'and in earlier stages of civilisation (it was) more common, to count time by *moons* than by years.'

It has indeed been suggested that the moon's use as a measurer of time was from the earliest ages so obvious that the Greek words *mēn* for month, *mēnē* for moon (less common, however, than *selēnē*), and the Latin *mensis* for month, should be associated with the Latin verb *to measure* (*metior, mensus sum*, &c.). Cicero says that months were called *menses*, 'quia *mensa spatia conficiunt*,' because they complete measured spaces. Other etymologists, says Whewell, connect these words 'with the Hebrew *manah*, to measure.' Note also the measure of value, manch,—' twenty shekels, five-and-twenty shekels, fifteen shekels shall be your *manch*, or *mna*' (Ezek. xlv. 12). Again, the name *manna* is given to the food found in the desert, by some interpreted 'a portion.' The word *mene*, or *mna*, in the warning, *Mene, tekel, pharcs*, was translated 'numbered.' With the same word is connected the Arabic *Al-manac*, or *Al-manach*. Whewell points out that 'if we are to attempt to ascend to the earlier conditions of language, we must conceive it probable that men would have a name for a most conspicuous object, *the moon*, before they would have a verb denoting the very abstract and general notion, to measure.' This is true; but it does not follow that the moon may not have received a name implying her quality as a measurer long after she was first named. For the idea of using the moon as a measurer of time must as certainly have followed the conception of the abstract idea of measurement, as this conception must have followed the recognition of the moon as an object of observation. It is noteworthy, indeed, that in the Greek the moon has two names—one, more usual, *sĕlēnē*, from which the Latins derived the name *luna*; the other, *mene*, certainly connected with *mēn*, for month. It seems almost certain that they, and those from whom they derived the usage, had come to regard the moon's quality as a time-measurer as distinct from her quality as an ornament of the night. To this second term for the moon Whewell's remark does not apply, or rather, his remark suggests the true explanation to be that very derivation of the words *mene*, *mensis*, *month*, *moon*, &c.,[1] from a word

---

[1] To these may be added the Sanskrit *mâsa*, the Zend *mao*, the Persian *mah*, the Gothic *mena*, the Erse *mios*, and the Lithuanian *mienu*.

signifying 'to measure,' which he oppugns. Even if this view be rejected, we may yet regard the words signifying mensuration (measurement and numbering) as derived from a name for the moon, months, &c.—a circumstance which would indicate the recognised character of the moon as a time-measurer even more significantly than the converse derivation.

It is noteworthy that of all the phenomena obvious to observation, the motions of the moon are those which most directly suggest the idea of measurement. The earth's rotation on her axis is in reality much more uniform than the moon's circling motion around the earth; but to ordinary observation the recurrence of day and night seems rather to suggest the idea of inequality than that of the uniform subdivision of time. For the lengths of day and night are seldom equal to each other, and are constantly varying. The daily motions of the fixed stars are more uniform than the moon's, and, if carefully noted, afford an almost perfect uniformity of time-measurement. But instruments of some kind are necessary to show that this is the case. The moon, on the other hand, measures off time in an obvious and striking manner, and, to ordinary observation, with perfect uniformity. In measuring time, the moon suggests also the idea of numerical measurement. And measures of length, surface, volume, and so forth, could more readily have been derived in ancient times from the moon's motions than in any other manner. In precisely the same way that now, in Great Britain, all our measures,[1] without exception, are derived from the daily motion of the stars, so in old times the more obvious motions of the moon could have been used, and were probably used, to give the measures required in those days.

[1] Even our measures of the value of money depend on the observed motions of the stars. As I pointed out in my essay 'Our Chief Timepiece Losing Time' (*Light Science for Leisure Hours*), 'when we come to inquire closely into the question of a sovereign's intrinsic value, we find ourselves led to the diurnal motion of the stars by no very long or intricate path.' For a sovereign is a coin containing so many grains of gold mixed with so many grains of alloy. A grain is the weight of such and such a volume of a certain standard substance—that is, so many cubic inches, or parts of a cubic inch, of that substance. An inch is determined as a certain fraction of the length of a pendulum vibrating seconds in the latitude of London. A second is a certain portion of a mean solar day, and is practically determined by a reference to what is called a sidereal day—the interval, namely, between the successive passages by the same star across the celestial meridian of any fixed place. This interval is assumed to be constant, and is in fact very nearly so. Strangely enough, the moon, the older measure of time, is, by her attraction on the waters of this earth, constantly tending to modify this nearly constant quantity—the earth's rotation. For the resistance of the tidal wave acts as a break, constantly retarding the earth's turning motion—though so slowly, that 1,500 millions of years would be required to lengthen the terrestrial day by one full hour.

P

If, then, the names of the 'moon,' 'months,' and so forth, were not originally derived from the idea of measurement, it is nevertheless certain that the moon must, from the very earliest times, have been regarded as *par excellence, the measurer.* The *à priori* reasons for expecting that the moon's name, or one of her names, would be thus derived, seem to me to add greatly to the probability of this derivation, which has been inferred from the actual co-existence of such names as *mene* for the moon ; *men, mensis,* &c. (see previous note), for the month ; *mna, manch, mensus* (root *mens*) for measurement.

The circling motion of the moon round the earth being noted from the very earliest time, it is certain that, very soon after, men would think of subdividing the moon's circuit. The nights when there was no moon would be distinguished in a very marked way from those in which the moon was full, or nearly so, and thus the lunar month would be obviously marked off into two halves, each about a fortnight in length. Something analogous to this first subdivision is to be recognised in a circumstance which I may one day have to deal with more at length, the subdivision of the year into two halves—one in which the Pleiades were above the horizon and visible at sunset, the other when they were below the horizon. There would be the bright half and the dark half of the month (so far as the nights were concerned) ; and it must be remembered that these would not be unimportant distinctions to the men of old time, nor mere matters of scientific observation. To the shepherd the distinction between a moonlit and a moonless night must have been very noteworthy. All his cares would be doubled when the moon was not shining, all lightened when she was nearly full. A poet in our time singing the glories of the moonlit night might be apt to forget the value of the light to the herdsman ; but in old times this must have been the chief thought in connection with such a night. Thus we find Homer, after describing the beauty of a moonlight night, in a noble passage (mis-translated by Pope, but nobly rendered by Tennyson), closing his description with the words—

> The shepherd gladdens in his heart.

We can well understand, indeed, that, according to tradition, the first astronomers in every nation were shepherds.

It might seem at a first view that the division of the months into two parts would be most conveniently marked by the moon (1) coming to full and (2) disappearing. But apart from the consideration just mentioned, showing the probability that the first division would be into the bright half and the dark half, it is easily seen that neither the full phase, nor what is called technically 'new' (in reality the absolute disappearance of the moon), could be conveniently determined with anything like precision. The moon looks full a day or two before and a day or two after she really is full. The time of the moon's coming to the same part of the sky as the sun, again, though it can be inferred by noting when she first disappeared and when she first reappeared, is not obviously indicated,—or, which is the essential point, so manifested as to afford, *at the time*, an indication of the moon's reaching that special stage of her progress. If a clock were so constructed that time were indicated by the rotation of a globe half white half black, and so situated that the observer could not be certain when the white side was fully turned towards him, it is certain he would not observe that phase for determining time exactly. If he were not only uncertain when the black side was fully turned towards him, but could not ascertain this at all until some little time after the white side began to come into view again on one side (having disappeared on the other shortly before), he would be still less likely to observe the black phase as an epoch.

If we consider what the owner of such a time-piece would be apt to do, or rather would be certain to do, we shall not be long in doubt as to the course which the shepherds of old time would have followed. The only phases which such a clock would show with anything like precision would be those two in which one half the globe exactly would be white and the other black. Not only would either of these be a perfectly definite phase marked unmistakably by the straightness of the separating line between black and white, but also the rate of change would at these times be most rapid. The middle of the separating line, or terminator in the moon's case, is at all times travelling athwart the face of our satellite, but most quickly when crossing the middle of her disc. Apart, then, from the consideration already mentioned, which would lead the first observers to divide the month into a dark and a light half, the aspect of the moon's face so varied before their eyes as to suggest, or, one may say, to force upon them, the plan of dividing her course at the quarters, when she is half full increasing and half full diminishing.

Let us pause for a moment to see whether this

first result, to which we have been led by purely *à priori* considerations, accords with any evidence from tradition. We might very well fail to find such evidence, simply because all the earlier and less precise ways of dividing time (of which this certainly would be one), giving way, as they must inevitably do, to more exact time-measurers, might leave no trace whatever of their existence. It is, therefore, the more remarkable and in a sense fortunate, that in two cases we find clear evidence of the division of the lunar month into two halves, and in the precise manner above indicated. Max Müller, remarking on the week, says that he has found no trace of any such division in the ancient Vedic literature of the Hindoos, but the month is divided into two according to the moon · the *clear* half and the *obscure* half.[1]   (Flammarion, from whom I take the reference to Max Müller, says, 'the *clear* half from new to full, and the *obscure* half from full to new;' but this is manifestly incorrect,

---

[1] It is noteworthy that in the Assyrian tablets lately deciphered by Mr. G. Smith (which are copies of Babylonian originals older probably than the books of Job and Genesis), we find in the account of the creation of the sun, moon, and stars, from which the account in Genesis was probably abridged, special reference to the moon's change from the horned to the gibbous phase · 'At the beginning of the month, at the rising of the night, his horns are breaking through, and shine on the heaven; on the ninth day to a circle he begins to swell.'

the half of the month from new to full having neither more nor less light by night than the half from full to new.) A similar division has been found among the Aztecs.

The next step would naturally be the division of each half, the bright and the dark half, into two equal parts. In fact, this would be done at the same time, in most cases (that is, among most nations), that the month was divided into two. The division at half full increasing and half full decreasing would be the more exact ; but once made would afford the means of determining the times of 'full' and 'new.' During the first few months after men had noticed closely the times of half full, they would perceive that between fourteen and fifteen days separated these times, so that 'full' and 'new' came about seven days after the times of half-moon.

All this would be comparatively rough work. Herdsmen, and perhaps the tillers of the soil in harvest time, would perceive that the lunar month, their ordinary measure of time, was naturally divisible into four quarters, two epochs (the half-moons) limiting which were neatly defined, while the intermediate two could be easily inferred. They would fall into the habit of dividing the months into quarters in this rough way long before they began to look for some connection between the length of the month and of the day, precisely as men (later, no doubt) divided the year roughly into four seasons, and the seasons into months, long before they had formed precise notions as to the number of months in years and seasons. We shall see presently that in each case, so soon as they tried to connect two measures of time—the month and day in one case, the year and month in the other—similar difficulties presented themselves. We shall see also that while similar ways of meeting these difficulties naturally occurred to men, these natural methods of dealing with the difficulties were those actually followed in one case certainly, and (to show which is the object of the present paper) most probably in the other also.

Men, at least those who were given to the habit of enumeration, would have found out that there are some $29\frac{1}{2}$ days in each lunar month, not long after they had regarded the month as divided into four parts, and long before they had thought of connecting months and days together. After a while, however, the occasion of some such connection would arise. It might arise in many different ways. The most likely occasion, perhaps, would be the necessity of apportioning work to those employed as herdsmen or in tilling the soil. They would be engaged probably (so soon as the simplest of all engagements, by the day, required some extension) by the month. In fact, one may say that certainly the hiring of labourers for agricultural and pastoral work must have been by the month almost from the beginning.[1]

But from the beginning of hiring also, it must have become necessary to measure the month by days. Herdsmen and labourers could not have had their terms of labour defined by tl.e actual observation of the lunar phases, though these

---

[1] The earliest record we have of hiring is that contained in Genesis, chap. xxix. We read there that Jacob 'abode with Laban *the space of a month,*' serving him without wages. Then Laban said to Jacob, 'Because thou art my brother, shouldst thou therefore serve me for nought? tell me, what shall thy wages be?' At this time, it is worth noting, the number seven had come to be regarded as convenient in hiring, for Jacob said, 'I will serve thee seven years for Rachel thy younger daughter. . . . And Jacob served seven years for Rachel; and they seemed unto him but a few days, for the love he had to her.' It is obvious that the length of service was regarded by the narrator as a special proof of Jacob's love for Rachel. For an ordinary wage a man would work seven days; for his love Jacob worked seven years. That this was so is shown by Laban's calling the term a week. After giving Leah instead of Rachel, he says, 'Fulfil her week, and we will give thee this also for the service which thou shalt serve with me yet seven other years. And Jacob did so, and fulfilled her week.' The week must have been a customary term of engagement long before this, or it would not be thus spoken of. Servants (the herdsmen of Abram's cattle, and the herdsmen of Lot's cattle) are mentioned somewhat earlier. The word 'week' is not used earlier than in the passage just quoted; and there is no reference to a weekly day of rest before the Exodus.

might have shown them, in a rough sort of way, how their term of labour was passing on.

Thus, at length, a month of days and its sub-divisions must have come into use. The subdivisions would almost certainly correspond with the quarters already indicated ; and the week of seven days is the nearest approach in an exact number of days to the quarter of a month. Four periods of eight days exceed a lunar month by two and a-half days ; while four periods of seven days exceed a lunar month by only one and a-half days.

Now there would be two distinct ways in which the division of the month into four weeks might be arranged.

First, the month might be taken as a constant measure of time, and four weeks, of seven days each, suitably placed in each month, so that the extra day and a-half, or (nearly enough) three days in two months, could be intercalated. Thus in one month a day could be left out at the time of new moon, and in the next two days, one day alternating with two in successive months : if the remaining part of each month were divided into four equal parts of seven days in each, the arrangement would correspond closely enough with the progress of the months to serve for a considerable time before fresh intercalation was required. Two lunar months would thus be counted as fifty-nine days, falling short of the truth by one hour, twenty-eight minutes, and nearly eight seconds. On four lunar months the difference would be nearly three hours, and in thirty-two lunar months nearly one day. So that if in the first month two days, in the second one, in the third two, in the fourth one, and so on—in the thirty-first two, and in the thirty-second *two* (instead of one), were intercalated, the total error in those thirty-two months, or about two years and five calendar months of our present time, would be only about half-an-hour.

We find traces of a former arrangement by which the time of new moon was separated, as it were, from the rest of the lunar month. The occurrence of new moon marked in most of the old systems a time of rest and religious worship, probably, almost certainly, arising originally from the worship of the heavenly bodies as deities. But the chronological arrangements, probably connected with this usage at first, have left few traces of their existence. The usage presents manifest imperfections as part of a chronological system, and must soon have been abandoned by the more skilful of those who sought among the celestial bodies for the means of measuring time. The Greeks adopted such an arrangement as I have above indicated.

'The last day of each lunar month,' Whewell says, 'was called by them " the old and new," as belonging to both the waning and the reappearing moon, and their festivals and sacrifices, as determined by the calendar, were conceived to be necessarily connected with the same periods of the cycles of the sun and moon.' 'The laws and oracles,' says Geminus, 'which directed that they should in sacrifices observe three things, months, days, and years, were so understood.' With this permission, a correct system of intercalation became a religious duty. Aratus, in a passage quoted by Geminus, says of the moon—

> As still her shifting visage changing turns,
> By her we count the monthly round of morns.

But the religious duty of properly intercalating a day every thirty-two months, to correct for the difference between two lunar months and fifty-nine days, would seem not to have been properly attended to, for Aristophanes in the 'Clouds' makes the moon complain thus :—

CHORUS OF CLOUDS.

> The moon by us to you her greeting sends,
> But bids us say that she's an ill-used moon,
> And takes it much amiss that you should still

Shuffle her days, and turn them topsy-turvy ;
And that the gods, who know their feast-days well,
By your false count are sent home supperless,
And scold and storm at her for your neglect.

The second usage would be the more convenient. Perceiving, as they would by this time have done, that the lunar month does not contain an exact number of days, or of half-days, men would recognise the uselessness of attempting to use any subdivision of the month, month by month, and would simply take the week of seven days as the nearest approach to the convenient subdivision, the quarter-month, and let that period run on continually, without concerning themselves with the fact that each new month began on a different day of the week. In fact, this corresponds precisely with what has been done in the case of the year.

The necessity of adopting some arrangement for periodical rest would render the division of time into short periods of unvarying length desirable. And, as herdsmen and labourers were early engaged by the lunar month, and afterwards by its subdivision the quarter-month, it is very probable that the beginning of each month would first be chosen as a suitable time for a rest, while later one day in each week would be taken as a rest day. This would not be by any means inconsistent with the

belief that from very early times a religious significance was given to the monthly and weekly
resting days. Almost every observance of times,
and seasons, and days had its first origin, most
probably, in agricultural and pastoral customs. It
was only after a long period had elapsed that
arrangements, originally adopted as convenient,
became so sanctioned by long habit that a religious
meaning was attached to them. Assuredly, whatever opinion may be formed about the Sabbath
rest, only one can be formed about the ' new moon '
rest. *That* certainly had its origin in the lunar
motions and their relation to the convenience and
habits of outdoor workers. It seems altogether
reasonable, apart from the evidence *à priori* and *à
posteriori* in favour of the conclusion, to adopt a
similar explanation of the weekly rest, constantly
associated as we find it with the rest at the time of
new moon.

This explanation implies that the week would
almost certainly be adopted as a measure of time
by every nation which paid any attention to the
subject of time-measurement. Now we know that
no trace of the week exists among the records of
some nations, while in others the week was at
least only a subordinate time-measure. Among
the earlier Egyptians the month was divided into

periods of ten days each, and hitherto no direct evidence has been found to show that a seven-day period was used by them.[1] The Chinese divided the month similarly. Among the Babylonians the month was divided into periods of five days, six such periods in each month, and also into weeks of seven days. The same double arrangement was adopted by the Hebrews.

It is easy to show, however, that the division of the month into six equal or nearly equal parts, five days in each, was not arrived at in a similar way to the division into four parts, and was a later method. We have seen how the quarters of the lunar orbit are determined at 'half-full,' by the boundary between the light and dark half crossing the middle of the moon's disc. Content at first to determine this ocularly, observers would after a time devise simply methods of making more exact determinations. Such devices as Ferguson, the self-taught Scottish peasant, employed to determine the positions of the stars, would be likely to occur to the Chaldæan shepherds in old times. That astronomer (for he well merits the name,

---

[1] Laplace asserts of the Egyptians that they used a period of seven days ; but he misunderstood the account given by Dion Cassius, who referred to the astronomers of the Alexandrian school, not to the ancient Egyptians.

when we consider under what disadvantages he
achieved success) constructed a frame across which
slender threads could be shifted, so that their inter-
sections should coincide with the apparent places
of stars.   A frame similarly constructed might be
made to carry four such threads forming a square,
which properly placed would just seem to enclose
the moon's disc, while a fifth thread parallel to two
sides of the square and midway between them
could be made to coincide with the straight edge
of the half-moon,—and thus the exact time of half-
moon could be easily determined.   Now when the
separating line or arc between light and darkness
fell otherwise, the fifth thread might be made to
show exactly how far across this separating arc
(that is, its middle point) had travelled, and thence
how far the month had progressed,—*if* the observer
had some little knowledge of trigonometry.   If he
had no such knowledge, but were acquainted only
with the simpler geometrical relations of lines and
circles, there would only be two other cases, besides
that of the half-moon, with which he could deal by
this simple method, or some modification of it.
When the middle point of the arc between light
and darkness has travelled exactly one-fourth of
the way across the moon's disc, the moon has gone
one-third of the way from 'new' to 'full.'   When

that middle point has travelled exactly three-fourths of the way across, the moon has gone two-thirds of the way from 'new' to 'full.' Either stage can be determined almost as easily with the frame and threads, or some such contrivance, as the time of half-moon, and similarly of the corresponding stages from 'full' to 'new.' Thus, including new and full, we have six stages in the moon's complete circuit. She starts from 'new;' when she has gone one-sixth of the way round, the advancing arc of light has travelled one-fourth of the way across her disc; when she has gone two-sixths round, it has travelled three-fourths of the way across: then comes 'full,' corresponding to half-way round; then, at four-sixths of the way round, the receding edge is one-fourth of the way back across the moon's disc; at five-sixths it is three-fourths of the way back; and lastly she completes her circuit at 'new' again. Each stage of her journey lasts one-sixth of a lunar month; or five days, less about two hours. Thus five days more nearly represents one of these stages than a week represents a quarter of a lunar month. For a week falls short of a quarter of a month by more than nine hours, while five days exceeds a sixth of a month by rather less than two hours. Moreover, while six periods of five days exceed a month by less than half-a-day, four weeks fall short of a month by more than a day and a-half.[1]

We can very well understand, then, that the division of the lunar month into six parts, each of five days, or into three parts, each of ten days, should have been early suggested by astronomers, as an improvement on the comparatively rough division of the month into four equal parts. We can equally understand that where the latter method had been long in use, where it had become connected with the system of hiring (one day's rest being allowed in each quarter-month), and especially where it had become associated with religious observances, the new method would be stoutly resisted. It would seem that a contest between advocates of a five days' period and those of a seven days' period arose in early times, and was carried on with considerable bitterness. There are those who find in the Great Pyramid of Egypt the record of such a struggle, and evidence that finally the seven days' period came to be distinguished, as a sacred time-measure, from the five days' period,

---

[1] The five days' period has as great an advantage over the week in more exactly dividing the year, as it has in dividing the month, since, while fifty-two weeks fall short of a year by nearly a day and a-quarter, seventy-three periods of five days only fall short of a year by a quarter of a day. But the number 52 has the great advantage over 73 of being subdivisible into four thirteens.

which was regarded doubtless as a profane though perhaps a more exact and scientific subdivision. In the Jewish religious system, however, both subdivisions appear.

A singular piece of evidence has quite recently been obtained respecting the week of the Babylonians, which, while illustrating what I have above shown about the week and the five days' period, seems to afford some explanation of the week of weeks. So far as I know, it has not been considered in this particular light before. We learn from Professor Sayce that the Babylonians called the 7th, 14th, 19th, 21st, and 28th days of each month *sabbatu*, or day of rest. Here clearly the 7th, 14th, 21st, and 28th correspond to the same day of the week; but how does the 19th fall into the series? It appears to me—though I must admit that I only make a guess in the matter, knowing of no independent evidence to favour the idea—that the 19th day of a month became a day of rest as being the forty-ninth day from the beginning of the preceding month. It was, in fact, from the preceding month, the seventh seventh day, or the sabbath of sabbaths. So to regard it, however,—that is, to make the 19th day of one month the forty-ninth from the beginning of the preceding,—it is necessary that the length of the month should be regarded as thirty days (the difference between forty-nine days and nineteen).

While in any nation the month and its sub-divisions would thus, in all probability, be dealt with,—the week almost inevitably becoming, for a while at least, a measure of time, and in most cases remaining so long in use as to obtain an unshaken hold on the people from the mere effect of custom,—another way of dealing with the moon's motions would certainly have been recognised.

Watching the moon, night after night, men would soon perceive that she travels among the stars. It is not easy to determine, from *à priori* considerations, at what particular stage of observational progress the stars, which are scattered over the background on which the heavenly bodies travel, would be specially noticed as objects likely to help men in the measurement of time, the determination of seasons, and so forth. On the whole it seems likely that the observation of the stars for this purpose would come rather later than the first rough determinations of the year, and therefore considerably later (if the above reasoning is just) than the determination of the month. The suitability of the stars for many purposes connected with the measurement of time is not a circumstance which obtrudes itself on the attention. Many

years might well pass before men would notice
that at the same season of the year the same stars
are seen at corresponding hours of the night; for
this is less striking than the regular variation of the
sun's altitude, &c., as the year progresses. This
would be true even if we assumed that from the
beginning certain marked star groups were recognised and remembered at each return to particular
positions on the sky. But it is unlikely that this
happened until long after such rough observations
as I have described above had made considerable
progress. There is only one group of stars respecting which any exception can probably be made,—
viz. the Pleiades, a group which, being both conspicuous and unique in the heavens, must very early
have been recognised and remembered. But even
in the case of the Pleiades (though almost certainly
it was the first known star group, while most
probably it was the object which led to the first
precise determination of the year's length) a con
siderable time must have passed before the regular
return of the group, at times corresponding to particular parts of the year of seasons, was recognised
by shepherds and tillers of the soil. Certainly the
moon's motions must have been earlier noted.

So soon, however, as men had begun to study
the fixed stars, to group them into constellations,

and to watch the motions of these groups athwart the heavens, hour by hour, and (at the same hour) night by night, they would note with interest the motions of their special time-measurer, the moon, amongst the stars.

They would find first that the moon circuits the stellar heavens always in the same direction, namely, from west to east, or in the direction contrary to that of the apparent diurnal motion which she shares with all the celestial bodies. A very few months would show that, speaking generally, the moon keeps to one track round the heavens ; but possibly, even in so short a time, close observers would perceive that she had slightly deviated from the course she at first pursued. After a time this would be clearly seen, and probably the observers of those days may have supposed for a while that the moon, getting farther and farther from her original track, would eventually travel on a quite different path. But with the further progress of time, she would be found slowly to return to it. And in the course of many years it would be found that her path lies always, not in a certain track round the celestial sphere, but in a certain zone or band, some twenty moon-breadths wide— to which no doubt a special name would be given. It was in reality the mid-zone of the present zodiac, which is about thirty-five moon-breadths wide. The central track of the moon's zone, which may be called the lunar zodiac, is in reality the track of the sun round the heavens. But the recognition of the moon's zone would long precede either the determination of the sun's path among the stars or that of the zodiac or planetary highway. The distinction between the sun and moon in this respect is well indicated in Job's words, ' If I beheld the sun when it shined, or the moon walking in brightness,'—the brightness of the sun preventing man from determining his real course till astronomy as a science had made considerable progress : whereas the track of the moon among the stars is obvious to every one who watches the moon, either from night to night or even for a few hours on any one night. The motions of the planets, again, and indeed the very recognition of these wandering stars, belong to an astronomy much more advanced than that which we have been here dealing with.

Watching the moon's progress along her zone of the stellar heavens night after night, the observers would perceive that she completes the circuit in less than a month. Before many months had passed they would have determined the period of these circuits as between twenty-seven and twenty-eight days. It is very likely that at first, while their estimate of the true period was as yet inexact, they would suppose that it lasted exactly four weeks. We must remember that the natural idea of the early observers would be that the motions of the various celestial bodies did in reality synchronise in some way ; though how those motions synchronised might not easily be discovered. They would suppose, and as a matter of fact we know they did suppose, that the sun and moon and stars were made to be for signs and seasons, and for days and months and years. To imagine that the celestial machinery contrived for man's special benefit was in any sense imperfect would have appeared very wicked. They would thus be somewhat in the position of a person for whom a clockmaker had constructed a very elaborate and ingenious clock, showing a number of relations, as the progress of the day, the hour, the minute, the second, the years, the months, the seasons, the tides, and so forth, but with no explanation of the various dials. The owner of the clock would be persuaded that all the various motions indicated on the dials were intended for his special enlighten- ment, though he would be unable for a long time to make out their meaning, or might fail altogether. So the first observers of the heavens must have been thoroughly assured that the movements of

the sun, moon, planets, and stars were for measures
of time, and therefore synchronised (though in long
periods) with each other. We recognise a wider
system (a nobler scheme, one might say, if this
did not imply a degree of knowledge which we do
not really possess) in the actual motions of the
celestial bodies. But with the men of old times it
was different.

Most probably, then, perceiving that the moon
completes her circuit of the stellar heavens in a day
or two less than a lunar month, they would suppose that it was *this* motion which the moon completes in twenty-eight days. Nor would they
detect the error of this view so readily as the
student of modern astronomy might suppose. The
practice of carrying on cycle after cycle till a
great number have been completed in order to
ascertain the true length of the cycle, obvious
though it now appears to us, would not be at all
an obvious resource to the first observers of the
heavens. Of course, if this method had been employed, it would soon have shown that the moon's
circuit of the stellar heavens is accomplished in
less than twenty-eight days. The excess of two-
thirds of a day in each circuit would mount up to
many days in many circuits, and would then be
recognised,—while after very many months the

exact value of the excess would be determined. This, however, is a process belonging to much later times than those we are considering. Watching the moon's motions among the stars during one lunation, the observer, unless very careful, would note nothing to suggest that she is travelling round at the rate of more than a complete circuit in twenty-eight days. If he divided her zone into twenty-eight equal parts, corresponding to her daily journey, and as soon as she first appeared as a new moon began to watch her progress through such of these twenty-eight divisions as were visible at the time (those on the sun's side of the heavens would of course not be visible), she would seem to travel across one division in twenty-four hours very nearly. As she herself obliterates from view all but the brighter stars, it would be all the more difficult to recognise the slight discrepancy actually existing,— the fact really being that she requires only twenty-three hours and about twenty-six minutes to traverse a station, a discrepancy large enough in time, but corresponding to very little progress on the moon's part among the stars. Then in the next month the observation would simply be repeated, no comparison being made between the moon's position among the stars when first seen in one month and that which she had attained when last

seen in the preceding month. If this were done—
and this seems the natural way of observing the
moon's motions among the stars when astronomy
was yet but young—the discrepancy between the
period of circuit and four weeks would long remain
undetected. So long as this was the case, the
moon's roadway among the stars would be divided
into twenty-eight daily portions.

Accordingly, we find, in the early astronomy of
nearly all nations, a lunar zodiac divided into
twenty-eight constellations or lunar mansions. The
Chinese called the zodiac the Yellow Way, and
divided it into twenty-eight *nakshatras*. These
divisions or mansions were not neatly or precisely
defined, but, precisely as we should expect from
the comparative roughness of a system of astronomy in which alone they could appear at all, were
irregular divisions, straggling far on either side of
the ecliptic, which should be the central circle of
the lunar roadway among the stars. The mansions
were named from the brightest stars in each ; and
we are told that the sixteenth mansion was named
Vichaca, from a star in the Northern Crown, a constellation almost as distant from the ecliptic as the
horizon is from a point half-way towards the point
overhead.

A similar division of the older zodiac was

adopted by Egyptian, Arabian, Persian, and Indian astronomers. The Siamese, however, only reckoned twenty-seven, with from time to time an extra one, called *Abigiteen*, or the intercalary mansion. It would appear, however, from some statements in their books, that they had twenty-eight lunar constellations for certain classes of observation. Probably, therefore, the use of twenty-seven, with an occasional intercalary mansion, belonged to a later period of their astronomical system, when more careful observations than the earlier had shown them that the moon circuits the stellar heavens in about twenty-seven and one-third days.

It is important to observe that astronomers were thus apt to change their usage, dropping either wholly or in great part the use of arrangements found to be imperfect. For, noting this, we shall have less difficulty in understanding how the twenty-eight lunar mansions of the older astronomy gave place entirely among the Chaldæans to the twelve signs of the zodiac—that is, the parts of the zodiac traversed day by day by the moon gave place to the parts of the zodiac traversed month by month by the sun. Because the Chaldæan astronomy has not the twenty-eight lunar mansions, it is commonly assumed that this way of dividing the zodiac was never used by them. But this conclusion cannot safely be adopted. On the contrary, what we have already ascertained respecting the Chaldæan use of the week, besides what we should naturally infer from *à priori* considerations, suggests that in the first instance they, like other nations, divided the zodiac into twenty-eight parts; but that later, recognising the inaccuracy of this arrangement, they abandoned it, and adopted the solar zodiacal signs.

This corresponds closely with what the Persian astronomers are known to have done. We read that ' the twenty-eight divisions among the Persians (of which it may be noticed that the second was formed by the Pleiades, and called *Pervis*) soon gave way to the twelve, the names of which, recorded in the works of Zoroaster, and therefore not less ancient than he, were not quite the same as those now used. They were the Lamb, the Bull, the Twins, the Crab, the Lion, the Ear of Corn, the Balance, the Scorpion, the Bow, the Sea Goat, the Watering Pot, and the Fishes. The Chinese also formed a set of twelve zodiacal signs, which they named the Mouse, the Cow, the Tiger, the Hare, the Dragon, the Serpent, the Horse, the Sheep, the Monkey, the Cock, the Dog, and the Pig.

It appears to me not unlikely that the change

from lunar to solar astronomy, from the use of the month and week as chief measures of time to the more difficult but much more scientific method of employing the year for this purpose, was the occasion of much ceremonial observance among the Chaldæan astronomers. Probably elaborate preparations were made for the change, and a special time chosen for it. We should expect to find that this time would have very direct reference to the Pleiades, which must have been the year-measuring constellation as certainly as the moon had earlier been the time-measuring orb. It has long seemed to me that it is to this great change, which certainly took place, and must have been a most important epoch in astronomy, that we must refer those features of ancient astronomy which have commonly been regarded as pointing to the origin of the science itself. I cannot regard it as a reasonable, still less as a probable assumption, that astronomy sprung full formed into being, as the ordinary theories on this subject would imply. Great progress must have been made, and men carefully trained in mathematical as well as observational astronomy must for centuries have studied the subject, before it became possible to decide upon those fundamental principles and methods which have existed from the days of the

Chaldæan astronomers even until now. As to the epoch of the real beginning of astronomy, then, we have, in my opinion, no means of judging. The epoch to which we really can point with some degree of certainty—the year 2170 B.C., or thereabouts—must belong, not to the infancy of astronomy, but to an era when the science had made considerable progress.

I have said that we should expect to find the introduction of the new astronomy, the rejection of the *week* as an astronomical period in favour of the *year*, to be marked by some celestial event having special reference to the Pleiades, the year-measuring star-group. Whether the *à priori* consideration here indicated is valid or not, may perhaps be doubtful; but it is certain the epoch above mentioned *is* related to the Pleiades in a quite unmistakable manner. For at that epoch, *quam proximè*, through the effects of that mighty gyrational movement of the earth which causes what is termed the precession of the equinoxes, the star Alcyone, the brightest of the Pleiades and nearly central in the group, was carried to such a position that when the spring began the sun and Alcyone rose to their highest in the southern skies at the same instant of time.

Be this, however, as it may, it seems abundantly clear that quite early in the progress of astronomy, the more scientific and observant must have recognised the unfitness of the week as an astronomical measure of time. With the disappearance of the week from astronomical systems (the lunar 'quarters' being retained, however) the week may be considered to have become what it now is for ourselves, a civil and in some sense a religious time-measure. That it should retain its position in this character was to be expected, if we consider the firm hold which civil measures once established obtain among the generality of men, and the still greater constancy with which men retain religious observances. A struggle probably took place between astronomers and the priesthood when first the solar zodiac came into use instead of the lunar stations, and when an effort was made to get rid of the week as a measure of time. This seems to me to be indicated by many passages in certain more or less mythological records of the race through whom (directly) the week has descended to us. But this part of the subject introduces questions which cannot be satisfactorily dealt with without a profound study of those records in their mythological sense, and a thorough investigation of philological relations involved in the subject. Such researches, accom-

panied by the careful discussion of all such astronomical relations as were found to be involved,
would, I feel satisfied, be richly rewarded. More
light will be thrown on the ancient systems of
astronomy and astrology by the careful study of
some of the Jewish Scriptures, and clearer light
will be thrown on the meaning of these books by
the consideration of astronomical and astrological
relations associated with them, than has heretofore
been supposed. The key to much that was mysterious in the older systems of religion has been
found in the consideration that to man as first he
rose above the condition of savagery, the grander
objects and processes of nature—earth, sea, and
sky, clouds and rain, winds and storms, the earth-
quake and the volcano, but, above and beyond all,
the heavenly bodies with their stately movements,
their inextricably intermingled periods, their mystical symbolisms—all these must have appeared as
themselves divine, until a nobler conception presented them as but parts of a higher and more
mysterious Whole. In all the ancient systems of
religion we have begun to recognise the myths
which had their birth in those first natural concep-
tions of the Child man. To this rule the ancient
religious system of the Hebrew race was no exception ; but from their Chaldæan ancestors they de-

rived a nature-worship relating more directly to
the heavenly bodies than that of nations living
under less constant skies, and to whom other phenomena were not less important, and therefore not
less significant of power, than the phenomena of
the starry heavens. So soon as we thus recognise
that Hebrew myths would, of necessity, be more
essentially astronomical than those of other nations, we perceive that the Hebrew race was not
unlike other early races in having no mythology,
as Max Müller thought, but possessed a mythology less simply and readily interpreted than that
of other nations.

IN one of the most striking passages of his 'Study
of Sociology,' Herbert Spencer considers what
might be said of our age 'by an independent observer living in the far future, supposing his statements translated into our cumbrous language.'

'"In some respects," says the future observer.
" their code of conduct seems not to have advanced
beyond, but to have gone back from the code of a
still more ancient people from whom their creed
was derived. . . . The relations of their creed to
the creed of this ancient people are indeed difficult
to understand. . . . Not only did they, in the law
of retaliation, outdo the Jews, instead of obeying
the quite opposite principle of the teacher they
worshipped as divine, but they obeyed the Jewish
law, and disobeyed their divine teacher in other
ways,—as in the rigid observance of every seventh
day, which he had deliberately discountenanced.
. . . Their substantial adhesion to the creed they

professedly repudiated, was clearly demonstrated by this, that in each of their temples they fixed up in some conspicuous place the Ten Commandments of the Jewish religion, while they rarely, if ever, fixed up the two Christian Commandments given instead of them. And yet," says the reporter, after dilating on these strange facts, "though the English were greatly given to missionary enterprises of all kinds, and though I sought diligently among the records of these, I could find no trace of a society for converting the English people from Judaism to Christianity."'

It is, indeed, a strange circumstance that Christian teachings in our time respecting the observance of each seventh day should be at variance, not only with what is known of the origin of the observance of Sunday, as distinguished from the Sabbath of the Jews, but even more emphatically with the teachings of Christ, both as to the purpose of a day of rest, and as to the manner in which the poor should be considered. Our Sunday is in fact, if not in origin, the Sabbath of the Jews, not the Lord's Day of the Apostles ; it is regarded, not as a day set apart to refresh those who toil, but as though man were made for its observance ; while the soul-wearying doom of the day is so ordered as to affect chiefly the poorer classes, who want rest from work and anxiety, not rest from the routine of social amusements, which are unknown to them. But although the thoroughly non-Christian nature of our seventh day is remarkable in a country professedly Christian, and although it is a serious misfortune for us that an arrangement which might be most beneficial to the working classes is rendered mischievous by the way in which it is carried out, I certainly have no purpose here to dis.uss the vexed question of Sunday observance. There are some points, however, suggested by Spencer's reference to the origin of our weekly resting day, which are even more curious than those on which he touches. We take our law of weekly rest from Moses; we practically follow Jewish observances in this matter: but in this, except in so far as the contrast between Judaism and Christianity is concerned, there is nothing incongruous. For the Jewish nation was of old the sole Eastern nation whose priesthood taught the worship of one God, and resisted the tendency of the people to worship the gods of other nations. But the real origin of the Jewish Sabbath was far more singular. The observance was derived from an Egyptian, and primarily from a Chaldæan source. Moreover, an astrological origin may be recognised in the practice; rest being enjoined by Egyptian priests on the seventh day, simply because they regarded that day as a *dies infaustus*, when it was unlucky to undertake any work.

It needs no very elaborate reasoning to prove that the Jewish observance of the Sabbath began during the sojourn in Egypt. Without entering into the difficult question of the authorship and date of the Pentateuch, we can perceive that the history of Abraham, Isaac, and Jacob, in the Elohistic portion of the narrative, is introductory to the account of the Jews' sojourn in Egypt and exodus thence under their skilful and prudent commander, Moses. It is incredible that the person who combined these two accounts into one history, including an exact record of the rules for observing festivals, should have failed to add some reference to the seventh day of rest when quoting (from the Elohist) the ordinances which Abraham and the other patriarchs were so carefully enjoined to obey, if it really had been a point of duty in patriarchal times to keep holy the seventh day. In every injunction to the Israelites after they left Egypt, the duty of keeping the Sabbath is strongly dwelt upon. It not only became from this time one of the commandments, but 'a sign between the Lord and the children of Israel for ever.' In the patriarchal times, on the contrary, we find no mention of it: the test of righteousness was the worship of one God—the God of Abraham, Isaac, and Jacob. In the book of Job, again, no reference whatever is made to the observance of the Sabbath; and this is the more remarkable because Job makes 'solemn protestation of his integrity' in several duties. He claims integrity in the worship of God: 'If I beheld the sun when it shined,' he says, 'or the moon walking in brightness, and my heart hath been secretly enticed, or my mouth hath kissed my hand' (the token of worship), 'this also were an iniquity to be punished by the judge: for I should have denied the God that is above.' But he says no word about the observance which, after the exodus, is so specially associated with the worship of God.

It is, indeed, somewhat singular that the observance of the Sabbath should be derived from far remoter times, by those who insist on the literal exactness of the Bible record, seeing that the Bible distinctly assigns the exodus from Egypt as the epoch when the observance had its origin. For Moses, in solemnly reminding all Israel of the covenant of Horeb, says:—

'Remember that thou wast a servant in the land of Egypt, and that the Lord thy God brought thee out thence, through a mighty hand and by a stretched-out arm : therefore the Lord thy God commanded thee to keep the Sabbath-day.' — (Deut. v. 15.)

And these words occupy the position in the Fourth Commandment which, in Exodus xx. 11, is occupied by the words, 'For in six days the Lord made heaven and earth,' &c.

Assigning the origin of the first Jewish observance of the Sabbath to the time of the exodus, we are forced to the conclusion that the custom of keeping each seventh day as a day of rest was derived from the people amongst whom the Jews had been sojourning more than two hundred years. It is unreasonable to suppose that Moses would have added to the almost overwhelming difficulties which he had to encounter in dealing with the obstinate people he led from Egypt, the task of establishing a new festival. Such a task is at all times difficult, but at the time of the exodus it would have been hopeless to undertake it. The people were continually rebelling against Moses, because he sought to turn them from the worship of the gods of Egypt, in whom they were disposed to trust. It was no time to establish a new festival, unless one could be devised which should correspond with the customs they had learned in Egypt. Moses would seem indeed to have pursued a course of compromise.[1] Opposing manfully the worship of the Egyptian gods, he adopted, nevertheless, Egyptian ceremonies and festivals, only so far modifying them that (as he explained them) they ceased to be associated with the worship of false gods.

We have also historical evidence as to the non-Jewish origin of the observance of the seventh day, as decisive of the arguments I have been considering. For Philo Judæus, Josephus, Clement of Alexandria, and others, speak plainly of the week as not of Jewish origin, but common to all the Oriental nations. I do not wish, however, to make use of such evidence here, important though it is— or rather because it is so important that it could not properly be dealt with in the space available to

----

[1] There is a passage in Jeremiah which, as it seems to me, cannot otherwise be reconciled with the Pentateuch—viz. chapter vii. 21–23, where he says, 'Thus saith the Lord of Hosts, the God of Israel ; Put your burnt offerings unto your sacrifices, and eat flesh. For I spake not unto your fathers, nor commanded them in the day that I brought them out of the land of Egypt, concerning burnt offerings or sacrifices ; but this thing commanded I them, saying, Obey my voice, and I will be your God, and ye shall be my people ; and walk ye in all the way that I have commanded you, that it may be well unto you.' It seems plainly intimated here that (in Jeremiah's opinion, at any rate) the ordinances relating to burnt-offerings and sacrifices on the Sabbath and new moons were not commanded by God, however plainly the account in the Pentateuch may seem to suggest the contrary ; and the two accounts can scarcely be reconciled except by supposing that the Mosaic laws on these points were intended to regulate and also to sanction an observance not originally instituted by Moses.

me. I wish to consider only the evidence which
lies directly before us in the Bible pages, combining it with the astronomical relations which are
involved in the question. For it is to an astronomical or rather an astrological interpretation that
we are led, so soon as we recognise the non-Jewish
origin of the Sabbath. Beyond all doubt, the week
is an astronomical period, and that in a twofold
sense ; it is first a rough sub-division of the lunar
month, and in the second place it is a period
derived directly from the number of celestial bodies
known to ancient astronomers as *moving* upon the
sphere of the fixed stars.

The astronomical origin of the Sabbath is shown
by the Mosaic laws as to festivals, illustrated by
occasional passages in other parts of the Bible. In
the 28th chapter of Numbers we find four forms of
sacrifice to be offered at regular intervals—first,
the continual burnt-offering to be made at sunrise
and at sunset (these epochs, be it noted, being
important in the astrological system of the Egyptians) ; secondly, the offering on the Sabbath ;
thirdly, the offering in the time of the new moon ;
and fourthly, the offering at the luni-solar festival
of the Passover. That is, we have daily, weekly,
monthly, and yearly offerings. An attempt has
been made to show that in the beginning of the

Mosaic rule the months were not lunar ; but, apart from all other evidence, repeated references to 'Sabbaths and new moons' negative this view, and show that, as Spencer (Rit. iii. 1) maintains, the Hebrews began their month when the new moon first appeared. It is also clear from the nature of the offerings made, that the festival of the new moon was held in equal esteem with the Sabbath ; and although the observances were different, yet both days were strictly religious in character. For when the Shunammite woman said to her husband that she would 'run to the man of God,' he answers (supposing she went to hear the sacred books read), 'Wherefore wilt thou go to him to-day? it is neither new moon nor Sabbath.' And again, the new moon resembled the Sabbath in being a day when sale was prohibited. 'Hear this,' says Amos, 'O ye that swallow up the needy, even to make the poor of the land to fail, saying, When will the new moon be gone, that we may sell corn ? and the Sabbath, that we may set forth wheat ?' It seems also, as Tirin has pointed out, that servile work was prohibited, for we read (1 Samuel xx. 18, 19) that Jonathan said to David, 'To-morrow is the new moon and thou shalt be missed, because thy seat will be empty. And when thou hast stayed three days, then thou shalt go down quickly, and come to the place where thou didst hide thyself *when the business was in hand,'* or, as in the Douay translation, 'in the day when it is lawful to work.' [1]

We have evidence equally clear to show that the seven days of the week were connected with the seven planets, that is, with the seven celestial bodies which appear to move among the stars. It was by no mere accidental agreement between the number of the days and the number of planets that so many of the Oriental nations were led to name the days of the week after the planets. The arrangement of the nomenclature is indeed so peculiar that a common origin for the practice must be admitted, when we find the same arrangement adopted by

---

[1] Tirin also asserts that the Jews observed the lunar system, and that their months consisted of 29 and 30 days alternately (29½ days, within about three-quarters of an hour, being the length of the mean lunar month). Hence the feast of the new moon came to be called the thirtieth Sabbath, that is, the Sabbath of the thirtieth day. Thus Horace (Sat. I. ix.) 'Hodie tricesima sabbata : vin' tu Curtis Judæis oppedere?' Macrobius mentions that the Greeks, Romans, Egyptians, Arabians, &c., worshipped the moon (Sat. I. xv.)? and it is probable that despite the care of Moses on this point, the Jews were prone to return to the moon-worship, whence the feast of the new moon had its origin. We must not, however, infer this from the passage in Jeremiah vii. 17, 18, 'Seest thou not what they do in the cities of Judah and in the streets of Jerusalem ? The children gather wood, and the fathers kindle the fire, and the women knead their dough, to make cakes to the queen of heaven, and to pour out drink-offerings unto other gods.' For the queen of heaven is Athor, parent of the universe.

nations otherwise diverse in character and habits.
Moreover, the arrangement is manifestly associated
with Sabaism on the one hand, and with astrological
superstitions on the other ; and we find the clearest
evidence in the Bible not only that Sabaism and
astrology were known to the Jews, but that Moses
had extreme difficulty in separating the observances
he enjoined (or permitted ?) from the worship of
the Host of Heaven. He was learned, we know,
in all the wisdom of the Egyptians (Acts vii. 22), and
therefore he must have known those astronomical
facts, and have been familiar with those astrological superstitions, which the Chaldæans had imparted to the Egyptians of the days of the
Pharaohs.[1] It is noteworthy, too, that the first
difficulties he met with in the exodus arose from
the wish of the Jews to return to Sabaism. This
is not manifest in the original narrative ; but the
real meaning of the account is evident from the
following passage (Acts vii. 40), where Stephen,
speaking of Moses, says, 'This is he . . . whom
our fathers would not obey, but thrust him from

[1] He showed considerable skill, if Dr. Beke was right, in his
application of such knowledge (combined with special knowledge
acquired during his stay in Midian), so that his people should cross
a part of the Gulf of Suez during an exceptionally low tide. For
though the Egyptians may have been acquainted with the general
tidal motion in the Red Sea, it may well be believed that the army
of Pharaoh would be less familiar than Moses with local peculiarities affecting (in his time) the movements of that sea.

them, and in their hearts turned back again into
Egypt, saying unto Aaron, Make us gods to go
before us ; for as for this Moses, which brought us
out of the land of Egypt, we wot not what is
become of him. And they made a calf in those
days, and offered sacrifice unto the idol, and rejoiced
in the works of their own hands. Then God turned,
and gave them up to worship the host of heaven ;
as it is written in the book of the prophets . . .
Ye took up the tabernacle of Moloch, and the star
of your god Remphan, figures which ye made to
worship them.'[1]

[1] This passage, and the passage from Amos, to which the proto-
martyr refers, are curious in connection with the special subject of
this paper, as indicated by its title. For where Stephen says
Remphan, Amos says Chiun.   Now it is maintained by Grotius that
Remphan is the same as Rimmon, whom Naaman worshipped, and
Rimmon or Remmon signifies 'elevated' (lit. a pomegranate), and
is understood by Grotius to refer to Saturn, the highest of the planets.
(The student of astronomy will remember Galileo's anagram on the
words '*Altissimum planetam tergeminum observavi.*')   Now Chiun,
which denotes a 'pedestal,' is considered to be equivalent in this
place to Chevan, or Kevan, the Saturn of the Arabians.   (Park-
hurst mentions that the Peruvians worshipped Choun.)   Moloch, of
course, signifies king.   Because children were sacrificed to Moloch,
Bonfrère considers this god to be the same as Saturn, described as
devouring his own children.   If so, the words 'tabernacle of Moloch
and the star of Remphan' relate to the same special form of
Sabaism—that, namely, which assigned to Saturn the chief place
among the star-gods.   I must remark, however, that this point is
by no means essential for the main argument of this paper, which is
in reality based on the unquestioned fact that amongst all the nations
which used the week as a division of time, the seventh day was

Now I might pass from what has here been shown, to the direct inference that the Sabbath corresponded with the day which Oriental Sabaism consecrated to the planet Saturn ; because we have the clearest possible evidence that all nations which adopted the week as a measure of time named the seven days after the same planets. But I prefer, at some risk of appearing to weaken the argument by introducing matters less certain, to consider the evidence we have as to the position of the god corresponding to the Latin Saturn in the Assyrian mythology.

Many years since, Colonel (then Major) Rawlinson, in a paper read before the Royal Asiatic Society, referring to an inscription beginning, ' This the Palace of Sardanapalus, the humble worshipper of Assarach,' made the following remarks :—

' There can be no doubt,' he said (I quote from a report not professing to be *verbatim*), 'that this Assarach was the Nisroch mentioned in Scripture, in whose temple Sennacherib was slain. He was most probably the deified father of the tribes, the Assur of the Bible. This Assarach was styled in

associated with the planet Saturn. It is necessary to call attention to this point, because not unfrequently it happens that some subsidiary matter, such as that touched on in this note, is dealt with as though the whole question at issue turned upon it.

all the inscriptions as the king, the father, and the
ruler of the gods, thus answering to the Greek
god, Chronos, or Saturn, in Assyrio-Hellenic mythology.'

Again Layard, speaking of Assyrian mythology,
says :—

' All we can now venture to infer is that the
Assyrians worshipped one supreme God as the
great national deity, under whose immediate and
special protection they lived, and their empire existed.　The name of this god appears to have been
Asshur, as nearly as can be determined at present
from the inscriptions.　It was identified with that
of the empire itself, always called "the country of
Asshur."　With Asshur, but apparently far inferior
to him in the celestial hierarchy, although called
the great gods, were associated twelve other deities.
. . . These twelve gods may have presided over
the twelve months of the year.'—(*Nineveh and
Babylon*, p. 637.)

In a note, Layard refers to doubts expressed
by Colonel Rawlinson respecting the identity of
Asshur and Nisroch, presumably removed by Rawlinson's later reading of the inscription referred to
above.　He remarks that this supreme god was
represented sometimes under a triune form ; and
' generally, if not always, typified by a winged

figure in a circle.' Plate XIII. of my treatise on Saturn shows how these two descriptions are reconcilable ; for there are shown in it two figures of Nisroch, both winged and within a ring, but one only triune.[1]

Amongst the twelve great gods were included six corresponding to the remaining planets, though doubts exist as to the gods associated with the different celestial bodies. It seems probable that Shamash corresponded with the Sun ; Ishtar (Astarte or Ashtar) with the Moon ; Bel with Jupiter,[2] Mero-

---

[1] I do not here dwell on the curious coincidence—if, indeed, Chaldæan astronomers had not discovered the ring of Saturn—that they showed the god corresponding within a ring, and triple. Galileo's first view of Saturn, with feeble telescopic power, showed the planet as triple (*'ergeminus*) ; and very moderate optical knowledge, such indeed as we may fairly infer from the presence of optical instruments among Assyrian remains, might have led to the discovery of Saturn's ring and Jupiter's moons. (Bel, the Assyrian Jupiter, was represented sometimes with four star-tipped wings.) But it is possible that these are mere coincidences. Saturn would naturally come to be regarded as the God of Time, on account of his slow motion round the ecliptic ; and thus the ring (a natural emblem of time) might be expected to appear in figures of the god corresponding to this planet. It is curious, however, that the ring is flat, and proportioned like Saturn's.

[2] Layard associates Bel, ' the father of the great gods,' with Saturn, and Mylitta, the consort of Bel, with Venus, but without giving any reasons, and probably merely as a guess. He elsewhere remarks, however, that from Baal came the Belus of the Greeks, who was confounded with our own Zeus or Jupiter, and apart from the clear evidence associating Nisroch with Saturn, the evidence connecting Bel with Jupiter is tolerably satisfactory. The point is not important, however, in relation to the subject of this paper.

dach with Mars; Mylitta with Venus; and Nebo
with Mercury.   But the question would only be of
importance in its bearing on my present subject,
if we knew the Assyrian time-measurement, and
especially their arrangement of the days of the
week.   Since we have to pass to other sources of
information on this point, the only really important
fact in the Assyrian mythology, for our purpose,
is the nearly certain one that their supreme god
Asshur or Nisroch corresponded to the 'highest'
or outermost planet Saturn.   He was also the
Time God, thus corresponding to Chronos.   But it
is necessary to notice here that mythological relations must to some degree be separated from astrological considerations, in dealing with the connection between various Assyrio-Chaldæan deities and
the planets.   For instance, it is important in
mythology to observe that the Greek god Chronos
and the Latin god Saturn are unlike in many of
their attributes, yet the association between the
planet Saturn and the Assyrian deity Nisroch is
not on that account brought into question, although we can only connect Nisroch with Saturn
by means of the common relation of both to
Chronos.

On etymological grounds, Yav, the fifth of the great gods, may perhaps be associated with Zeus, identical with the Sanscrit Dyaus, and
the Latin root 'Jov;' also with Yahveh, the tribal god of the Jews.

Many circumstances point to the Chaldæan origin of Egyptian astronomy. The Egyptian zodiac corresponded with the Dodecatemoria of the Chaldæans, and though some of the Chaldæan constellations were modified in Egyptian temples, yet sufficient general resemblance exists between the Egyptian arrangement and that which other nations derived from the Chaldæans, to show the real origin of the figures which adorn Egyptian zodiac temples.[1] The argument derived from

[1] In an essay on the 'Shield of Achilles' (*Light Science for Leisure Hours*, first series), I called attention, seven years ago, to the probability that the description of the Shield, a manifest interpolation, related originally to a zodiac temple, erected by star-worshippers long before Homer's time. Some of the Egyptian zodiac temples exist to this day, though probably they belong to a much later date, and were only copies (more or less perfect) of the ancient Chaldæan temples. That Homer, if he had visited such a temple, and had composed a poem descriptive of its sculptured dome, would have 'worked in' that description if he saw the opportunity when singing the Iliad, all Homeric students will be ready to admit. Like every improvisatore, the glorious old minstrel knew the advantage of the rest afforded by an occasional change from invention to recitation. In so using it, he appears to have pruned the description considerably; for in the *Shield of Hercules* (manifestly taken from the same Homeric poem, though sometimes attributed to Hesiod) we find, along with much almost identical matter, several passages which are omitted from the Achillean description. Very curious evidence of the nature of the original poem is found in one of these passages. In a zodiac temple, the constellation of the Dragon (whatever the age of the temple) would occupy the boss or centre of the dome, for the north pole of the zodiac falls in the middle of that constellation. Now in the *Shield of Hercules—*

astrological fancies is even stronger, for the whole system of astrological divination is so artificial and peculiar that it must of necessity be ascribed to one nation. To find the system prevailing among any people is of itself a sufficient proof that they were taught by that nation. Nor can any question arise as to the nation which invented the system. The Egyptians themselves admitted the superiority of the Chaldæan astrologers, and the common consent of all the Oriental nations accorded with this view. We know that in Rome, although Armenians, Egyptians, and Jews were consulted as astronomers, Chaldæans were held to be the most proficient. 'Chaldæis sed major erit fiducia,' says Juvenal, of the Roman ladies who consulted fortune-tellers: 'quicquid Dixerit astrologus, credent a fonte relatis Ammonis,'—whatever the Chaldæan astrologers may say, they trust as though it came from Jupiter Ammon. Another argument in favour of the Chaldæan origin of astronomy and astrology is derived from the fact

---

' The scaly horror of a dragon coil'd
  Full in the central field, unspeakable
  With eyes oblique retorted, that aslant
  Shot gleaming flame.'

(The very attitude, be it noted, of the Dragon of the Star sphere.) There is much more evidence of this kind to which, for want of space, I cannot here refer.

that the systems of astronomy taught in Egypt, Babylon, Persepolis, and elsewhere, do not correspond with the latitude of these places ; but this argument (which I have considered at some length in Appendix A. to my treatise on Saturn) need not detain us here. It is sufficient to observe that in Egypt the astrological system was early received and taught :—

'Egypt,' says a modern writer, 'a country noted for the loveliness of its nights, might well be the supporter of such a system. . . . To each planet was attributed a mystic influence, and to every heavenly body a supernatural agency, and all the stars that gem the sky were supposed to exert an influence over the birth, and life, and destiny of man ; hence arose the casting of nativities, prayers, incantations, and sacrifices, — of which we have traces even to the present day in those professors of astrology and divination, the gipsies, whose very name links them with the ancient country of such arts.'[1]

One of the cardinal principles of astrology was this : that every hour and every day is ruled by its proper planet. Now, in the ancient Egyptian

---

[1] This may be questioned. It is said, however, that when the gipsies first made their appearance in Western Europe, about the year 1415, their leader called himself Duke of Lower Egypt.

astronomy there were seven planets ; two, the sun
and moon, circling round the earth, the rest circling
round the sun. The period of circulation was
apparently taken as the measure of each planet's
dignity, probably because it was judged that the
distance corresponded to the period. We know
that some harmonious relation between the distances
and periods was supposed to exist. When Kepler
discovered the actual law, he conceived that he had
in reality found out the mystery of Egyptian
astronomy, or, as he expressed it, that he had
'stolen the golden vases of the Egyptians'
Whether they had clear ideas as to the nature of
this relation or not, it is certain that they arranged
the planets in order (beginning with the planet of
longest period) as follows :—

<table>
<tr><td>1. Saturn.</td><td>5. Venus.</td></tr>
<tr><td>2. Jupiter.</td><td>6. Mercury.</td></tr>
<tr><td>3. Mars.</td><td>7. The Moon.</td></tr>
<tr><td>4. The Sun.</td><td></td></tr>
</table>

The hours were devoted in continuous succession
to these bodies ; and as there were twenty-four
hours in each Chaldæan or Egyptian day, it follows
that with whatever planet the day began, the cycle
of seven planets (beginning with that one) was
repeated three times, making twenty-one hours,

and then the first three planets of the cycle completed the twenty-four hours, so that the fourth planet of the cycle (so begun) ruled the first hour of the next day Suppose, for instance, the first hour of any day was ruled by the Sun—the cycle for the day would therefore be the Sun, Venus, Mercury, the Moon, Saturn, Jupiter, and Mars, which, repeated three times, would give twenty-one hours; the twenty-second, twenty-third, and twenty-fourth hours would be ruled respectively by the Sun, Venus, and Mercury, and the first hour of the next day would be ruled by the Moon. Proceeding in the same way through this second day, we find that the first hour of the third day would be ruled by Mars. The first hour of the fourth day would be ruled by Mercury; the first hour of the fifth day by Jupiter; of the sixth by Venus; and of the seventh by Saturn. The seven days in order, being assigned to the planet ruling their first hour, would therefore be—

1. The Sun's day (Sunday).
2. The Moon's day (Monday, Lundi).
3. Mars's day (Tuesday, Mardi).
4. Mercury's day (Wednesday, Mercredi).
5. Jupiter's day (Thursday, Jeudi).
6. Venus's day (Friday, Veneris dies, Vendredi).
7. Saturn's day (Saturday; *Ital.* il Sabbato).

Dion Cassius, who wrote in the third century of our era, gives this explanation of the nature of the Egyptian week and of the method in which the arrangement was derived from their system of astronomy. It is a noteworthy point that neither the Greeks nor Romans in his time used the week, which was a period of strictly Oriental origin. The Romans only adopted the week in the time of Theodosius, towards the close of the fourth century, and the Greeks divided the month into periods of ten days; so that, for the origin of the arrangement connecting the days of the week with the planets, we must look to the source indicated by Dion Cassius. It is a curious illustration of the way in which traditions are handed down, not only from generation to generation, but from nation to nation, that the Latin and Western nations receiving the week along with the doctrines of Christianity, should nevertheless have adopted the nomenclature in use among astrologers. It is impossible to say how widely the superstitions of astrology had spread, or how deeply they had penetrated, for the practices of astrologers were carried on in secret, wherever Sabaism was rejected as a form of religion ; but that in some mysterious way these superstitions spread among nations professing faith in one God, and that even to this day they are secretly accepted in Mahometan and even Christian communities, cannot be disputed. How much more must such superstitions have affected the Jews, led out by Moses from the very temple of astrology? Knowing what we do of the influence of such superstitions in our own time, can we wonder if three thousand years ago Moses found it difficult to dispossess his followers of their belief in 'the host of heaven,' or if, a few generations later, even the reputed prophetess Deborah should have been found proclaiming that 'the stars in their courses' had fought against the enemies of Israel?[1]

[1] We are apt to overlook the Pagan origin of many ideas referred to in the Bible, as well as of many ceremonies which Moses at least *permitted*, if he did not enjoin. The description of the Ark of the Covenant, of the method of sacrifices, of the priestly vestments, &c., indicate in the clearest manner an Egyptian or Assyrian origin. The cherubim, for instance - figures which united, as Calmet has shown, the body of the lion or ox with the wings of an eagle—are common in Assyrian sculptures. The oracle of the temple differed only from some of the chambers of Nimrod and Khorsabad, in the substitution of 'palm trees' for the sacred tree of Assyrian sculptures, and open flowers for the Assyrian tulip-shaped ornament. Layard (*Nineveh and Babylon*, p. 643) states further that 'in the Assyrian halls, the winged human-headed bulls were on the side of the wall, and their wings, like those of the cherubim, "touched one another in the midst of the house." The dimensions of these figures were in some cases nearly the same—namely, fifteen feet square. The doors were also carved with cherubim and palm trees, and open flowers, and thus, with the other parts of the building, corresponded with those of the Assyrian palaces On the walls at Nineveh, the only addition appears to have been the introduction of the human form and the image of the king, which were an abomination to the

That the Egyptians dedicated the seventh day of the week to the outermost or highest planet, Saturn, is certain ; and it is presumable that this day was a day of rest in Egypt.   It is not known, however, whether this was ordained in honour of

Jews.   The pomegranates and lilies of Solomon's temple must have been nearly identical with the usual Assyrian ornament, in which —and particularly at Khorsabad—the pomegranate frequently takes the place of the tulip and the cone.'   After quoting the description given by Josephus of the interior of one of Solomon's houses, which even more closely corresponds with and illustrates the chambers in the palace of Nineveh, Layard makes the following remark : 'To complete the analogy between the two, edifices, it would appear that Solomon was seven years building the temple, and Sennacherib about the same time building his great palace at Kouyunjik.'   The introduction into the Ark of figures so remarkable as the cherubim can hardly be otherwise explained than by assuming that these figures corresponded with some objects which the Jews during their stay in Egypt had learned to associate with religious ceremonies. That the Egyptians used such figures, placing them at the entrance of their temples, is certain.   Neither can it be doubted that the setting of dishes, spoons, bowls, shewbread, &c., on the table within the Ark, was derived from Egyptian ceremonials, though direct evidence on these points is not (so far as I know) available.   We know, however, that meats of all kinds were set before Baal (see *Apocrypha,* Bel and the Dragon).   The remarkable breast-plate worn by the Jewish high priest was derived directly from the Egyptians.   In the often-repeated picture of judgment the deceased Egyptian is seen conducted by the god Horus, while 'Anubis places on one of the balances a vase supposed to contain his good actions, and in the other is the emblem of truth, a representation of Thmèi, the goddess of Truth, which was also worn on the judicial breast-plate.'   Wilkinson, in his *Manners and Customs of the Ancient Egyptians,* shows that the Hebrew Thummim is a plural form of the word Thmèi.   The symbolism of the breast-plate is referred to in the *Apocrypha,* Book of Wisdom, lxviii. 24.

the chief planet—that is, their supreme deity—or because it was held unlucky to work on that day. It by no means follows from the fact that Nisroch, or his Egyptian representative, was the chief deity, that he was therefore regarded as a beneficent ruler. Rather what we know of Oriental superstitions would lead us to infer that the chief deity in a system of several gods was one to be propitiated. And, indeed, the little we know of Egyptian mythology suggests that the beneficent gods were those corresponding to the sun and moon— later represented by Osiris and Isis (deities, however, which had other interpretations). Saturn, though superior to the sun and moon, not only in the sense in which modern astronomers use the term superior, but also in the power attributed to him, was probably a maleficent if not a malignant deity. We may infer this from the qualities attributed to him by astrologers—' If Saturn be predominant in any man's nativity, and cause melancholy in his temperature,' says Burton, in his 'Anatomy of Melancholy,' 'then he shall be very austere, sullen, churlish, black of colour, profound in his cogitations, full of cares, miseries, and discontents, sad and fearful, always silent and solitary.' We may not unreasonably conclude, therefore, that either rest was enjoined on Saturn's day as a religious observance to propitiate this powerful but gloomy god, or else because bad fortune was expected to attend any enterprise begun on the day over which Saturn bore sway. The evil influence, as well as the great power attributed to Saturn, are indicated in the well-known lines of Chaucer :—

> . . . Quod Saturne,
> My cors, that hath so wide for to turne,
> Hath more power than wot any man ;
> * * * * *
> I do vengeaunce and pleine correction
> While I dwell in the signe of the leon ;
> * * * * *
> Min ben also the maladies colde,
> The darke tresons, and the castes olde ;
> My loking is the fader of pestilence.

It is, however, possible that the idea of rest on the day dedicated to Saturn may have been suggested to Egyptian astrologers and priests by the slow motion of the planet in his orbit, whereby the circuit of the ecliptic is only completed in about twenty-nine years.

However this may be, we know certainly that on the Sabbath of the Jews rest was enjoined for a different reason. Moses adopted the Egyptian week, and allowed the practice of a weekly day of rest to continue. But in order that the people whom he led and instructed might not fall into the worship of the host of heaven, he associated the observance of the seventh day with the worship of that one God in whom he enjoined them to believe, the God of their forefathers, Abraham, Isaac, and Jacob. So far as appears from the Bible narrative, there is no scriptural objection to this view. On the contrary, strong scriptural reasons exist for accepting it. If the account of the creation given in the first chapter of Genesis could be accepted as literally exact, it nevertheless would not follow that the seventh day of rest was enjoined before the time of the exodus. And we have seen that the Bible account itself assigns the departure from Egypt as a reason for the observance, so that whatever view we form respecting the real origin of the seventh day of rest, we have no choice as to the time we must assign for the commencement of its observance by the Jews, unless Deuteronomy v. be rejected as not even historically trustworthy.

Nothing, therefore, that I have shown in this paper need be regarded as necessarily opposed to the faith of those who honestly believe in the literal exactness of the reason assigned in Exodus xxxi. 17 for the observance of the Sabbath of the Jews. Such persons may accept the week as of

Pagan origin, and the original observance of
Saturn's day as of astrological significance, while
believing in the reason given by Moses for the
adoption of the practice by his followers, that ' in
six days the Lord made heaven and earth, and
on the seventh day He rested and was refreshed.'
(The idea of rest, accepted literally, accords neither
better nor worse with the conception of an
Almighty Creator, than the idea of work.)   But
it seems to me that those who thus regard the
Jewish Sabbath as a divinely instituted compromise between the worship of the seven planets as
gods, and the worship of one only God the
Creator of all things, may yet find in what I have
here shown a new reason for Christianising our
seventh day of rest, even if we must still continue
to miscall it the Sabbath.   Since it was permis-
sible for Moses to adopt a Pagan practice (to
sanction, if not to sanctify, a superstition), it may
well be believed that the greater than Moses was
entitled to change the mode of observance of the
seventh day of rest.   We know that in Christ's
time the Sabbath (of its very nature a convenient
ceremonial substitute for true religion) had become
a hideous tyranny ; nay, that many, wanting real
goodness, were eager to prove their virtue by in-
flicting the Sabbath on those who most needed

'to rest and be refreshed' on that day. Whether in the obedience to the teaching of Christ, who (we learn) rebuked those hypocrites, all this has been changed in our time, is a point which may be left to the reflection of the reader.

ASTRONOMY AND THE JEWISH FESTIVALS.

IN the essay on the 'Origin of the Week,' I have shown that so soon as a people began to rise above the savage state, and to require some means of measuring time-periods other than the day and the year (if, indeed, the year ever was even roughly measured until long after the month and week had been used as time-measures), they must have used the moon for this purpose, and must soon after have been led to divide time into periods of seven days. It is no mere accident that all the nations of antiquity used the week of seven days as a measure of time, though some, later, employed the astronomically more exact division of time into periods of five and ten days. The moon naturally suggests by her movements precisely this division of time into periods of seven days, though a more careful study of her motions suggests the division of the lunar month into six periods of five days each, rather than into four periods of seven days each. Nor is it a mere accident that in one of the books of that little library of Hebrew works we call the Old Testament, we find as the very earliest division of time used for the hiring of labour the week of seven days. Even those nations, if any such there were (which I doubt), who did not in the beginning of their existence worship either the sun or the moon, or both, and often the other heavenly bodies as well, yet adopted the belief that the sun and moon and stars were set in the heavens for signs, and for seasons, and for days and years. And as I have shown, all the names for the moon which do not refer to her light, indicate her use as a time-measurer.[1] I may also repeat here, that the times of half-moon alone would be observed with any exactitude, the time of full, like the time of new moon, not being determinable with anything like the same degree of accuracy. Moreover, I have shown that soon after the use of the month and its quarters for measuring time had been commenced, it would be found necessary to employ successive

---

[1] This is true of nearly all the Indo-European languages, though in some, as in Greek, we have two names for the moon, one relating to her brightness, the other to her time-measuring use; while in some, as in Latin, the latter name has disappeared, save as it remains in derivations as *mensis*, the month, the connection of which word with *mensuration* was noticed even by the Romans, as by Cicero and others.

T

weeks of seven days without reference to their agreement or not with the four quarters of successive lunar months. In other words, since the week and the month are not exactly synchronous, it would be found necessary to use them separately, just as the lunar month and the year not being synchronous have had to be used separately, and as, in like manner, the day not being synchronous with either the lunar month or the year, has had to be used apart from them, though all four periods, day, week, month, and year, are associated together.

In the essay on the Jewish Sabbath I have shown how the seven days came to be associated with the seven planets. The twenty-four hours of each day were devoted to those planets in the order of their supposed distance from the earth,— Saturn, Jupiter, Mars, the Sun, Venus, Mercury, and the Moon. The outermost planet, Saturn, which also travels in the longest period, was regarded in this arrangement as of chief dignity, as encompassing in his movement all the rest, Jupiter as of higher dignity than Mars, and so forth. Moreover, to the outermost planet, partly because of Saturn's gloomy aspect, partly because among half-savage races the powers of evil are always more respected than the powers that work for good, a maleficent influence was attributed. Now, if we assign to the successive hours of a day the planets as above-named, beginning with Saturn on the day assigned to that powerful deity, it will be found that the last hour of that day will be assigned to Mars,—the lesser infortune, as Saturn was the greater infortune of the old system of astrology,— and the first hour of the next day to the next planet, the Sun,[1] the day following Saturday would thus be Sunday. The last hour of Sunday would fall to Mercury, and the first of the next to the Moon; so Monday, the Moon's day, follows Sunday. The next day would be the day of Mars, who, in the Scandinavian theology, is represented by Tuisco; so Tuisco's day, or Tuesday (Mardi), follows Monday. Then, by following the same system, we come to Mercury's day (Mercredi), Woden's day, or Wednesday; next to Jupiter's day, Jove's day (Jeudi), Thor's day, or Thursday; to Venus's day, Vendredi (Veneris dies), Freya's day, or Friday, and so to Saturday again. That the day devoted to the most evil and most powerful of all the deities of the Sabdans should be set apart—first as one on which it was unlucky to work, and afterwards as one on which it was held to be

---

[1] The sun and moon were both regarded as planets by astrologers who, it must be remembered, were of old the only astronomers.

sinful to work—was but the natural outcome of the superstitious belief that the planets were gods ruling the fates of men and nations.[1]   It is, however, obvious that the Jews, or rather those from whom they derived their special religious observances, were taught to find a worthier motive for their Sabbath rest.   Yet, of the connection between the Jewish and the astrologic and sabaistic Sabbath,. there could be no manner of doubt, even were there not the evidence now to be considered, which indicates that all the Jewish festivals and fasts were of astronomical origin.

It must, in the first place, be obvious to any one who considers the matter with the least degree of attention, that the Jewish ceremonial worship, with all its complicated arrangements, must have been in existence long before the exodus.   No reasoning mind can for a moment imagine that such a system could have been devised in a lifetime, or a generation, far less during such a period as that in

---

[1] In like manner the day of Venus, Friday, was a day for marrying and giving in marriage ; and though our modern customs make the day of marriage the day also for starting on a journey (even that, however, showing evidence of astronomical origin, in its customary length as the ' moon of honey '), it was the reverse in ancient times, so that Friday would be of all days in the week the one regarded as least suited for starting on a journey.   We see some trace of this association in Deuteronomy, chap. xx. v. 7, ' What man is there that hath betrothed a wife ? let him go and return unto his house.'

which the Jewish people were wandering between
Egypt and Palestine—assuming the description of
the exodus to be in its outlines true, however manifestly inexact in details. But we are not left to
infer this, from the obvious considerations suggested
by experience as the origin of ceremonial observances among other people. There is abundant
evidence to show that the Jewish ceremonial system
was derived either directly from the Assyrians (who
may have received it still earlier from Hindoo
sources), or, more probably, from Assyria through
the Egyptians. As I have pointed out at pp. 265,
266, 'the description of the Ark of the Covenant, of
the method of sacrifices, of the priestly ornaments,
&c., indicates in the clearest manner an Egyptian
or Assyrian origin.'

And now let us examine the Jewish sacrifices
offered up at various feasts and fasts, or otherwise
at stated times. We may conveniently follow the
account given in the Book of Numbers, chaps.
xxviii. and xxix., though the reader will do well to
consult also Leviticus, chaps. xxiii., xxv., &c., and
Deuteronomy, chaps. xv. and xvi. These accounts,
though probably written by different persons, and
at widely different times, agree substantially
together—and, indeed, would seem to have passed
under revision by one person (before the time of

Ezra the scribe.　See the Book of Nehemiah, chap. viii.).

At the very outset, we find evidence that the sacrifices were not originally offered to the Almighty Being, who works in and through all things, but were devised as parts of a system of nature worship (primarily, it would seem, a system of Sun worship).　For we read, 'The Lord spake unto Moses, saying, Command the children of Israel, and say unto them, My offering and my bread for *my sacrifices made by fire, for a sweet savour unto me*, shall ye observe to offer unto me in their due season.'　The conception that the savour of cooked flesh could be sweet to an Almighty, All-wise, and Omnipotent Being, belongs as completely to the childhood of religion as does the idea that such a Being could under any conditions need the rest and refreshment mentioned in Exodus, chap. xxxi. v. 17.　The use of fire also in sacrificial observances belongs essentially to Sun worship and the associated system of Fire worship.

The first sacrifice is the daily sacrifice, or the continual burnt offering.　'This is the offering made by fire which ye shall offer unto the Lord : two lambs of the first year without spot day by day, for a continual burnt offering; the one lamb shalt thou offer in the morning, and the other lamb shalt thou offer at even.' Flour and oil also were offered for the continual burnt offering. There was also, precisely as in Pagan sacrifices, a libation— ' In the holy place shalt thou cause the strong wine to be poured unto the Lord for a drink offering.'

We have here manifestly those sacrifices to the rising and setting sun which formed so characteristic a feature of Sun worship.

Secondly, on the Sabbath-day, besides the continual burnt offering, there were offered ' two lambs of the first year without spot, and two tenth deals of flour for a meat offering, mingled with oil and the drink offering thereof.' This may be regarded as partly derived from sacrifices originally offered to Saturn ; partly from the worship of the moon, which certainly was not unknown to the Jewish people. In fact, it is noteworthy that in the Book of Job, where no mention whatever is made of the Sabbath and Sabbath rest, the worship of the sun and moon is referred to in terms implying that it was common in Job's time, though Job himself had risen superior to the superstitions of Sabaism. (See p. 248, &c.) Moreover, it is evident from the various reasons assigned for keeping the Sabbath holy, that the observance had originally belonged to another cult than that in which the lawgivers of Leviticus, Numbers, and Deuteronomy endeavoured to train the Jewish people. In Leviticus xxiii. they were simply told that the day is an holy convocation, the Sabbath of the Lord ; just as in chap. xxv. they were told that the seventh year was a Sabbath for the Lord, and that the jubilee was to be holy unto them. In Exodus xxii. 11 they were told that the day was to be kept holy because the All-powerful God rested on the seventh day. In Deuteronomy v. 14 they were told that God commanded them to keep the Sabbath day because He had brought them out of the land of Egypt 'through a mighty hand, and by a stretched-out arm.'

In passing, it may be noticed that the Assyrian tablets indicate a weekly resting-day, called the Sabbat, but it was of much earlier date than the Jewish, belonging to the time before the week and the month had been separated. Thus, the 7th, 14th, 21st, and 28th days of each month were days of Sabbat, or rest, and also the 19th day, or the 49th day from the beginning of the previous month, so that this 19th, or mid-month rest, corresponded to the Jewish 'week of weeks.'

In the third place, sacrifices were offered in the beginning of the months, that is, at the time of new moon.

So far as the offerings at the feast of the new moon were concerned, we might infer that the Sabbath of the new moon was originally held to be more important than the week-day Sabbath. Instead of two lambs, as at the weekly Sabbath, there were offered at the feast of the new moon two young bullocks, and one ram, and seven lambs; instead of two tenth deals of flour, fifteen tenth deals; instead of half a hin of wine, more than two hins were offered at the monthly Sabbath. Even if we take into account the greater frequency of weekly Sabbaths (in about the proportion of 59 to 14), we still find that the monthly offerings taken throughout the year, or throughout a number of years, considerably surpassed the weekly offerings.

We come next to the two most important festivals of the Jewish year—the feast of the passover, and the feast of tabernacles—on the fifteenth days of the first and of the second months respectively.

We might safely infer, that these two feasts were astronomical from the circumstance that one is assigned to the time when the sun crosses the equator from south to north, and the other to the time when he crosses the equator from north to south, in other words, to the times of the spring

and autumn equinox. We should be confirmed in
this opinion in remembering that among other
nations these epochs had been regarded as of espe-
cial significance, and that where Sabaistic worship,
and Sun worship, in particular, had prevailed (and
there have been few races which have not at one
time or other adopted these forms of worship), the
time of Easter [1] and the corresponding autumn's
epoch had been times of ceremonial observance
long before, and long after, the feast of the passover and the feast of tabernacles had been regulated by the Jewish lawgivers. But there is also
evidence of the astronomical character of these
two festivals in the nature of the sacrifices offered
on these occasions. It was no mere accident that
during the seven days of unleavened bread, at the
time of the passover, the daily sacrifice was the
same as for the feast of the new moon, except that
in addition to the 'two young bullocks, one ram,
and seven lambs,' 'one goat' was offered 'for a sin
offering,' to make an atonement for the people. So
also during the eight days of the feast of tabernacles, two rams and fourteen lambs were offered
every day, but on the other days, in succession,
thirteen bullocks, twelve, eleven, and so forth,
thirteen (as eminent Jewish writers have pointed

---

[1] The very word signifies *uprising*.

out) being the nearest whole number to the number
of lunar months in a year.

It is noteworthy that even in the day of the
first fruits, the one festival not directly of astronomical origin (though indirectly so, as a seasonal
festival), the offerings were the same as at the feast
of the new moon—viz. two bullocks, one ram, and
seven lambs, ' one kid of the goats ' being added,
' to make an atonement ' for the people.

Now the feast of the passover, and the feast
of tabernacles, corresponding thus exactly with
the two solar passovers, the nodal passages of the
equator,—whatever subsequent interpretation was
given by the Jewish lawgivers to one (at least) of
their festivals,—we are justified in recognising the
real origin of both in the Sabaistic system of
worship, from which the whole system of Jewish
ceremonial was manifestly derived. It is to be observed that each part of the evidence strengthens
the rest ; we might be in doubt (though for my
own part, after studying the subject in the light of
known astronomical facts, I cannot myself entertain any doubt) as to the astronomical origin of
Sabbath observance, if we did not find it associated, on the one hand, with the manifestly astronomical observances at the time of sunrise and
sunset, and, on the other, with the manifestly astro-

nomical festival of the new moon. But when we find, in addition, that the two principal annual festivals of the Jews (the only remaining festivals except the seasonal feast of the first fruits) corresponded with the two most marked epochs of the year—the passages of the sun across the equator at the time of the vernal and autumnal equinox— we find it altogether impossible to resist the inference, that the entire system of sacrificial observance was based on astronomical considerations.

But we can infer more than this. Seeing that these festivals remained religious festivals, even when the Jews had been taught no longer to worship the host of heaven, we perceive that they must originally also have been not simply astronomical but religious. They could therefore have been nothing, as first devised, but Sabaistic observances, for Sabaism is the only form of religion which is based solely on astronomical principles.

We can understand, then, the great difficulty experienced by the Jewish lawgivers in weaning the Jews from the worship of the sun, moon, and stars, for the whole sacrificial system of the Jews shows us that in preceding times the people had been imbued with Sabaistic ideas.

There are some who go much farther than this, finding in festivals supposed to be peculiarly

Christian (which Easter, be it observed, is not) an astronomical significance. Thus, Osiris, Mithra, Bacchus, and Chrishna are represented as having been born on December 25 (or rather at the moment of midnight, between Christmas Eve and Christmas Day) in a cave or stable. Now, although at the present time the only peculiarity of this part of the year is, that it corresponds with the time when the sun is just beginning to rise above his lowest mid-winter descent below the equator, yet at the time when the zodiac was first formed, to which time probably the myths in question may be referred, the constellation Virgo had just risen above the eastern horizon [1] while the sun was entering the constellation Capricorn, which also bore the name of the Augeas. It is singular also, as showing how our modern festivals have been dated according to these old Sabaistic ideas, that August 8, which was about the time when the sign Virgo is lost in the sun's light, is the date assigned by the Catholic Church to the festival of the Assumption of the Virgin, while the Nativity of the Virgin is assigned to September 8, which followed

---

[1] In reality, the sign Virgo had just so risen, meaning by that the 30 degrees of the ecliptic preceding the autumnal equinoctial point, where the sign Libra – the Scales—begins, or what is technically called the first point of Libra.

the epoch when the middle of the sign of Virgo passes the sun by just the same interval as that by which Christmas Day followed the mid-winter solstice. However, it would take us too far to follow out all the analogies which have been traced between solar myths and the fasts and festivals of the modern calendar. Many of these are very doubtful, and some are more than doubtful, whereas no doubt whatever seems to rest on the astronomical origin of the Jewish sacrificial observances.

THE HISTORY OF SUNDAY.

IT is rather singular that two of our small wars with Africa, those with the Ashantees and the Zulus, should have presented an illustration of the influence which the observance of special days may have on human conduct. In one case a foolish superstition was involved, in the other what many regard as a most weighty religious duty. It is worth noticing that the superstition prevailed,— the religious duty was for the time being set on one side.

At a rather critical epoch in the Ashantee war, when it was a matter of extreme importance that certain military stores should be forwarded to the British army with as little delay as possible, it so chanced that all preparations for loading the ship which was to convey those stores were completed late on Thursday night. In the ordinary course of things the ship would have sailed early on Friday morning. But it is well known that sailors have a superstitious objection against beginning a journey

on a Friday.   It is even whispered that this idiotic
superstition is not limited to ordinary seamen, but
is entertained by many among their officers who
might be expected to have more sense.   Whether
at the Admiralty such nonsensical notions are
believed in, I do not know.   But certain it is that
the stores so much required were not despatched
until the Saturday, though the delay involved the
risk of serious mischief to the British forces in
Ashantee.   I do not say that the delay was unwise
on the part of the authorities, assuming always that
it was not directly based on the foolish superstition
about Friday sailing.   So long as sailors are
ignorant enough and silly enough to believe in
such superstitions, their folly must be taken into
account as one of the factors which their officers
and those yet higher in authority have to deal with.
It might probably have been far more mischievous
to have despatched the ship on Friday, with a dis-
heartened crew, than it was to lose twenty-four
precious hours for the sake of encouraging those
gallant but feeble-minded simpletons.   Whether it
was for this reason that the ship was delayed, or
because (as some have said) the Friday superstition
extends to the quarter-deck and farther yet, certain
it is that this superstition was allowed to prevail,
and a great nation waited in the midst of hurried

military preparations till a *dies infausta* should be overpast.

Five years passed, and again the British nation was engaged in hurried preparations for war against African savages. Every hour was of importance, for reinforcements and military stores were to be sent in all haste to save Natal from the warriors of Cetywayo. And now another 'day' to which a widespread opinion attaches special significance is reached before the preparations can be completed. Up to Saturday night the work of preparation has gone busily forward. But the morrow is Sunday, on which, according to the teaching of nine-tenths of our clergy and the professions at any rate of ninety-nine hundredths of our people, we should do 'no manner of work.' What the people from whom that law is ostensibly derived would have done under such circumstances we may partly infer from the well-known episode in the history of the Maccabees. If a thousand Jews, including many fighting men, would allow themselves to be slain rather than do work on the Sabbath-day by which their lives might have been saved,[1] we can understand that they would have interrupted on the Sabbath-day such work as fitting ships, collecting stores, &c. (which our military and naval folk had in hand

---

[1] Maccabees, Book I. chap. ii. 32–39.

U

at the time I am writing about) and would only have resumed work when the Sabbath was fairly over. Our authorities did not so act; they acted, to say truth, far more sensibly. They regarded the work of preparation as a labour of necessity. Its object was not, indeed, precisely to save life, as in a case which a certain Jewish teacher considered : for unquestionably the military and naval preparations made when the news of the disaster in Zululand reached England would grievously have disappointed expectation if they had not resulted in the destruction of many more lives than they saved. But if such preparations have to be made, they cannot be made too quickly. Stopping them on the Sunday would have been straining out an exceedingly small gnat after several most monstrous camels had been swallowed. Whatever the considerations may have been which influenced the Government, certain it is that the religious observance was for the time being set on one side as 'not convenient,' and the work of preparation was pushed on as busily through the Sunday as on the Saturday which preceded and on the Monday which followed it.

It is possible that during the discussions likely to take place before long on the question of opening our museums, art galleries, and so forth on Sundays, we may hear something more of the sensible decision of the Government to omit for awhile the observance of Sunday when warlike preparations were in progress. It may occur to our lawmakers that possibly if Sunday may be used as a day for preparing weapons whereby the bodies of men may be conveniently destroyed, it may almost as righteously be used as a day on which the minds of men may be conveniently nourished and instructed. I have not told the two stories, however, which illustrate so strikingly the relative positions assigned by the authorities to superstitious and to religious observances, for the purpose of enforcing any argument in favour of freeing the Sunday, but simply as a convenient way of introducing some considerations respecting the Sunday of Christianity and the Sabbath of Judaism which are worthy of attention in the approaching discussions on Sunday observance. There is not much of novelty in the points I shall have to advance on this subject, but a useful purpose may be subserved by bringing together within the compass of a single essay arguments and considerations heretofore advanced in lengthy treatises, or even scattered through several volumes.

The idea commonly entertained respecting Sunday is, that from the time of the Apostles or thereabouts, the observance of the Jewish Sabbath

—the seventh day in the week—was replaced by the observance of the Lord's day—the first in the week. As we still retain among the Commandments that one which specially refers to the seventh day, it must be assumed that the Church teaches the observance in our time of one day in the week in the manner appointed for the Jewish Sabbath, and also considers that the people require no special information as to the manner in which the seventh day has been replaced by the first. At least, this way of viewing the matter reduces to a minimum the inherent absurdity of teaching one law while another law is to be practised. The absurdity, even when thus reduced to a minimum, remains, in the judgment of all who are acquainted with the facts, a monstrous one ; but it would be far more monstrous if it were to be assumed that, as respects even the manner of observance as well as respects the day to be observed, the law thus constantly repeated amongst us has been abrogated; or again, if it were assumed that the laity really understood how incorrect is the notion on which they for the most part base their observance of Sunday.

A brief sketch of the gradual displacement of the Jewish Sabbath by the Christian Sunday will show how the question rests so far as the authority and action of the Church are concerned.

We do not find in any writer during the first five centuries of the Christian era, or in any ecclesiastical or civil public document, the slightest hint of a transfer of the obligations indicated in the Fourth Commandment from the Sabbath-day to the Sunday. Both days were observed as days of worship and as days of rest. The author of the 'Constitutions' says that Peter and Paul ordered that servants should work on five days in the week, and rest on the Sabbath in memory of the Creation, and on the Lord's day in memory of the Resurrection. The Council of Laodicea (363 A.D.) orders Christians to work on the Sabbath, giving preference to the Lord's day, and if possible resting on it ; but they are to be accursed if they keep it in the Jewish fashion. And Augustine, Bishop of Hippo Regius, so far from taking the Fourth Commandment as the basis of Sunday observance, says that to fast on Sunday as on the Sabbath ' is a grave scandal.'

Even regarded apart from its imagined relation to the Fourth Commandment, Sunday during the first centuries of the Christian era was not observed as Sunday now is. It was originally a day to be observed only by those who wished to observe it. It was to be observed, if at all, as a day of gladness. Tertullian condemned as unlawful not only Sunday fasting, but the use of a kneeling posture in Sunday services.   'Die Dominico,' he says, 'jejunium nefas ducimus vel de geniculis adorare.'

The first law which forbade work of any sort on Sunday was passed by that most Christian and exemplary emperor, Constantine (321 A.D.).   For reasons best known to himself he allowed field labourers to work on Sundays, but city people, artisans, and judges were enjoined to rest on 'the venerable Day of the Sun.'   This was a high compliment to the Christian religion, for Constantine was thus extending to Sunday the suspension of business which heretofore had only been customary on civil festivals, including his own birthday, which he had probably regarded, and continued to regard, as far more 'venerable' than any day of merely religious significance.   That the law was intended to be civil, not religious, is confirmed by the edict of Theodosius (386 A.D.), in which Sunday and other Christian festivals are set apart, in company with the days of the founding of Rome and Constantinople, the days of the birth and accession of the emperors, and the traditional festivals of heathen Rome, as days on which no business was to be transacted.

Until this time no law had been passed which tended directly to prohibit amusements on Sunday, or indeed on the Sabbath either.   But the edict of

Theodosius prohibited not only secular business, but theatrical amusements, horse racing, and the baiting of animals. A few years later the Council of Carthage expressed in a canon regret that the multitude preferred flocking to the circus than to the church on Sundays. At length, in 425, Theodosius the Younger issued a prohibition against Sunday work and Sunday sports, which was expanded forty-four years later into the famous law of Leo and Anthemius, ordaining that on Sunday ' no office of the law should be executed, no persons summoned or arrested as sureties, no pleading or judgment take place, and that also there should be no theatrical shows, or games in the circus, or baiting of wild beasts.'

Such was the beginning of Sunday observance, though time was required to develop fully the Sunday as now known.

In the time of Leo the Philosopher (889–910) Sunday field-work, which had hitherto been permitted as a work of necessity—for nature does not observe any Sabbath rest—was forbidden by an imperial law. Athelstane, Edgar, and Canute forbade all Sunday tradings ; and it appears from one of Edgar's laws that in those days Sunday was held to begin at three o'clock on Saturday afternoon, and to continue till dawn on Monday. Soon after, hunting on Sunday was forbidden.　In the reign of Richard II., tennis, football, gambling, and putting the stone, were included among forbidden Sunday amusements.　Attempts were made at this time to enforce the laws for closing all shops on Sundays, especially barbers' shops; for then, as now, barbers were great offenders against Sunday laws —whether because beards *will* continue to grow during Saturday night and Sunday morning, or for some other as yet undetermined reason, I do not know.　Eustace, Abbot of Flay, in 1201, maintained the duty of observing Sunday most strictly; and he was able (probably as a reward for his great virtues, and especially, it should seem, his great veracity) to put in documentary evidence on this point in the form of a letter from Christ, miraculously 'delivered' on the altar of St. Simeon at Golgotha: by this letter all kinds of work were forbidden from three on Saturday until Monday morning.

'It is said also,' says a writer in the 'Westminster Review' (who puts one of the following stories so delicately that I cannot do better than follow him), 'that certain miraculous penalties visited those who paid no heed to this prohibition. One woman weaving after three o'clock on Saturday was struck with the dead palsy; whilst another, who had put some paste into an oven, when she thought it was baked found it paste still. A man, too, made a cake during the forbidden hours, from which blood flowed when he began to eat it on Sunday ; and an unfortunate Jew of Tewkesbury, who fell on the Sabbath into a place from which extrication was difficult, and had scruples about letting himself be drawn out on that day, whilst the Duke of Gloucester had similar scruples about drawing him out on Sunday, was dead when they came to his assistance on Monday.'

The Duke of Gloucester's scruples show him to have been a man of very delicate conscience (of course we are not to imagine the possibility that the unfortunate Jew might have been a creditor of his) ; manifestly, he would have been shocked if any one had advanced the easy doctrine that a man, having an ox or a sheep fallen into a pit, might without sin take it out on the Sabbath-day.

But as in the days of the Christianised Roman emperors the laws for the observance of Sunday were placed on the same footing only as those relating to the observance of imperial birthdays and Pagan festivals, so in the days before the Reformation Sunday was placed on no higher a level than was assigned to saints' days.

'Sunday,' says the 'Westminster' reviewer

very truly, 'was as holy as the deposition of St. Wulfstan, or the day of St. Lawrence the Martyr, but no more; so that if (as, historically, it seems we must do) we ascribe the binding authority of Sunday to the institution of the Church, we are equally bound to observe the numerous saints' days, which have exactly the same authority and grew up in exactly the same way. If, for instance, tennis and football are wrong on Sunday, they are equally wrong upon any of the saints' days to which the Act of Richard II. applied. For the canons and statutes upon which our statute is based did not take Sunday exclusively under their protection; and if we acknowledge their authority at all, we must acknowledge it *in toto.* We have no right to elect which of the holy days created by the Church we shall retain and which we shall discard; for, if we discard some, why should we not discard all? At least, we must be prepared with reasons for our preference; and, it is submitted, no good reasons can be given. It is useless to appeal to what the Reformation did; the question is, Had it any grounds for what it did? If it acknowledged no sanction for the saints' days, what sanction remains for Sunday? The sanction only of subsequent statutes.'

But let us pass on to the time of the Reformation,

and see whether—though we can obtain no means of separating one set of holidays sanctioned by the Church from another equally sanctioned—we may not find the Sunday of our time sanctioned by the special approval of the Reformation. In other words, though we cannot logically deduce our Sunday observances from the authority of the Church before the Reformation, we may find that at the time of the Reformation it was thought well to establish such Sunday observances as at present exist, and thus, for want of older and perhaps better authority, we may be able to take the authority of the Reformed Church.

But we find no help whatever in this direction. The teaching of the Reformers was as definitely opposed as it could be to the teaching of modern Sabbatarians. Said Luther, ‘If anywhere any one sets up the observance of Sunday on a Jewish foundation, then I order you to work on it, to ride on it, to dance on it, to do anything which shall remove the encroachments on Christian liberty.’ In the Augsburg Confession, again, the Protestants say, ‘Those who judge that, in place of the Sabbath, the Lord’s day was instituted as a day to be necessarily observed, do greatly err. Scripture abrogated the Sabbath, and teaches that the Mosaic ceremonies may be omitted now that the

Gospel is revealed.' As to the Reformation in England, it is commanded in the twenty-fourth injunction of Edward VI. that *the holy day* be wholly given to God, in hearing His Word read and taught, and in private and public prayers ; but parishioners are to be instructed that it is lawful in harvest-time to labour on holy and festival days, and to save that which God has sent, and that ' if, for any scrupulosity or grudge of conscience, men should superstitiously abstain from working on those days, then they would grievously offend and displease God.' (What a comfort it must have been to the preachers of those times to know so well what God wanted men to do !) Again, in 5 and 6 Edward VI., cap. 3, Sunday is specially included among holy days, respecting which section 6 specifies that it shall be lawful for every husbandman, labourer, fisherman, and all and every other person or persons of any estate, degree, or condition (upon the days before mentioned), at harvest or any other time, when necessity shall so require, to labour, ride, fish, or work any kind of work, at their free will or pleasure.' Cranmer speaks of Sunday and other holy days as ' mere appointments of the magistrates,' which he considers, however, to be a sufficient reason for their observance. But, as the writer in the 'Westminster Review,' from whose excellent paper on 'Sunday and Lent' the above account of the Reformers' views has been abridged, remarks justly, the most striking exposition of the Reformation doctrine is Tyndale's answer to Sir T. More's dialogue, where he says :—

'As for the Sabbath, *we be lords* over the Sabbath, and may yet change it into Monday, or into any other day, as we see need, or may make every tenth day holy day only as we see cause why. We may make two every week if it were expedient, and one not enough to teach the people. Neither was there any cause to change it from the Satur-day, but to put a difference between ourselves and the Jews ; neither need we any holy day at all, if the people might be taught without it.'

Yet, before long, the Sunday of our time began to grow out of the more reasonable (though in one sense less logical) Sunday of the early Reformers. The Puritans, even in the time of Elizabeth, began to be as superstitious about Sunday observance as the Catholics had been in the time of Richard II. ; and after a time the Reformation, which had in the first instance repudiated as too Judaised the Sun-day of the Catholics, adopted a method of Sunday observance which even surpassed in strictness the old rabbinical observance of the Sabbath.

'Even Elizabeth,' says the 'Westminster' reviewer, 'was prevailed upon by the magistrates of London to interdict plays and games on Sunday within the liberties of the city. The Reformers were in advance of their age, and, in some respects, of our own. But Puritanism rapidly got the better of them. It is recorded that it was preached in Somersetshire that to throw a ball on the Sabbath was as great a sin as to kill a man; in Norfolk, that to make a feast or a wedding dinner on Sunday was as great a sin as for a father to cut his child's throat with a knife; in Suffolk, that to ring more bells than one was a crime equivalent to murder.[1] Then came, in 1595, Nicholas Bounde's great work on Sabbatarianism, which began a controversy that has never since ended. Few books are to be compared with his for their permanent influence on our social life. Our own Sunday has much more of Bounde in it than of Tyndale or Cranmer; and the Scotch Sabbath itself is really due to Bounde, not to Calvin or Knox. For, as

---

[1] Fuller, Book ix. s. 8, 22. It will hardly be believed, but within the last few years views as ludicrous in one aspect and as horrible in another have been promulgated respecting Sunday observance. A foolish clergyman, at a meeting when the question of playing cricket upon the village green on Sunday afternoons had been discussed, got up with great warmth to express his conviction that in God's eyes there was no difference between the man who could thus break the Fourth Commandment and one who broke the Sixth.

Dr. Hessey has clearly shown, Sabbatarianism in Scotland was not so much the work of the last-named Reformers as of the English Puritans ; and he mentions an existing tradition that Knox, being one day on a visit to Calvin, found that worthy theologian engaged in a game of bowls.'

That the English Puritans, and not the Scotch Reformers, were the inventors of the rigidest forms of Sabbatarianism, is further shown by the results of English Puritanism where it worked unchecked. Detestable as the Scotch Sunday is (not detestable, be it understood, because of its unreasonable character, but because of the mischief that it has worked and continues to work), the New England Sunday was even more abominable. In the twenty-eighth article of the code drawn up for Newhaven in 1656 we find the following article, which for folk who had fled from the abuse of authority is sufficiently severe :—' Whosoever shall profane the Lord's day, or any part of it, by work or sport, shall be punished by fine or corporally. But if the court, by clear evidence, find that the sin was proudly, presumptuously, and with a high hand committed against the command and authority of the blessed God, such person therein despising and reproaching the Lord *shall be put to death.'* The thirty-eighth article is rather ridiculous than atrocious, like the twenty-eighth.   It runs simply, 'If any man shall kiss his wife, or wife her husband, on the Lord's day, the party in fault shall be punished at the discretion of the court of magistrates ;' and as the magistrates were of the same kidney as the law-makers, it will be conceived what 'punishment at *their* discretion signified,' for discretion they had none, neither did they know what mercy or justice meant.

It is, indeed, clear that very early after the Reformation the Puritans in the old country itself were beginning to observe Sunday as dismally as the Scotch now do.   Thus, in 1635, or thereabouts, Dr. Heylin found occasion to rebuke the gloomy asceticism of some rigid Puritans : ' People,' he says, ' should not be so superstitiously fearful (of breaking the Sabbath) that they dare not kindle a fire, or dress meat, or visit their neighbours, sit at their own door, or walk abroad, no, nor so much as talk with one another, except it be—in the poet's words—

> Of God, grace, and ordinances,
> As if they were in heavenly trances.

In Scotland, only a few years later, the strict observance of Sunday had begun to be regarded as a matter for the attention of the magistrates. In 1644 the six sessions forbade all walking in the streets on Sunday after the noonday sermon. In 1645 the magistrates were ordered to cause English soldiers to lay hold of both old and young whom they might find in the streets either before or after the sermon. In 1650 the magistrates of Edinburgh ordered that the city gates should be closed from 10 P.M. on Saturday till 4 A.M. on Monday, except for one hour in the morning and one in the evening for the watering of horses. About the same time Margaret Dickson, a widow, had to pay two marks for having ' spits and roasts at the fire in time of sermon.'

Such being, in brief, the history of the steps by which the Sunday observance of our time has come into existence, it remains that we should consider what actual authority we have for modern Sabbatarianism, regarded as a religious question. No one will care to take the Puritans of the seventeenth century as the sole or the chief authority for keeping Sunday holy after a stricter fashion than that in which the Jews held that the Sabbath should be observed. For the Sabbath was a day of abstinence from labour, not of abstinence from amusement. If the Puritans had simply said the Sunday shall be our Sabbath, and shall be observed in all respects even as the Sabbath of the Jews was observed, we could understand their position as

X

authorities in this matter. We should still have to regard them as absolutely the only authorities we have for Judaising Sunday ; but we might at least understand that many would consider the observance of one day in seven as ordained by a higher authority, by the highest indeed of all conceivable authorities. We must believe, however, if we regard the Puritans as our sufficient guide in this matter, that not only were they right in insisting on Sunday as a substitute for the Jewish Sabbath, but also in assigning a number of new Sabbath regulations, such as the Jews, and the teacher, whoever he may have been, from whom the Jews received their Sabbath laws, had never thought of enjoining. No one, I should imagine, considers the Puritans of sufficient authority to countenance teachings of this sort. The most outspoken among them, those who exerted greatest influence, were as ignorant as they were bigoted, as cruel as they were crafty—the last men in the world from whom a cultured people would care to take their religious observances.

But if we do take the Puritans as our authorities in this matter, we ought in all reason to take their views as they stood. We have no right, if they really were commissioned to lay down the law for us in such matters, to accept a part of their teaching and reject the rest. The punishment for Sunday labour, presumptuously and with a high hand carried on, should be death now, as the Puritans (when free from the trammels of civil control) taught in the seventeenth century that it should be. The kissing of a wife by her husband, or of a husband by a wife on Sunday, should still be an offence punishable at civil law. And now, as two thousand years ago, soldiery or police should be enjoined to allow none to remain in the streets either before or after the hours of noonday service.

But if we do not accept the Puritans as authority, we find equal difficulty when we turn to the Catholic Church in pre-Reformation times. If that Church really had power to bind and loose men with regard to Sunday observance, then we should pay the same respect to that Church's ordinances about saints' days and other Church holidays; apart always from the fact that for several centuries the Catholic Church enjoined no such strict observance of Sundays as afterwards she insisted upon.

A similar difficulty is met with if, going farther back, we take Constantine as our authority. We have the same authority for the observance of Constantine's birthday and the kalends of January. Whatever reason may be used to show that Constantine was a sufficient authority in one matter, establishes his authority in the other also.

But lastly, if we go back to Moses, and rejecting the opinion of those who considered in old times that the Jewish Sabbath was abrogated, and the opinion also of those others who considered that the Christian Sunday should not resemble the Jewish Sabbath, whether this last were abrogated or not, adopt the opinion that the Fourth Commandment should now be understood as transferred from the Sabbath to Sunday, how does the matter then stand? Have we any reason for selecting this one special day from among all the other days that Moses commanded the people to observe? If we are to hold, at least with regard to the Sabbath, that not one jot or tittle of the law of Moses has passed away, how can we escape the obligation of observing other days and other seasons about which the Mosaic law was equally definite? Moses said, ' Six days shalt thou do thy work, and in the seventh day thou shalt rest ;' but he also said, ' Six years thou shalt sow thy land, but the seventh year thou shalt let it rest and be still.' Are we to keep this law of the seventh year or the law of the year of jubilee, as well as the law of the seventh day?

Yet once more, we know that Moses commanded the people to observe the festival of the New Moon, and this festival should be observed by us now, if the law of Moses is really to be regarded as of authority over us. So far as we can judge from the sacrifices respectively appointed for this festival and the Sabbath-day, the former was held to be of at least equal importance with the latter. On the Sabbath-day the sacrifices were 'two lambs of the first year without spot, and two tenth deals of flour for a meat offering, mingled with oil, and the drink offering thereof: this is the burnt offering of every Sabbath, beside the continual burnt offering and his drink offering.' On the feast of the New Moon, 'in the beginnings of your months, ye shall offer,' says the Mosaic law, 'a burnt offering unto the Lord ; two young bullocks, and one ram, seven lambs of the first year without spot ; and three tenth deals of flour for a meat offering, mingled with oil, for one bullock ; and two tenth deals of flour for a meat offering, mingled with oil, for one ram ; and a several tenth deal of flour, mingled with oil, for a meat offering unto one lamb ; for a burnt offering of a sweet savour, a sacrifice made by fire unto the Lord. And their drink offerings shall be half an hin of wine unto a bullock, and the third part of an hin unto a ram, and a fourth part of an hin unto a lamb : this is the burnt offering of every month throughout the months of the year. And one kid of the goats for a sin offering unto the Lord shall be offered, beside the continual burnt offering and his drink offering.' The continual burnt offering mentioned here, and in the description of the Sabbath offering, is the morning sacrifice, all these ceremonies, daily, weekly, monthly, and the yearly sacrifice of the Passover, being survivals of the practices of the star-worshipping ancestors of the Jews. Indeed, if we accept the Jewish law of the Sabbath, we ought not only to accept with it the festival of the New Moon, and other festivals (the Passover we have very little modified), but the principle of sacrifices, offerings of meat and drink to God, or to a god supposed to care for such things, and moreover, the recognition of the heavenly bodies as deities, which, however skilfully disguised by Moses and other Jewish lawgivers, in reality underlies the entire ceremonial system of the Jewish religion.

Then also the observance of Sunday, if really based on the Fourth Commandment, should correspond more closely than is actually the case with the observance of the Jewish Sabbath. It corresponds too closely, in many respects, already with Sabbath observance. But the correspondence should be exact if the Sunday really has replaced the Sabbath. I wonder, indeed, that some of the superstitious abuses of the Jewish Sabbath should not have commended themselves ere this to the modern Sabbatarian, so closely does their spirit accord with that in which he urges the observance of the Lord's day. The Doritheans, for instance, taking the precept of Moses, 'Abide ye every man in his place,' interpreted it to mean that every man should remain throughout the Sabbath day in whatever attitude he chanced to be in on the Sabbath morning: 'If he was sitting, he must continue to sit ; if lying, he must continue to lie down.' 'The rabbinical doctors,' we are told, 'met this by saying that as a man's place was 2,000 cubits all round him, he did not break the Mosaical command provided he kept himself within that distance. The rabbins were unrivalled in such sophistry. They invented thirty-nine negative precepts relative to the Sabbath ; for instance, people were not to walk on the grass, for walking on it would bruise it, and such bruising amounted to *a kind of threshing.* Shoes without nails might be borne ; but shoes with nails were a burthen.' And so forth.

ASTROLOGY.

WE are apt to speak of astrology as though it
were an altogether contemptible superstition, and
to contemplate with pity those who believed in it
in old times ; and yet, if we consider the matter
aright, we must concede, I think, that of all the
errors into which men have fallen in their desire to
penetrate into futurity, astrology is the most
respectable, one may even say the most reasonable.
Indeed, all other methods of divination of which I
have ever heard are not worthy to be mentioned in
company with astrology, which, delusion though
it was, had yet a foundation in thoughts well
worthy of consideration. The heavenly bodies *do*
rule the fates of men and nations in the most unmistakable manner, seeing that without the con-
trolling and beneficent influences of the chief
among these orbs—the sun—every living creature
on the earth must perish. The ancients perceived
that the moon has so potent an influence on our
world, that the waters of the ocean rise and fall in
unison with her apparent circling motion round

the earth. Seeing that two among the orbs which move upon the unchanging dome of the star-sphere are thus potent in terrestrial influences, was it not natural that the other moving bodies known to the ancients should be thought to possess also their special powers? The moon, seemingly less important than the sun, not merely by reason of her less degree of splendour, but also because she performs her circuit of the star-sphere in a shorter interval of time, was seen to possess a powerful influence, but still an influence far less important than that exerted by the sun, or rather than the many influences manifestly emanating from him. But other bodies travelled in yet wider circuits if their distances could be inferred from their periods of revolution. Was it not reasonable to suppose that the influences exerted by those slowly moving bodies might be even more potent than those of the sun himself? Mars circling round the star-sphere in a period nearly twice as great as the sun's, Jupiter in twelve years, and Saturn in twenty-nine, might well be thought to be rulers of superior dignity to the sun, though less glorious in appearance; and since no obvious direct effects are produced by them as they change in position, it was natural to attribute to them influences more subtle, but not the less potent.

Thus was conceived the thought that the fortunes of every man born into the world depend on the position of the various planets at the moment of his birth. And if there was something artificial in the rules by which various influences were assigned to particular planets, or to particular aspects of the planets, it must be remembered that the system of astrology was formed gradually and perhaps tentatively. Some influences may have been inferred from observed events, the fate of this or that king or chief guiding astrologers in assigning particular influences to such planetary aspects as were presented at the time of his nativity. Others may have been invented, and afterwards have found general acceptance because confirmed by some curious coincidences. In the long run, indeed, any series of experimental predictions must have led to some very surprising fulfilments, that is, to fulfilments which would have been exceedingly surprising if the corresponding predictions had been the only ones made by astrologers. Such instances, carefully collected, may at first have been used solely to improve the system of prediction. The astrologer may have been careful to separate the fulfilled from the unfulfilled predictions, and thus to establish a safe rule. For it must be remembered that, admitting the car-

dinal principle of astrology, the astrologer had
every reason to believe that he could experi-
mentally determine a true method of prediction.
If the planets really rule the fate of each man,
then we have only to calculate their position at
the known time of any man's birth, and to consider
his fortunes, to have facts whence to infer the
manner in which their influence is exerted. The
study of one man's life would of course be altogether insufficient. But when the fortunes of many
men were studied in this way, the astrologer
(always supposing his first supposition right) would
have materials from which to form a system of
prediction.

Go a step farther. Select a body of the ablest
men in a country, and let them carry out continuous
studies of the heavens, carefully calculate nativities
for every person of note, or even for every soul born
in their country, and compare the events of each person's life with the planetary relations presented at his
birth. It is manifest that a trustworthy system of
prediction would, in the long run, be deduced by
them, if astrology have any real basis in fact.

I do not say that astrologers always proceeded
in this experimental manner. Doubtless in those
days, as now, men of science were variously con-
stituted, some being disposed to trust chiefly to

observation, while others were ready to generalise, and yet others evolved theories from the depths of their moral consciousness. Indeed, what we know of the development of astrology in later times, as well as the way in which other modes of divination have sprung into existence, shows that the natural tendency of astrologers would be to 'nvent systems rather than to establish them by careful and long-continued observation. Within a very few years of the discovery of the spots on the sun a tolerably complete system of divination was founded upon the appearance, formation, and motions of these objects. Certainly this system was not based on observation, nor will any one suppose that the rules for ' reading the hand' had an observational origin, or that fortune-telling by means of cards was derived from a careful comparison of the result of shuffling, cutting, and dealing, with the future fortunes of those for whose enlightenment these important processes were performed.

But we must not forget that astrology was originally a science, though a false one. Grant the truth of its cardinal idea, and it had every right to this position. No office could be more important than that of the astrologer, no services could be more useful than those he was capable of rendering according to his own belief as well as that of those who employed him. It is only necessary to mention the history of astrology to perceive the estimation in which it was held in ancient times.

As to the extreme antiquity of astrology it is perhaps needless to speak ; indeed, its origin is so remote that we have only imperfect traditions respecting its earliest developments. Yet it may be worth while to mention some of these traditions, seeing that, whether true or not, they show clearly enough the great antiquity attributed to astrology, even in times which to ourselves appear remote. Philo asserts that Terah, the father of Abraham, was skilled in all that relates to astrology ; and, according to Josephus, the Chaldæan Berosus attributed to Abraham a profound knowledge of arithmetic, astrology, and astronomy, in which sciences he instructed the Egyptians. Diodorus Siculus says that the Heliadæ, or children of the sun (that is, men from the East), excelled all other men in knowledge, particularly in the knowledge of the stars. One of this race, named Actis (a ray), built Heliopolis, and named it after his father, the sun. Thenceforward the Egyptians cultivated astrology with so much assiduity as to be considered its inventors. On the other hand Tatius says that the Egyptians taught the Chaldæans astrology. The people of Thebais, according to Diodorus Siculus, claimed the power of predicting every future event with the utmost certainty; they also asserted that they were of all races the most ancient.

However, we have, both in Egypt and in Assyria, records far more satisfactory than these conflicting statements to prove the great antiquity of astrology, and the importance attached to it when it was regarded as a science. The Great Pyramid in Egypt was unquestionably an astronomical, that is (for in the science of the ancients the two terms are convertible) an astrological building. The Birs Nimroud,[1] supposed to be built on the ruins of the tower of Babel, was also built for astrologers. The forms of these buildings testify to the astronomical purposes for which they were erected. The Great Pyramid, like the inferior buildings copied from it, was most carefully oriented, that is, the four sides were built facing exactly north, south, east, and west. The astronomical use of this arrangement is manifest. By

[1] Every brick hitherto removed from this edifice bears the stamp of King Nebuchadnezzar. It affords a wonderful idea of the extent and grandeur of the buildings raised by the tyrants of old times, that the ruins of a single building on the site of Babylon (Rich's Kasr) has 'for ages been the mine from which the builders of cities rising after the fall of Babylon have obtained their materials.' Layard's *Nineveh.*

looking along either of the two long straight sides lying east and west the astronomer could tell the true east or west points of the horizon, and determine when the sun rose in the east [1] exactly, or set exactly in the west. By looking along the straight sides lying north and south, the astronomer could tell when the sun, or any other celestial body, was in the meridian. Proclus informs us that the pyramids terminated at the top in a platform, on which the priests made their celestial observations.

The figure of the Babylonian temple of astronomy was probably different, though it is possible that Nebuchadnezzar altogether modified the proportions of the original temple. We may infer the nature of the earlier use of such temples from later usages. We learn from Diodorus Siculus that, in the midst of Babylon, a great temple was

[1] A good story is told about the rising of the sun in the east, the point of the joke being different, perhaps, to astronomers than to others :—A certain baron was noted for never replying directly, even to the simplest questions, and a wager was laid that, if he were asked whether the sun rises in the east and sets in the west, he would not answer directly, even though told of the wager. The question was put, and he began—'The terms east and west, gentlemen, are conventional, but admitting that —;' the rest of the reply was lost, the wager being won, which was all the inquirers cared for. If this worthy had answered simply 'Yes,' the wager would have been lost, but the reply would not have been correct ; for the sun never has risen in the east and set in the west, exactly, at any place or on any day since the world began. If the sun rises due east on any day, he does not set due west, and *vice versâ*.

erected by Semiramis, and dedicated to Belus or Jupiter, 'and that on its roof or summit the Chaldæan astronomers contemplated, and exactly noted, the risings and settings of the stars.'

If we consider the manner in which the study of science, for its own sake, has always been viewed by Oriental nations, we must admit that these great buildings, and these elaborate and costly arrangements for continued observation, were not intended to advance the science of astronomy. Only the hope that results of extreme value would be obtained by observing the heavenly bodies could have led the monarchs of Assyria and of Older Egypt to make such lavish provision of money and labour for the erection and maintenance of astronomical observatories. So that, apart from the evidence we have of the astrological object of celestial observations in ancient times, we find in the very nature of the buildings erected for observing the stars the clearest proof that men in those times hoped to gain results of great value from such work. Now, we know that neither the improvement of navigation nor increased exactness in the surveying of the earth was aimed at by those who built those ancient observatories : the only conceivable object they can have had was the discovery of a perfectly trustworthy system of prediction from the study of the motions of the heavenly bodies. That this was their object is shown with equal clearness by the fact that such a system, according to their belief, was deduced from these observations, and was for ages accepted without question.

Closely associated with astrological superstitions was the widespread form of religion called Sabaism, or the worship of the host of heaven (Sabaoth). It is not easy to determine whether the worship of the sun, moon, and planets preceded or followed the study of the heavens as a means of divination It is probable that the two forms of superstition sprang simultaneously into existence. The shepherds of Chaldæa, who —

> Watched from the centres of their sleeping flocks
> Those radiant Mercuries, that seemed to move,
> Carrying through æther in perpetual round,
> Decrees and resolutions of the gods,

can hardly have regarded the planetary movements as *indicating*, without believing that those movements actually *influenced*, the fate of men and nations ; in other words, the idea of planetary power must from the very beginning, it would seem, have been associated with the idea of the significance of planetary motions. Be this as it may, it

is certain that in the earliest times of which we
have any historical record, belief in astrology was
associated with the worship of the host of heaven.
In the Bible record we find the teachers and rulers
of the Jewish nation compelled continually to
struggle against the tendency of that people to
follow surrounding nations in forsaking the worship
of the God of Sabaoth for the worship of Sabaoth,
turning from the Creator to the creature. They
would seem even, as the only means of diverting
the people from the worship of those false gods, to
have adopted all the symbols of Sabaism, explain-
ing them, however, with sole reference to the God
of Sabaoth.   Moses adopted, in this way, the four
forms of sacrifice to which the Jewish people had
become accustomed in Egypt—the offerings to the
rising and setting sun (Numbers xxviii. 3, 4) ; the
offerings on the day dedicated to the planet
Saturn, chief of the seven star-gods (Numbers
xxviii. 9) ; the offerings to the new moon (Numbers xxviii. 11); and the offerings for the luni-solar
festival belonging to the first month of the sun's
annual circuit of the zodiacal constellations (Numbers xxviii. 16, 17). All these offerings were in a
sense sanctified by the manner in which he enjoined
them, and the new meaning he attached to them ;
but that the original offerings were Sabaistic is

scarcely open to question. The tenacity, indeed, with which astrological ceremonies and superstitions have maintained their position, even among nations utterly rejecting star-worship, and even in times when astronomy has altogether dispossessed astrology, indicates how wide and deep must have been the influence of those superstitions in remoter ages. Even now the hope on which astrological superstitions were based, the hope that we may one day learn to lift the veil concealing the future from our view, has not been altogether abandoned. The wiser reject it as a superstition, but even the wisest have at one time or other felt its delusive influence.

PRINTED BY
SPOTTISWOODE AND CO., NEW-STREET SQUARE
LONDON

The ORBS AROUND US; a Series of Essays on the Moon and Planets, Meteors and Comets, the Sun and Coloured Pairs of Suns. With Chart and Diagrams. Crown 8vo. 5s.

OTHER WORLDS than OURS; the Plurality of Worlds Studied under the Light of Recent Scientific Researches. With 14 Illustrations. Crown 8vo. 5s.

The MOON : her Motions, Aspects, Scenery, and Physical Condition. With Plates, Charts, Woolcuts, and Lunar Photographs. Crown 8vo. 6s.

UNIVERSE of STARS; presenting Researches into and New Views respecting the Constitution of the Heavens. With 22 Charts and 22 Diagrams. 8vo. 10s. 6d.

LIGHT SCIENCE for LEISURE HOURS; Familiar Essays on Scientific Subjects, Natural Phenomena, &c. 3 vols. Crown 8vo. 5s. each.

CHANCE and LUCK : a Discussion of the Laws of Luck, Coincidence, Wagers, Lotteries, and the Fallacies of Gambling; with Notes on Poker and Martingales (or Sure (?) Gambling Systems). Crown 8vo. 5s.

LARGER STAR ATLAS for the Library, in Twelve Circular Maps, with Introduction and 2 Index Plates. Folio, 15s. or Maps only, 12s. 6d.

NEW STAR ATLAS for the Library, the School, and the Observatory, in 12 Circular Maps (with 2 Index Plates). Crown 8vo. 5s.

TRANSITS of VENUS; a Popular Account of Past and Coming Transits, from the First Observed by Horrocks in 1639 to the Transit of 2012. With 20 Lithographic Plates (12 Coloured) and 38 Illustrations engraved on Wood. 8vo. 8s. 6d.

STUDIES of VENUS-TRANSITS; an Investigation of the Circumstances of the Transits of Venus in 1874 and 1882. With 7 Diagrams and 10 Plates. 8vo. 5s.

ELEMENTARY PHYSICAL GEOGRAPHY. With 33 Maps, Woodcuts, and Diagrams. Fcp. 8vo. 1s. 6d.

LESSONS in ELEMENTARY ASTRONOMY; with an Appendix containing Hints for Young Telescopists. With 47 Woodcuts. Fcp. 8vo. 1s. 6d.

FIRST STEPS in GEOMETRY : a Series of Hints for the Solution of Geometrical Problems, with Notes on Euclid, useful Working Propositions, and many Examples. Fcp. 8vo. 3s. 6d.

EASY LESSONS in the DIFFERENTIAL CALCULUS; indicating from the outset the Utility of the Processes called Differentiation and Integration. Fcp. 8vo. 2s. 6d.